Texan's Wedding-Night Wager
by Charlene Sands

THE TEXAS TATTLER
All The News You Need To Know...And More!

Who remembers four years back, when Texas mogul Kevin Novak was happily married? Didn't think there were many of us. But one has to recall the fervour of the rumour mills when his wife decided to leave her billionaire breadwinner. Everyone was taking bets to see who'd become the next Mrs Novak.

Except that was not an option – for anyone. The Novaks never divorced. Did the powerful Kevin refuse to finalise their estrangement? Or did he always have something else in mind? (He is brilliant, after all.) Because the little woman has finally returned!

D0237365

TEXAN'S WEDDING-NIGHT WAGER
BY
CHARLENE SANDS

THE OILMAN'S BABY BARGAIN
BY
MICHELLE CELMER

Published in Great Britain 2010
Harlequin Mills & Boon Limited,
Eton House, 18-24 Paradise Road, Richmond, Surrey TW9 1SR

The publisher acknowledges the copyright holders of the individual works as follows:

Texan's Wedding-Night Wager © Harlequin Books SA 2009
The Oilman's Baby Bargain © Harlequin Books SA 2009

Special thanks and acknowledgement are given to Charlene Sands and Michelle Celmer for their contributions to the Millionaire's Club series.

ISBN: 978 0 263 88179 0

51-0910

Harlequin Mills & Boon policy is to use papers that are natural, renewable and recyclable products and made from wood grown in sustainable forests. The logging and manufacturing processes conform to the legal environmental regulations of the country of origin.

Printed and bound in Spain
by Litografia Rosés S.A., Barcelona

The Oilman's Baby Bargain
by Michelle Celmer

THE TEXAS TATTLER
All The News You Need To Know...And More!

We all heard rumours that Mitch Brody had been plotting to help his brother marry the Texas senior senator's daughter. He'd even gone so far as to "visit" Alexis Cavanaugh multiple times – wining and dining her in elaborate establishments. But when Lance Brody upped and married his mousy secretary, it *seemed* that the Brody/Cavanaugh merger was off.

Now, rumours abound that the still-eligible Brody brother is back romancing Miss Cavanaugh. Could there have been more to their meetings than one might have imagined? Perhaps the Cavanaughs are so desperate to marry into the Brody family it doesn't matter which brother the groom is! Though we can certainly attest to Mitch Brody's appeal – the man is quite the charmer. Or...could there be something to that noticeable "bump" beginning to appear at Alexis's middle? Perhaps a Brody heir is on the way?

TEXAN'S WEDDING-NIGHT WAGER

BY
CHARLENE SANDS

Dear Reader,

I'm so glad to have been invited to write *Texan's Wedding-Night Wager* as part of the MILLIONAIRE'S CLUB series along with five other fabulous authors.

Set in the fictional town of Somerset, just outside of Houston, my story features dynamic, handsome Kevin Novak (think David Beckham) and his beautiful, feisty, soon-to-be-ex-wife, Cara. It's a story of true love and second chances. The two have been separated by distance and regret for four years, and when Cara returns to her home town to get a divorce, Kevin turns the tables on her.

That's when the fun begins in Maverick County! While Kevin snares Cara in his trap, he becomes a victim of intense attraction and admiration for the wife who abandoned him early in their marriage.

I hope you enjoy the story from beginning to end. In fact, I'll *wager* that you do.

Happy reading!

Charlene

Charlene Sands resides in Southern California with her husband, school sweetheart and best friend, Don. Proudly, they boast that their children, Jason and Nikki, have earned their college degrees. The "empty nesters" now enjoy spending time together on Pacific beaches, playing tennis and going to movies, when they are not busy at work, of course!

A proud member of Romance Writers of America, Charlene has written twenty-five romance novels and is the recipient of the 2006 National Readers' Choice Award, the 2007 Cataromance Reviewer's Choice Award and the 2008 Booksellers Best Award. *Romantic Times BOOKreviews* magazine nominated her book *Do Not Disturb Until Christmas* as the Best Desire of 2008.

Charlene invites you to visit her websites www.charlenesands.com, www.petticoatsandpistols.com and www.myspace.com/charlenesands, to enter her contests, check out her new releases and see what's up.

This book is dedicated to all of my friends
and fellow authors on Petticoats and Pistols.
I've never met a smarter, more wonderful, more
gregarious group of authors. Thanks to Pam Crooks,
Stacey Kayne, Cheryl St John, Kate Bridges,
Linda Broday, Mary Connealy, Pat Potter, Karen Kay
and Elizabeth Lane for being great Western blog
pardners. Y'all make it fun!

The Millionaire's Club

August 2010
Taming the Texas Tycoon
Katherine Garbera
&
One Night with the Wealthy Rancher
Brenda Jackson

September 2010
Texan's Wedding-Night Wager
Charlene Sands
&
The Oilman's Baby Bargain
Michelle Celmer

October 2010
The Maverick's Virgin Mistress
Jennifer Lewis
&
Lone Star Seduction
Day Leclaire

One

Cara shut down the ballroom lights and stood in the middle of the floor of Dancing Lights, flanked by a wall of mirrors and elegant surroundings that she'd insisted upon when designing her studios. A smile emerged just as Elton John's voice carried over the speakers. The song stirred up vivid memories and Cara slowly closed her eyes. She moved her hips, swaying to the rhythm and the poetic lyrics.

> *There's a calm surrender to the rush of day*
> *When the heat of the rolling world can be*
> *turned away*

An enchanted moment, and it sees me through
It's enough for this restless warrior just to be
with you

And can you feel the love tonight
It is where we are
It's enough for this wide-eyed wanderer
That we got this far
And can you feel the love tonight

"Can you feel the love, Cara?" Kevin had said to her the day they'd married.

Kevin had brought her hand to his mouth and nibbled, his dark blue eyes piercing hers. She'd tingled with excitement from that single gesture. Cara *had* felt his love, with every heart-stopping glance, every tender touch and each tantalizing kiss.

"Yes, I feel it, honey," she'd replied.

He'd kissed her lips, whispering, "This is our song, babe."

They'd hung on to each other and sung the lyrics along with Elton's smooth tones, moving to the music as their family and friends looked on. She thought she'd married her Prince Charming, her college sweetheart who could make her laugh one moment and sizzle the next.

Cara's heart swelled thinking back on her wedding day, thinking of being in Kevin's arms, of loving him for all she was worth and hoping for the same kind of happy life she'd wished for so many of her dance students through the years.

She'd had such big dreams.

"Why, Kevin?" she whispered in the silence of the Dallas ballroom.

Gorgeous Kevin Novak, with the penetrating blue eyes and short blond hair, had often been mistaken for David Beckham. She and Kevin had their own private joke about it since, with her curly blond hair and sky-blue eyes, she hardly looked like Posh Spice. Cara smiled briefly at the memory.

They'd had such good times in the beginning, until Kevin had decided building his real estate empire was more important than building their marriage. He'd become a die-hard workaholic, neglecting her needs in favor of the next big deal. He'd broken her heart—hearing their song again brought it all back. The happiness she'd hoped for with Kevin had eluded them. Cara still felt the ache in the pit of her stomach.

She'd moved on with her life, leaving Somerset to start a new life in Dallas, but she hadn't escaped the deep hurt and anguish Kevin had caused.

Cara snapped her eyes open and stared at the fading shadows in the mirror. Her silhouette reflected back the new, confident woman she'd become. She was a businesswoman now, owner of a chain of dance studios, and a choreographer and dance instructor as well.

No longer that optimistic, hope-filled girl who'd wanted a life and children with Kevin, it was long past time for Cara to rectify her situation.

She punched off the CD player and headed to the

phone to call the man she hadn't spoken with in over four years. She'd waltzed around this issue long enough.

It was time to divorce her husband.

Kevin Novak chalked the cue stick with slow, deliberate twists, contemplating his next shot. He was one of the best pool players at the Texas Cattleman's Club, but his pal Darius Franklin was making him sweat for the win. "You know darn well Montoya is responsible for setting the fire."

Kevin bent over the carved-oak vintage pool table and took his shot, the solid orange cue ball angling into the corner pocket. He knew darn well Darius didn't believe Alejandro Montoya was responsible for the damaging blaze set at Brody Oil and Gas. But he wasn't above using distraction to earn a win.

"I don't know that for a fact, Kev. The fire was definitely an act of arson, but I'm not pointing fingers yet."

"Montoya has always been a pain in the ass."

Kevin missed his next shot and Darius lifted his cue stick, eyeing the pool table. "True, but arson? That's an accusation I'm not ready to make. It looks like a professional job and if that's the case, I'd have to rule him out."

"I say he's guilty." Lance Brody, another of Kevin's old frat brothers from the University of Texas, chimed in. Kevin's four best friends were all members of Texas Cattleman's Club in Maverick

County. They watched the game, sipping drinks and cajoling from the sidelines of the club's game room.

"I'm with Lance," Mitch Brody said, agreeing with his brother. "Montoya's got an ax to grind."

Justin Dupree nodded, taking a swig of beer. "I think Montoya is guilty, too. He's got issues with Lance. Always has."

Lance scoffed. "*I* have issues with him." Their rivalry went back to high-school days.

Darius eyed the striped blue ball and took his shot. The ball rolled into the side pocket and Kevin winced.

"Nice shot."

Darius laughed. "It hurt you to say that, didn't it?"

"Like a knife in my heart."

Darius shook his head. "You're a sore loser, Kev."

"I haven't lost yet."

And when Darius missed his next shot, Kevin went full throttle, unwilling to give an inch. His competitive nature wouldn't allow a loss. He sank the next four solid-color balls, then the eight ball, winning the game.

Satisfied, Kevin shook his friend's hand. "You gave me a run for my money."

Darius slapped a twenty in his palm. "I'll get you next time." He lowered his voice, setting his cue stick into its case. "So you really think Montoya set the fire?"

"I'm thinking he did. I also think he's behind blocking my project in downtown Somerset. He's got it in for the Brody brothers and their friends. Wasn't a coincidence to find the area I'd designated for a major development is being declared an historic district. He's got to be behind the rezoning. It's all a little too suspicious."

Lance walked up and put his arms around their shoulders. "Come on, you two. Let's forget about Montoya for a minute. We need to set a date for my wedding reception. Kate deserves more than the Las Vegas elopement she got."

Kevin grinned. "Yeah, you really know how to impress a girl."

Justin added, "Lance really pulled out all the stops on that one."

"Funny, guys." Lance pulled a frown, but Kevin knew he didn't mind their teasing. He'd found his soul mate in Kate and wanted to provide her a beautiful reception.

When the game-room phone rang, Lance walked over to pick it up. "Cara? Is it really you? It's good to hear your voice."

Kevin froze. All heads turned his way and he met with four pairs of curious eyes. Emotions washed through his system. A tic worked his jaw while he stood rigid and waited.

"Okay, I'll get him. He's right here." Lance nodded his way, holding the phone up. "It's…Cara. She wants to speak with you."

Kevin strode across the room to take the phone. Before speaking, he turned to look at his friends, and with a quick gesture signaled them to continue playing and butt out.

The guys turned around and Kevin spoke into the receiver. "Cara?"

"Hello, Kevin."

So formal.

God, he hadn't heard her voice in four years. Not once. Not since she'd left him high and dry and made a new life for herself in Dallas. He'd kept up on her through friends and what little he'd read in the newspapers about her successful dance studios.

She sounded the same—sassy if not a little stiff. There was an awkward moment of silence.

"I guess it's time for us to end it," she said.

Images of Cara getting remarried immediately entered his mind. After four years, why else would she call? Had she fallen in love with another man?

Kevin didn't know how he'd feel about that. She'd walked out on him and their marriage. She'd tried to file for divorce but Kevin had sent the papers back to her. He'd given her an ultimatum— if she wanted out, she would have to come back and face him.

"I'm coming to Somerset. I'd like to make an appointment with you to discuss the…divorce."

"Fine." Kevin's lips tightened.

"It's business, Kevin. You should understand that. I need an expansion loan for my studios. The bank recommends… Well, let's face it. We both need to get on with our lives."

It's business.

How many times had he said that to her when he couldn't make it home for dinner? When he'd come in so late that he'd plopped into bed beside her and held her tight until they'd fallen asleep? She'd wanted children and Kevin had asked for her patience. His business had come first, but only because he'd wanted to provide a good life for her. He'd made his millions, but she never understood that he'd done it all for her. And how had she showed him her undying love? She'd packed up in the middle of the night and left him. Just like that. After five years of marriage.

Damn her.

"I'm good with that," he said. "When are you coming in?"

"Tomorrow?"

Kevin turned to find all four of his friends silently watching him. "Tomorrow is good. Meet me at the office at five."

Kevin hung up the phone and contemplated his next move. Cara wasn't going to get away with breezing into his life for a day to get her divorce. No, he wouldn't make it so easy for her.

A plan began to formulate in his head and his lips lifted. "Cara's coming to town tomorrow," he said needlessly. "She wants to finalize the divorce."

"I've seen that expression on your face before," Darius said. "What's got you looking so damn smug?"

"Nothing," he replied innocently.

"Like the nothing that nearly got us expelled from UT? Remember when we stole Professor Turner's prized Shakespeare bust from his classroom?" Lance asked, narrowing his eyes. "That kind of nothing?"

Kevin shrugged.

"I don't like it," Lance said. "You looked fit to be tied when she called, and now you're looking like a fat cat who just lapped up a pint of milk."

Kevin only smiled and finished his beer. "I'd better get going."

"I feel for Cara already. That girl won't know what hit her," Darius added.

Kevin walked to the door of the game room, shaking his head. "That *girl* is my *wife*. And she deserves everything she gets."

Darius shot him a warning look. "I always liked Cara."

"Yeah," Kevin said on a deep breath, before exiting the room. "So did I."

As the elevator closed to take Cara up to Kevin's office, she caught sight of herself in the doors' reflective surface. She must have glanced in the mirror a dozen times before leaving her Houston hotel room, making sure she looked just right for her meeting with Kevin. On any given day she wore her curly blond hair pulled back in a clip, but today she let the curls fall to her shoulders freely, glossed her lips with a light berry shade and made sure she wore a soft sapphire dress that accented her figure and her blue eyes.

Because it wasn't any given day.

Today, she'd see her husband for the first time in four years.

And a small part of her wanted him to see what he'd thrown away. She hadn't wilted like a delicate flower when they'd separated. She'd been broken but not beaten by his betrayal of trust. He hadn't cheated on her in the classic way, but he had shattered his vows by abandoning their love.

Cara had grown from that experience. Through her pain, she'd managed to create a successful business in a field she loved. She'd come here for Dancing Lights and that expansion loan she needed from the bank, but she'd also come for her own personal reasons.

She drew oxygen in as she exited the elevator and glanced around Kevin's new office space. He'd certainly come up in the world, from his smaller office on the outskirts of Houston to this impressive space on the tenth floor of a downtown high-rise building.

She walked to the reception desk and waited for the receptionist to finish her phone call.

"May I help you?" she asked.

"Yes, I'm Mrs. Novak. I have an appointment… with my husband."

The young woman's eyebrows shot up, surprise evident on her face. Kevin had replaced a great many things since she'd left and apparently sweet, aging Margie Windmeyer, his loyal secretary, hadn't fit in with the new decor.

Looking baffled, the receptionist paged through her appointment book.

"He's expecting me." Cara's nerves jumped at the edginess in her tone. She wanted to get this over with.

"Yes, Mrs. Novak." The receptionist gave up looking for her name on the books and pointed toward a set of double doors. "Right through there."

Cara nodded and stared at the doors for a second. Then, with her slim briefcase tucked under her arm, she entered the office.

Kevin stood with his back to her, staring out the arched window behind his desk. Both hands tucked into his suit pants, she was treated to a captivating view of his tight backside. His physique hadn't suffered through the years—that much she could determine right away.

As he angled toward her, his profile and the sharp, handsome lines of his face struck her with force. He turned fully around and stared at her, his gorgeous, piercing-blue eyes not giving anything away.

He cast her a half smile. "Cara."

She stood in the middle of the large office, refusing to let her nerves go raw. It was a shock to see him. She couldn't possibly have anticipated this moment—how she'd react to seeing him again. She'd imagined it a hundred times, but nothing compared to the reality. Seeing him brought back bittersweet memories of all they'd had and all they'd lost, which swept through her in a matter of seconds.

She got hold of her bearings and smiled a little. "Hello, Kevin."

Kevin eyed her up and down, the way he used to when he wanted to make love to her. Heat swelled and coursed through her body, a remnant of what they'd once shared coming to light. Suddenly, the enormity of her mission here struck her. She would put an ending note on the last chapter of their marriage.

"You look…well."

Kevin taunted her. "You look *beautiful*."

"Thank you." Cara held on to her defenses, despite the bitter way he offered up the compliment.

"Have a seat, Cara." He gestured and she sat in a brown leather chair facing him.

Cara fidgeted with her briefcase, finally setting it on Kevin's desk. She crossed her legs and tapped her fingers on the arms of the chair.

Kevin's gaze fell to her thighs, where the material of her dress gathered. She refused to squirm under his direct scrutiny. But she wished he'd sit down.

"Are you getting remarried?"

His blunt question surprised her. She shook her head. "No."

He nodded, folding his arms across his rigid body.

"It's just time, Kevin. We need to move on. I'm planning to expand my business and I need to get a large bank loan."

"You don't want my name on anything legal, right?" His eyes narrowed on her.

"You're a businessman," she responded with patience, wondering what happened to the Kevin Novak she'd married. This man seemed so different, so dark and contemptuous. She'd never seen this side of Kevin before. "You know how it works."

"Yeah, I know how it works." His cutting, derisive tone sobered the moment even more.

Kevin finally took a seat behind his desk. He braced his elbows on the chair arms and steepled his fingers. "Don't you find it strange that we're sitting here in my office, speaking formalities?"

"Strange?"

The corner of Kevin's mouth lifted in a wry smile. "Yeah, strange. Considering how we started out. Hot and heavy from the moment we laid eyes on each other."

Cara recalled her college sorority sister's birthday bash, with balloons and loud music and alcohol flowing. She'd taken one look at Kevin and fallen in love instantly. They'd spent the entire night flirting shamelessly. Cara had never been so aware of her own sensuality until that day. She and Kevin had blown off the party. They'd had a party of their own that night.

Heat crawled up her neck at the erotic memory. "That's the past, Kevin."

Kevin let her comment drop. He leaned back in his seat and stared into her eyes. "I understand your dance studios are doing very well."

Cara's heart sped up at his implication. She straightened in her seat and leaned forward a bit. "I'm not here for your money, Kevin." She glanced around the elaborate surroundings. Exquisite Southwest artwork adorned the walls of his very tastefully decorated office. "Though I see you've become a huge success. That was always most important to you."

Cara made her point and leaned back in her seat, content to put a name on the mistress who'd stolen her marriage from her. "I'm only here for your signature."

"And you'll get it," Kevin said.

Oh, boy. That was easy, Cara thought, sighing silently with relief.

"Under one condition. I want something from you, Cara."

So Kevin had terms. She'd be willing to hear him out. She wanted nothing more than to get this whole ordeal over and done with. "I'm willing to do anything, within reason."

Kevin grinned a little too widely. "Considering you abandoned me and our marriage, I think my request is quite reasonable."

Cara went numb. She didn't like the look on her husband's face. "You forced my hand, Kevin. I hung on to our marriage for years, hoping. But you gave me no option—"

"And I'm giving you no option now. If you want your precious divorce," he said, "you'll have to agree to my terms."

Two

Kevin watched Cara's sudden panic when his request finally sank in. Momentarily silenced, Cara blinked rapidly, giving him a chance to really look his wife over.

He hadn't realized what four years of separation had done to him. He'd never met a woman he admired more than Cara, or thought more beautiful or talented. Cara had it all. He'd always thought so, and everything he'd done, he'd done for her. He'd wanted to prove to her and her wealthy family that she'd married well. That he could give her all the things she deserved.

God, how he'd loved her.

Kevin inhaled sharply and Cara's head snapped up. "You can't be serious, Kevin."

"I'm not joking."

Cara stood abruptly and stared straight into his eyes. "No, I don't suppose you have a sense of humor anymore."

He caught a slight whiff of her exotic scent, the same fragrance she'd worn when they'd been truly man and wife. Memories of hot, erotic nights flooded his senses. Of her silky smooth skin against his flesh, her breath against his cheek, her soft, sensual body tucked under his.

He wanted her again. He'd given her no other choice but to accept his demand. He wouldn't let Cara have the last laugh. "On the contrary, babe. I have a great sense of humor, when something is funny. This, however, isn't funny."

"It's ridiculous! You want me to live with you for a week? Why, Kevin?"

Kevin arched his brows, but remained silent.

Her blue eyes sparked like raging fire when she caught on. She shook slightly and pointed her finger. "This is blackmail."

"You owe me for walking out."

Indignant, Cara raised her voice. "You walked out on *us!*"

Kevin's gut tightened. "No, Cara," he said with quiet calm. "I worked hard to give us a good start."

Cara shook her head so hard her blond curls whipped across her face. "No, no, no. I won't let you get away with that. I wanted *you.* I wanted a *family. Children.* You only wanted to amass a fortune. You were never there for me, Kevin."

He shrugged. He'd heard this all before and he'd never agreed with her take on their marriage. He'd asked for one thing from Cara—patience. He'd wanted to give her the world. "So your solution was to run away?"

Cara backed up a step and lowered her voice. "I couldn't do it anymore. I needed more from you."

"And leaving Somerset solved the problem for you." Kevin snapped his fingers. "Just like that, you were gone."

A sharp, stinging pain sliced through his gut. Kevin didn't think Cara had the power to hurt him anymore, but seeing her again brought back all the bitter memories. They'd argued the night before Cara had left and had gone to bed angry with each other, but that was nothing compared to the memory of finding that Cara had slipped out of the house before dawn, leaving only a note in her wake.

"It wasn't as easy as you make it seem." Cara's pretty mouth turned down. She filled her lungs with a fortifying breath and opened her slim attaché case, pulling out the divorce papers. "If you'll forget this nonsense and just sign the papers, you and I…"

"Will be done?"

Cara closed her eyes. "Yes. Please, Kevin. This is difficult enough."

She got that right. It was difficult seeing her again. All the old, hurtful feelings came tumbling back. Her leaving had cut him deep and left him bleeding. He'd hidden his injury from those around him until he'd become numb inside, then bitterness had emerged. He'd spent the next few years resenting Cara Pettigrew and trying to wash away her memory with an occasional one-night stand, women who would never measure up. He'd refused relationships and poured all his energy back into his business.

Kevin shrugged off his pain the way he'd learned to, from years of experience. He stood his ground. "I told you, I want one week with you, Cara. One week at my penthouse. And then I'll sign the divorce papers."

Cara's shoulders slumped. She shoved the papers back into the attaché case and snapped it shut. "I can't do that."

Kevin walked around his desk and approached her. Her eyes gleamed like diamonds and her skin appeared soft as a baby's, but it was her very kissable mouth, tight as it was at the moment, that had him moving in even closer. He'd never gotten over his anger with her, but he'd also never gotten over wanting her. And now that she was here, he wanted one last fling with his wife.

Before he ended their marriage for good.

He touched her wrist and slid his finger tenderly up her arm. Goose bumps broke out on her skin and Kevin felt a moment of satisfaction. "If you want the divorce, you're going to have to pay for it."

Breathless, Cara looked deep into his eyes. "You've changed, Kevin."

"I won't deny it."

Cara moved back a step and Kevin dropped his hand from her arm. She worked the inside of her lower lip in that adorable way that always made him hot for her.

"I'll make you a counteroffer."

Kevin smiled inside. He should have known his feisty wife wouldn't give in without a fight. It was a trait he'd always admired about her. "I'm listening."

"One night. You get one night and that's all."

Initially Kevin balked. One night wasn't nearly enough to exact his payback. He wanted more time with her. His plan was to romance her into falling in love with him again. The ultimate revenge for dumping him would be in his rejection of her. Then he'd sign her divorce papers.

A thought struck and Kevin acted swiftly. "You've got a deal. If and only if you agree that our one night will be two weeks from tonight."

"Two weeks? I can't possibly—"

"That's my offer. You stay in town for two weeks, and in exactly fourteen days you'll have your divorce. Take it or walk away now with those unsigned papers, babe."

Cara narrowed her eyes and crinkled her nose. She mulled it over for a few seconds, then finally gave him her uplifted chin. "Fine. But only because I need that bank loan. You've got me up against a wall."

Her scent drew him closer. She looked so darn beautiful when she was indignant. He arched a brow. "Baby, I've *had* you up against a wall. Remember?"

Recollection replaced the surprise on her face and her features softened with the memory. Kevin wrapped his hands around her slender waist and tugged her against him, his fingers splayed across her backside.

"Kevin," she whispered, before his mouth claimed hers.

Kevin could kiss and Cara fell into him for all she was worth. His expert lips teased and tempted her with little nibbles until sizzling heat built up. She tried a vain attempt to pull away, but Kevin only brought her up tighter, pressing her hips to his with a subtle grind that swept through her system. Her knees buckled, her heart slammed as the frenzied kiss overwhelmed her. She found it hard to breathe. And when she opened her mouth to take in oxygen, Kevin mated their tongues and the tantalizing thrill escalated.

He cupped her head in both hands and kissed her again and again, their breathing labored and intense. In the past, this kind of kiss had meant only one thing—a steamy night under the sheets. Kevin could always turn her inside out…

The sobering thought of his blackmail returned full force.

Damn him. Damn him. Damn him.

She didn't want this. She didn't want to be swayed by memories of hot, mind-blowing sex with her husband. She'd put those thoughts out of her mind, for the most part. She'd come here for a signature and instead got a near-orgasmic experience just from one kiss.

She pushed at his chest and broke off the kiss.

Kevin glanced at her lips, which she was sure were red and swollen, and smiled. "Two weeks is gonna be a long time."

"We could finish it here and now." Cara nearly died of mortification when Kevin noticed her glancing at the top of his uncluttered desk.

"Tempting," Kevin said, his gaze raking her over. "But we made a deal."

"Couldn't we undo that deal, Kevin?" She prayed her plea came through sure and steady, instead of desperate.

Kevin stepped away from her and shook his head. "The way you undid our marriage? No, Cara. This time you're not running away from me. In fact, I want you to have dinner with me tomorrow night. I'll pick you up at seven."

Cara jammed her hands on her hips. Who was this man? Certainly, he wasn't the man she'd fallen in love with and married nine years ago. "You can't issue orders like that to me, Kevin. I'm not at your beck and call."

Chagrined, Kevin scratched his head, acknowledging his mistake. "Sorry," he said. "Guess I'm out of practice wining and dining a lady."

His confession touched something deep in her heart. Furious with him as she was, it was nice to know that behind all his anger there was a glimmer of the man she'd once known. And to know that Kevin was out of practice with women instilled great comfort within her.

Kevin made a point of clearing his throat and beginning anew. "Cara, I'd like for you to join me for dinner tomorrow night. We have a lot to catch up on. And I could use your advice about something."

Curious, Cara raised her brows. "My advice?"

"Yes, you always had a level head and you know the parties involved. I want to run something by you. Will you join me for dinner?"

After raising her curiosity level a notch, Cara could hardly refuse. "Yes, okay. I'll have dinner with you. I'm staying at the Four Seasons."

Kevin nodded. "I'll pick you up at seven." He moved to his desk to retrieve her attaché, and without pause laid a hand to her back and walked her to the door. Handing her the briefcase, he looked into her eyes. "I'm looking forward to seeing you tomorrow night, Cara."

Cara nodded, biting her lip to keep from making a snarky retort like, *You're blackmailing me into this. What choice do I have?*

But in fact she did have a choice. She could've made up an excuse not to have dinner with him. Maybe that would have been the wiser move. Yet Cara had been curious, not only about the advice Kevin wanted, but to learn what had become of her friends in Somerset.

After leaving him, she'd lost touch with so many

people and she'd always regretted that. Maybe it was time to renew those friendships while she was here.

Cara bounded out of Kevin's office with a bounce in her step. This wasn't how she'd envisioned her encounter going—especially succumbing to Kevin's kiss the way that she had—but her goals were in sight.

And that was all that mattered to her.

Cara walked the distance to her hotel, willing to trudge the ten blocks in high heels rather than hailing a cab. It was a good way to cool off from Kevin's melt-your-heart kiss and his blatant blackmail. She didn't know which of the two disturbed her more.

She'd had little power over Kevin's kiss. From day one, she'd never been able to resist him. That's why she'd stolen off in the middle of the night four years ago, fearing that if she'd told him her plans he'd convince her to stay. He'd make his argument, as he had so many other times, and kiss her into oblivion.

But she'd thwarted his blackmail attempt. Somewhat. She could take some satisfaction in that. He'd wanted a week with her when it was clear their marriage was over, and she'd offered him *one* night. Some might not think it a victory, but Cara knew how determined Kevin was and his compromise certainly meant a win, small as it might be.

Cara clutched her briefcase and thought of the divorce papers inside. Soon, she'd have the independence she needed to expand her business without relying on her mother's money, which she'd managed to do so far. Since leaving Kevin, she'd looked forward to being her own woman and was proud of her accomplishments. Everything she'd achieved, she'd done on her own. Though her mother had offered to fund her dance studios, Cara wanted to make it on her own. So Cara viewed negotiating with Kevin to get him to sign the divorce papers as a business proposition—a means to achieving her goal.

"Soon, Cara-Bella," she whispered, smiling at the nickname her dance instructors had bestowed upon her, claiming she danced like a princess.

Soon, you'll have what you came here for.

As she moved along the sidewalk, taking in the sights and sounds of downtown Houston, gradually her steps slowed to a stroll. She calmed herself by window-shopping, glancing at the familiar storefronts, noting which had revamped their exteriors and which had gone out of business, replaced by newer, more upbeat trendy shops.

People moved along the sidewalks at a quick pace, but that didn't stop her from spotting Alicia Montoya across the street, bogged down with several shopping bags. She waved, trying to get her attention. "Alicia!"

Alicia swiveled her head and saw her. Surprised, she smiled and waved back, then gestured toward the street corner. Cara met her there after crossing the street.

"Cara, it's so good to see you!" She gave her a double-armed, shopping-bag hug.

Cara chuckled and knew the first moment of actual joy since coming to Houston. She hugged her back. "Alicia, I'm happy to see you, too. It's been years."

She and Alicia had become friends in her first years of marriage with Kevin, despite her brother's objections. Alex Montoya didn't want his family involved with any friends of either Lance or Mitch Brody. Both those men had been close to Kevin since their college days, along with Justin Dupree and Darius Franklin. Alex's extreme hatred carried over to anyone involved with the five men of the Texas Cattleman's Club.

"Yes, it has been. I wish we had stayed in touch," Alicia said quietly.

"I'm really sorry about that, Alicia. I went through a hard time. Leaving my home and everything I knew…wasn't easy. I needed to make a clean break."

Alicia's chocolate-brown eyes softened. "I understand. But you're here now."

"Yes, I'm here for two weeks. I'd actually planned on calling you, so I'm doubly glad I spotted you. Looks like you bought out the store."

Alicia glanced down at the shopping bags she held. "I know, I went a little crazy. I don't shop much, so I had some making up to do. Where are you staying?"

"In a hotel just down the street. Do you think we can get together while I'm here?"

"I was just going to suggest that. We can meet in Somerset for lunch."

"Sounds great." Cara handed Alicia her business card. "Here's my cell number. I'm looking forward to it."

Alicia smiled when she read the card designed with two dancing figures silhouetted by twinkling lights. "Dancing Lights. I like it, Cara. I'd heard you opened a dance studio."

Cara shrugged. "All my gymnastics and cheer-leading really paid off, I guess. We teach all kinds of dance at the studio. It keeps me out of trouble."

Thoughtful, Alicia glanced at the card again. "I'll call you at the end of the week. I have to meet Ale-jandro now. He's expecting me."

Cara nodded. She couldn't send a greeting to Alicia's brother. Not when he'd tried to break up her friendship with Alicia, simply because she'd married Kevin. Guilt by association didn't sit well with her.

"Okay, I'll see you soon. I'm really looking for-ward to it." The sentiment held true—Cara wanted to renew friendships she'd allowed to dissolve when she'd left town. Alicia was a sweetheart and had lent a compassionate ear to Cara when her marriage had fallen apart. She'd love to get acquainted with her again.

Cara stopped in the food court of the Galleria and picked up an Asian salad for dinner before heading to her hotel. When she entered her room, she kicked off her shoes and sat down on the bed, exhausted from the turmoil of the day.

Not two minutes later, a knock came at her door.

She groaned and lifted herself off the bed. "Yes," she said, opening the door to a hotel employee.

"Mrs. Novak? This came for you. Special delivery."

An "ohh" escaped from Cara before she realized it. The young man handed her a dozen black calla lilies and lavender orchids, beautifully arranged in a vase.

"Thank you," she said and gave him a tip before closing the door. Admiring the lilies, she set them down on the dresser and plucked the card out.

She read the note. "I didn't forget your favorite." Tears stung her eyes for a second. She knew the exotic flowers were from Kevin. Cara had a thing for the unique-colored lilies and it had been the one extravagance she'd requested for their wedding.

Emotion stirred in her stomach and she flopped onto the bed. Staring at the ceiling, her throat constricted and she whispered in the silence of the room, "You didn't forget, did you, Kevin."

Kevin sank the putt and eagled the eighteenth hole, then pumped his fist once, twice, in a fair imitation of Tiger Woods. The TCC's golf course wasn't exactly a tournament course but Kevin was too happy with the turn of events lately to give a damn. He liked winning.

"Lucky shot," Lance muttered with mocking disgust.

"Lucky, my ass. That's pure skill, Brody. That makes five wins to your two, this month."

"I had you beat until those last three holes," Lance

grumbled. "It's as if you can't wait to get off the course today."

At the reminder of time, Kevin glanced at his watch. He had to stop by his office, change and get ready to pick up Cara.

"Got a hot date or something, Kev?" Lance's mouth curled into a smirk.

Kevin set his putter into his golf bag. "I'm seeing Cara tonight."

Lance whistled low and long. "Is there an inkling of hope for you two?"

Kevin glanced at Lance. "Not even a chance."

Lance blinked. "You're saying that you're over her?"

Kevin gritted his teeth. Damn right, he was over her. No matter that seeing her yesterday had reminded him of good times they'd shared or that he looked forward to seeing her again tonight. "Yeah, I'm over her."

"But you're taking her out tonight, right?"

"Yeah, I'm taking her out."

"Hey, just tell me to butt out, buddy. But I saw the look on your face yesterday when she called. You were hopping mad. And anger means you still care. And it also means that you're up to something. I know you, Kevin."

"I'm having one last fling with my wife before I sign the divorce papers," Kevin said in his own defense. "There's no crime in that."

"Unless you have an ulterior motive."

Kevin shrugged. "She'll be here for a couple of weeks." Thanks to his blackmail.

After stowing their bags on the back end of the golf cart, he and Lance settled in the seats, Kevin taking the driver's side.

"So you plan on dating her, and then what?" Lance wouldn't give up.

Kevin stared at him thoughtfully and exhaled. Every one of his friends knew how much Cara had hurt him when she'd left. Though Kevin wouldn't openly admit his plan to anyone, it wouldn't be hard for any one of his friends to put two and two together.

"You're going to win her back and dump her, aren't you?" Lance said, his face twisting in disbelief. When Kevin didn't deny it, Lance shook his head. "Oh, man. Kev, if you have a second chance with someone special, take it. Don't blow it, the way I almost did with Kate."

Kevin tossed Lance's words back at him. "This is the part where I say, butt out, buddy."

He didn't need a lecture. Ever since Lance had married Kate, he seemed to want everyone else to follow suit. Only Kevin wasn't shopping for happily-ever-after anymore. He just wanted a little payback for all the heartache and humiliation Cara had caused him.

"Okay, fine," Lance said. "But don't say I didn't warn you."

Later that day, Kevin went to the office to look over some contracts before sending them to his legal department. He wanted a clear head when he picked up Cara. One of the things he'd learned over the past four years was to surround himself with employees he trusted, and delegate the work. He found that freed up more of his time for pleasurable endeavors, which lately amounted to a round of golf or a game of pool with his buddies.

Anticipation stirred his blood. Cara posed a greater challenge than beating Darius in pool or Lance at golf. And, hell, he had to face facts—he was looking forward to spending his nights with her again.

Just like old times, a voice in his head said.

Kevin left the office at five, drove to his apartment, showered, shaved and checked on the arrangements he'd made for his first date with Cara.

He arrived at her hotel room a little early and knocked on the door.

"Just a minute," she called from inside.

Kevin smiled just hearing the lilt of her sassy voice.

She opened the door wide and whispered, out of breath, "You're early."

She fixed a silver hoop earring to her lobe, looking a little flustered but beautiful all the same in a black silky dress that showed off her long, shapely dancer's legs. Her hair curled past her shoulders and was held up on one side by a crystal clip.

"You look gorgeous, Cara." He stepped into the room.

Cara looked him up and down, surprise registering on her face. And before she could comment on *his* attire, he shook his head and added, "It's a shame you're going to have to take off all your clothes."

Three

Dressed in jeans and wearing leather boots Kevin had provided, Cara sat upon Dream Catcher, the five-year-old mare who had been born at TCC's stables when Cara had been living with Kevin. Though she had grown up with horses on her parents' estate, Cara had forgotten how much she loved riding. She and Kevin had taken an occasional ride in their early years of marriage, before he'd been too obsessed with work to take the time.

The day Dream Catcher was born, Cara had rushed to the stables and the moment she'd seen the feisty little filly, she'd fallen a little bit in love. To sit upon the sweet mare and ride off into the hills of Maverick County with Kevin seemed almost like a dream.

The Texas sun lowered on the horizon and cast hues of orange-gold over the valley as they rode in silence. There was a quiet settle to the land, a peace like nothing Cara had experienced for a long time. She'd been so caught up in the fast pace of Dallas that she'd forgotten what it was like to be with nature. Kevin seemed to understand that, setting the slow pace and enjoying the scenery. There was an odd sense of comfort being here with him. She could almost forget his blackmail and his manipulation.

Almost.

She slid a glance his way and let go a little sigh. Looking just as comfortable atop a horse as he was cutting a deal in his downtown office, Kevin acclimated well. Dressed in solid Wranglers, a blue plaid shirt and black Stetson, her husband dressed down *very* nicely.

"You're staring at me," he said with a grin.

"Oh, you'd like to think so." Caught, Cara averted her gaze, hiding her own grin.

"I know so. See anything you like?"

Cara sobered at his question. "I don't know, Kevin. Do I?"

Kevin clucked his jaw a few times. "You need to lighten up, Cara. Enjoy the scenery."

"And you think you're part of that scenery?"

"Me?" he said, lowering the brim of his hat. "No, ma'am. I wouldn't presume."

Cara chuckled. Okay, maybe she should just lighten up. She didn't like Kevin's blackmail, but she could enjoy the ride. If for no other reason than that she was atop Dream Catcher on a glorious, late-summer evening.

"I see a whole lot I like," Kevin said quietly, after a minute.

Cara sensed his gaze on her, and a burning heat crawled up her neck. She didn't dare look at him. A lump formed in her throat. She didn't trust herself to respond.

They rode in silence until the dirt path led them to a rise. "Wait here," Kevin said mysteriously, and clicked his mare into a trot. He rode on about ten yards to the peak of the rise, then turned toward her. "Okay, come on up." He gestured with a wave.

Dream Catcher followed the path in a trot, until Cara met Kevin at the top of the rise. Looking into his eyes first, then following the direction of his gaze, Cara gasped at the view below. "Oh, Kevin. This is amazing."

A small, well-kept cottage on the TCC property was lit outside by at least a hundred pillar candles. A table, dressed in white linen, was set with fine china, crystal wineglasses and lilies of every variety.

"It's beautiful." Tears stung her eyes. Why couldn't he have done something like this years ago when their marriage was shaky, when she needed attention, when she needed to know she was more important than his business? *Oh, Kevin,* she thought, *why are you doing this now, when it's too late?* The question plagued her, but she pushed it out of her mind.

Lighten up, Cara. This is temporary.

"I'm glad you like it." Kevin pushed his horse on, and Dream Catcher followed him down the other side of the rise. When they reached the cottage, Kevin dismounted. He walked over to Cara and reached for her. She slid down the left side of the horse into Kevin's arms. He held her, their gazes entwined, as luminous candles lit the background.

"You were always gorgeous in candlelight, babe."

Cara smiled, the compliment warming her heart.

Kevin tilted his head, the brim of his Stetson grazing her forehead. She braced herself for the kiss, tightening up inside in anticipation.

Kevin brushed his lips over hers in the lightest feather-touch of a kiss, then backed away. Cara blinked, a little surprised.

He took her hand. "Have a seat." He guided her to the table and pulled out a chair for her. "I'll see to the horses."

She watched him take the reins of both horses and go behind the cottage. When he returned and sat down, a chef appeared at the table wearing a white coat and tall hat, a waiter standing just behind him. "I hope you enjoy the meal Mr. and Mrs. Novak," the chef said.

"I'm sure we will," Kevin returned, with a nod.

Cara sat quietly while the waiter served their first course, a little pastry puff filled with light cheese and raspberries. She took her first bite and closed her eyes. "Oh…this is heaven."

When she opened her eyes, Kevin's gaze was on her, watching her enjoy the pastry with a gleam in his eyes. "The chef came highly recommended."

Cara was again tempted to ask, why was he going to so much trouble? But she'd already decided that she would just go with the flow and see where that would take her, so she remained silent on the subject. "I can see why. He's already got my vote for Chef of the Year."

Kevin poured them each a glass of wine.

"You said something about needing my advice?" Cara sipped her wine and the smooth liquid warmed her inside. "But you haven't said a word about it yet."

Kevin lifted his glass to his lips and sipped. "It's not a pleasant subject, Cara. I hate to spoil the night, but yes, I do have something I'd like to tell you. It's regarding Alex Montoya and the recent fire at Brody Oil and Gas. I think it was set deliberately."

"You think Alex did it?" Cara's voice elevated with disbelief. Sure, the Brody brothers had issues with Alex, and vice versa, from their teen years, but Cara never thought Alejandro Montoya capable of something as criminal as arson.

"I do, Cara. I'd like your opinion about this. Hear me out."

Kevin gave a detailed description of what had transpired between Lance, Mitch and Alex through the years, and then added a final note about how Alex had managed to hamper his newest revitalization development. He explained how Alex had helped back a faction that had that particular area in Somerset declared historic, thus killing the project. "I have no proof regarding the fire, but you know everyone involved. What do you think?"

Cara shook her head. She thought about the accidental meeting she'd had with Alicia just yesterday. Alicia would be devastated if her brother was involved with the fire in any way. "My gut instincts tell me Alex wouldn't do anything so drastic. It's not his style, Kevin. Yes, I can see him behind the scenes, working to preserve the Somerset area. He may have even done that to spite you, but that's not a criminal act."

"No, it just caused me a major headache and financial losses."

"You may not agree with me," she said with a shake of her head, "but I don't think Alex had anything to do with the refinery fire."

"Okay, noted. You and Darius are the only ones. Lance, Mitch, Justin and I all think he's behind it."

Cara sipped her wine. "Maybe you're not being objective. Maybe you want to blame Alex. Maybe you're so pissed at him, you want him to be guilty." Kevin winced and Cara continued. "Revenge can be sweet, isn't that what you always said?"

"No, I never said that."

Cara blinked and leaned forward. "Oh, sorry, that must have been the *other* husband I married nine years ago."

"Must have been." With a smug look, Kevin lifted his glass and finished off his wine. He poured himself another glass as the waiter cleared their dishes and brought the next course.

"So, is that all you wanted to ask me?" Cara dived into her asparagus salad, her appetite flaring to life.

"Yes."

"Are you sorry you asked for my opinion?"

"No." Kevin spoke with an earnest tone. "I always valued your opinion. That hasn't changed."

Cara sat back in her seat and stared into Kevin's eyes. "You can be so charming—when you want to be."

"I want to be. Right now. With you."

Why? Cara didn't understand it, but the voice in her head told her to go with it and enjoy these last few days with Kevin. Soon enough, their marriage would be over.

When they finished all four courses of the main meal, Kevin suggested they go inside the cottage for coffee and dessert. "The chef made us something special."

"I should be full, but I can always fit in dessert," Cara said, feeling the zipper of her jeans expanding a bit. She was slender and, at five foot eight, she could afford to eat a decadent dessert once in a while.

Kevin stood and reached for her hand. With fingers entwined, they entered the cottage, climbing the steps, their boots scraping the wooden floors. Cara made a quick tour of the quaint cottage, noting the rustic stone fireplace, cozy chintz sofa and several swag-draped pane windows. "It's lovely here."

"It was the groundskeeper's home at one time. TCC let it go to ruin, practically. I renovated it and now it's available—"

"For impressing your dates?" she blurted, in a teasing tone.

Kevin whipped around and grabbed her by the waist, bringing her flush up against him. "You have a mouth on you, don't you?"

Cara pulled her head back to look at him fully. "You always liked my sassy mouth."

Kevin's gaze devoured her mouth. He cupped her head with one hand and pulled her close, his lips so near. "I still do."

Cara's heart pumped double time when he kissed her. He tasted of robust wine and warmth. He tasted familiar and fine. He tasted of all the sweet things in her life she missed. "Kevin."

"I love it when you whimper my name," he said between kisses.

"I didn't whimper," Cara protested mildly. Kevin cupped her derriere and tugged her in. Hip jamming hip, she felt his desire, rough against rough as their jeans brushed.

Kevin nibbled on her throat. "Really? Guess I'm gonna have to do something about that."

There were times when Kevin hated his methodical mind and this was one of them. Every instinct he possessed told him to seduce Cara, here and now, and take advantage of the remote, romantic cottage setting. But Kevin had a plan in mind, and the culmination of that plan had to happen later rather than sooner.

He'd kick himself tomorrow for his damnable obstinate nature and pay the price of losing out on a wild night of sex with his wife. Yet all wasn't lost. He needed more from Cara tonight and he'd take what little his plan allowed.

He nipped at Cara's lips over and over, sweeping his tongue through her mouth with frenzied heat. A little tiny moan escaped her throat that sent Kevin's straining erection into overdrive.

With an effort that took all of his will, he pulled away from her to look deep into her eyes. Her hazy-blue surrender unnerved him.

He needed to touch her and feel the softness of her skin, caress the firm mounds of her perfect breasts. Nothing was going to stop him, his plan be damned.

"Baby," he murmured, licking the soft center of her throat. "Let me touch you."

She trembled and whimpered helplessly.

Kevin kissed his way down to the first button of her blouse. With nimble fingers, he undid that button, then the next and the next. Her breasts, cupped in white cotton, spilled out, an invitation he couldn't ignore.

He palmed her breasts and closed his eyes, relishing the remembered feel of her, the way she fit so completely in his hand. His thumbs simultaneously caressed both erect tips, her nipples straining against her bra, until Kevin freed them from the torture.

"Ohh," she moaned, leaning closer to him with a need he knew he couldn't satisfy tonight.

"You feel as good as you look, baby. As good as I remember," he murmured.

Kevin bent his head and kissed the tips of her breasts, first one, then the other. Always responsive to his touch, she arched back and Kevin drew her deep into his mouth, suckling and teasing the rosy buds with his tongue.

He wanted to take her here and now, to ease the desire straining against his jeans, to begin to rectify four years of wanting her, despite his anger. It was hard to back off, to pull away from what she offered and what he wanted, but Kevin was determined to see his plan through.

"Did you hear that?" he asked quietly.

Breathlessly, she replied, "You mean the pounding of my heart?"

Kevin smiled and kissed her lips. "No, outside. Something spooked the horses. I'll go check."

Cara appeared a little surprised by his quick dismissal. He turned and walked out the front door. Behind the house, the horses calmly waited. Kevin leaned against the cottage wall, beside a hibiscus vine in full yellow bloom, and shut his eyes. "Harder than I thought," he whispered.

He waited just a few moments, until his breathing slowed and his internal thermostat cooled down. Then he untied the reins of both horses and guided them toward the front of the cottage. Cara waited on the porch steps. "False alarm," he said. "Must have just been a coyote howl off in the distance."

Thankfully, Cara had buttoned her blouse and straightened her unruly, honey-blond hair. He only had so much willpower where his wife was concerned. He tilted his head and sighed, without falsity. "We should go. It's getting late."

Cara blinked a few times, then nodded. "Of course."

Kevin helped Cara onto Dream Catcher and then bounded up onto his horse. They headed to the TCC stables in silence. Once they were safely back at the entrance, Kevin glanced at Cara. "We never had dessert."

Cara broke her silence with an acknowledging light in her eyes. "We'll have to lie to the chef and tell him it was fabulous."

He dismounted, then reached for her and, once again, she slid down the horse and into his arms. Kevin stared deep into her eyes, holding her loosely around the waist. "It *was* fabulous."

Cara searched his eyes. She had questions, but Kevin had only one answer. He kissed her soundly on the lips, tasting her once again. "Have dinner with me tomorrow night. I'll make up for the dessert we missed."

"How can you do that? I'm sure the chef is on to bigger and better things."

He chuckled, knowing Cara was messing with him. "Easy. I know what you crave."

Cara jammed her hands to her hips and shook her head in denial. "I bet you don't."

"Oh, no? Hot fudge over chocolate cake with vanilla ice cream and a dozen cherries."

"Tasty's?" Cara's smug expression changed to one of longing. "I haven't had Tasty's for—"

"Four and a half years? I took you there for your birthday, remember?"

A thoughtful look crossed her expression and she smiled sadly. "Yeah, I do remember."

"So, how about it? Burgers and dessert at Tasty's tomorrow night?"

Cara opened her mouth, then clamped it closed with a quick snap. He could always tell when she waged a war of decision in her mind.

"Don't overthink it, babe. Just go with it."

The comment opened her eyes wide and she made a quick decision. "Okay. But, Kevin," she began in a solemn tone, "maybe we shouldn't get in over our heads. We both know why I came to Somerset."

"Oh, don't worry. I haven't forgotten."

"G-good."

"But I'm not making any promises."

Cara's mouth tightened into a frown.

Kevin planted a brief kiss over her down-turned lips. "Come on, I'll drive you back to the hotel. You can think about Tasty's all the way home."

* * *

Cara didn't think about Tasty's all the way back to her hotel. She thought about Kevin. He'd touched her in ways she hadn't allowed another man since they'd split up. Sensual images flashed vividly in her head. Her body still prickled. Nope, no man since had even made her feel like trying. Oh, she'd dated at times, but nothing had ever come of it.

Kevin had been sweet and attentive all night and just minutes ago he'd nearly made her forget her own name.

It's Cara Pettigrew, she thought sourly. Not Cara Pettigrew-Novak.

She was still his wife, but in name only. She had stopped being a Novak four years ago.

Cara slipped out of her riding clothes, tugging off the new leather boots Kevin had given her. He'd remembered her shoe size, she realized. How many men would even know their wife's shoe size?

"Remember why you left him," Cara whispered in the quiet of her room. He'd been fun and loving for the first few months of their marriage and then he'd become obsessive and driven. For success? For money? For power? Cara wasn't sure of his motivation, since he'd made a decent living and she'd never complained. She hadn't asked for riches. She'd grown up wealthy. She'd seen how her own father had been driven and how much his obsession had hurt his marriage—and her. She'd been the daughter her father never had time for.

"Money doesn't guarantee happiness," she'd tell

Kevin. But her husband hadn't listened. His competitive nature made him want to prove his worth to Cara and her family. He wanted to measure up, she presumed, though she'd never once implied that he wasn't enough for her.

When the hotel phone rang, Cara was grateful for the interruption of her thoughts.

"Oh, hi, Mom."

Perhaps *grateful* was too strong a word. Her mom had been like a watchdog lately and she was the last person Cara wanted to speak with about Kevin. Especially after what had happened between them tonight. Ever since Cara had made her decision to divorce Kevin, her mother had been *overly* supportive.

"Did he sign the papers yet?"

Cara flinched. Her mother got right to the point. She couldn't possibly tell her mother the truth, that she'd been blackmailed into sleeping with her estranged husband before he'd sign on the dotted line. "No, Mom. Not yet. But we had a…meeting tonight. Kevin is cooperating."

"But, dear, I don't see why there's a problem. You're not asking for much. Actually, you're being quite fair with the settlement. What's the holdup?"

What was the holdup? She didn't know what purpose it served to hang around Somerset for two weeks, but she had to tell her mother something. "Well, Kevin is really busy."

"He hasn't changed," her mother chimed in bitterly. "Just like your father."

Cara swallowed that and continued, "Mom, you know I liked living in Somerset. I'm catching up with friends while I'm here. Taking a little vacation."

"Dear, a vacation is relaxing in a villa in Siena, not begging for signed divorce papers from your husband. I'm worried about you, Cara. You've done so well for yourself in Dallas."

"I was happy here, too, once upon a time."

Her mother's silence was quite telling. She couldn't blame her for being protective. Cara had been hurt by the separation. She'd really loved Kevin, and no mother wants to see her child in pain. Cara understood all that.

"I know, dear, that's why ending it quickly is better for you. It's been dragged out long enough."

"I agree with you, Mom. And I'll get back to Dallas as soon as I can."

"Well, all right. I hope to see you home soon. I love you, dear."

"Love you, too."

Cara hung up the phone and took a long pull of oxygen, thankful the conversation hadn't lasted too long.

When the phone rang again, Cara let it ring four times. She was through talking for the day. All she wanted to do was climb into bed and get to sleep.

But her curiosity got the better of her. She picked

up the receiver, hoping it wasn't her mother on the other end with more pearls of wisdom.

"Hello?"

"Hi, baby." The deep timbre of Kevin's voice oozed through the phone line. "What are you doing?"

"I'm getting out of my…uh, getting ready for bed."

"Yeah? Me, too. I just got out of the shower."

The visual image of Kevin's hard-ripped body wet from head to toe and wrapped in a skimpy towel swept through her mind. She mouthed a silent *oh,* thankful that the word didn't slip out accidentally.

She cleared her throat.

"What do you wear to bed these days?" Kevin asked.

The question was so audacious, Cara laughed. "Wouldn't you like to know?"

"I would, Cara," he said with quiet sincerity.

"Nothing."

Kevin let go a sexy groan.

"Much. Nothing much. I mean, just an old Dancing Lights T-shirt."

"I can picture you wearing that."

"Kevin, why are you calling so late?"

"Had a good time tonight, Cara. Just wanted you to know."

Cara nibbled on her lower lip. She squeezed her eyes shut, yet couldn't shake off images from tonight of Kevin's lips on hers, his mouth making love to her breasts, the tantalizing look of pure lust in his deep-blue eyes when he'd taken off her blouse. "Thank you." She paused, then added, "It was a good night. I enjoyed riding Dream Catcher."

"I thought you might."

"Why are you being so sweet to me?" Cara blurted. She couldn't figure out his motivation. "Our marriage is ending."

Kevin didn't miss a beat. "Yes, but there's no reason we can't be friends, Cara. No reason we can't end this on a happy note."

"Marriages usually don't end on happy notes, sweetheart."

He paused, and she realized she'd used his favorite endearment. "Ours could. We can be different from everyone else. So, are you picturing me dripping wet in my towel or what?"

Cara gasped and then laughed aloud. He'd caught her, but she'd rather die than admit it. "I see you haven't lost your sense of humor after all, Kevin."

"I've lost a lot of things, Cara." His playful mood suddenly changed. "But not my sense of humor."

Cara didn't want to deal with the serious tone of his voice now. Sudden panic developed and she searched for an escape. "Kevin, I'd better get to bed."

"Yeah, me, too. Sleep tight, babe. Dream good dreams."

Cara nearly choked out a quick good-night. She knew what would fill her dreams tonight.

Good or bad, they'd be of Kevin.

Wearing nothing but a small towel.

* * *

The next day the image of Kevin stayed with her all morning long. Restless from those thoughts, Cara left the Four Seasons and walked the Houston streets, stopping in at boutiques along the way— she was bored with the few changes of clothes she'd brought for a trip she had thought would only take two days.

She'd told her mother she'd be taking a little vacation and, though she'd had to rearrange her entire schedule to stay on in Houston, Cara decided, a shopping spree would do her good. Why not enjoy the city while she was here?

By the end of the day, she'd filled two shopping bags with gifts for her dance instructors, a Gucci French flap wallet for her mother and several new outfits for herself, including a scarlet dress to match the new Valentino slingbacks she'd purchased.

The time had flown by. She had just enough time to rush back to the hotel and shower before Kevin came knocking.

It bothered her that she'd changed her clothes three times before her date with him for burgers at Tasty's. Why was she trying to look pretty for Kevin?

But the minute she opened the door and saw the glint of appreciation in his eyes, she thought it was all worth it.

"Wow, you look great. Too good for Tasty's." Kevin toured her body up and down leisurely, and Cara knew a moment of satisfaction.

She'd tried on the dresses she'd picked up today, but decided instead on a pair of formfitting, black pants, very high black heels and a white, flowing, off-the-shoulder blouse belted at the waist with a gold-and-black twist rope. "Stop right there if you think you're gonna weasel your way out of taking me to Tasty's."

"Okay," Kevin said with a teasing twist of his lips. "If I have to. Are you ready to go or do you want to invite me in?"

He peeked over her shoulder and into her hotel room. His gaze focused on her king-size bed. Cara wasn't about to let him in. Her husband was a dangerous man and she'd never been able to resist him when he smiled and spoke with charm.

Kevin still had a perfect body, broad of shoulder and slightly muscular, enough to show his strength without overkill. Four years hadn't changed that. His grooming was impeccable, and darn if he didn't look like he belonged on the cover of *GQ*.

Right now, his blue eyes gleamed with the kind of mischief that could get them both into deep trouble. She shoved at his chest lightly and pushed him out the door. "I'm ready for a burger."

Kevin took her hand from his chest and entwined their fingers. He leaned over to whisper in her ear. "And I'm ready for dessert. It's been a long time, Cara. I need to satisfy my craving."

Four

Kevin helped Cara into his jet-black Jaguar, and then got in and started the engine. His Jag roared to life. All that power at his fingertips at one time had been a big turn-on. But now, Kevin looked across the seat to find his wife sitting beside him and he couldn't think of a bigger turn-on. Cara, dressed for a casual date with him in her classy style, took his breath away.

He gritted his teeth with determination. He wasn't going to make it easy for her to walk away from their marriage. Damn her, anyway. She'd been the primary reason he'd worked sixteen hours a day. She'd come from wealth, and his pride wouldn't allow her to climb down that ladder to marry someone who couldn't provide her the same sort of elevated life-style.

The success he'd achieved had been for her and for their marriage. But her patience had run out and she'd followed suit. He'd never forgive her for leaving him high and dry. The humiliation he'd suffered alone was reason enough for this retaliation. But it was more than that. He'd loved Cara. Really loved her. And she'd destroyed that love.

Cara glanced his way with a quizzical look. "You're quiet."

"It's been a long day."

Kevin snapped on the CD player and smiled. "Oldies, to get us in the mood."

Elvis came on and Cara turned up the volume to "All Shook Up." She knew all the words and sang along with the music. Her toes tapped in rhythm and she swayed her body back and forth. Graceful and elegant, Cara knew how to move.

He'd been resentful when he'd learned about her success with Dancing Lights, somehow seeing the studio as his competition. She'd moved from him to bigger things. Yet, from a purely professional stand-point, he secretly admired her acumen. She hadn't used her family's money for the start-up of her enterprise, but instead had taken out small-business bank loans to fund the studios. Now she was willing to end their marriage to expand her business.

Kevin pushed those bitter thoughts out of his mind. He was on a mission and couldn't forget his game plan.

By the time they reached Tasty's, his spirits had lifted and he grabbed Cara's hand as they bounded up the steps to the fifties diner. They sat in a red-vinyl corner booth and ordered cherry Cokes and Tasty Burgers.

The dated chrome jukebox stood in the opposite corner next to the long Formica lunch counter, and mini-jukeboxes anchored each booth. "Pick some songs," Kevin said as he put two quarters in.

They both leaned in close to view the playlist. "Oh, look. They have one-hit wonders! 'Pretty Little Angel Eyes' was one of my favorites." Cara punched in its number, along with a few other obscure songs from the past.

"What do you suppose happened to these artists?" she asked, her expression thoughtful.

He shrugged. "They tried and failed. They probably went on to lead productive lives in some other field."

Cara nodded. "One would hope. It'd be a shame not to do what you love to do, though."

"Most people don't, Cara. Most don't enjoy the work they do. They simply have to do it to survive."

Cara's sky-blue eyes softened. "I feel extremely lucky that I found something I love to do."

Kevin searched her expression for any sign of regret and found none. It irked him that she could dismiss their marriage so easily. "You were always good at everything you attempted."

"Thank you," she said. She sent him a smile that flattened quickly.

"What's wrong?" Kevin asked, curious about her change of expression.

She shook her head and looked down at the tabletop. "Nothing."

"Something," he prodded.

She lifted her shoulders. "It's just that, at times, I think I failed as…a wife."

Floored by her admission, Kevin furrowed his brow. "Why?"

Emotions surfaced on her face and her eyes narrowed with pain. "I don't know. Maybe because nothing I said or did kept you at home."

Kevin leaned way back in his seat and studied her.

She continued. "My mother had the same issue with my dad. He was never home. Always working, until the day he died. You know he died of a heart attack. Fell facedown on his desk at the office." Cara looked up for a second, holding back tears. "My mother said he died doing what he loved best."

Anger bubbled in his gut. Cara had it all wrong if she was comparing her father to him. Their situations were entirely different. Cara's father had had more wealth than he knew what to do with, while Kevin had had nothing and worked hard to bring their life up to a certain standard of living. He'd been determined to make his first million by age twenty-five.

For Cara.

Always for Cara.

"You think I didn't love you enough?" Kevin asked. "That I wasn't home because I wasn't…

what? Happy with you? Or because I found you lacking in some way?"

Cara shrugged. "It doesn't matter now, Kevin."

They'd had this argument before, but never with so much raw honesty. "I say it does—"

"Hey, Novak." Lance walked in with Darius and both strode to their table. Kevin winced. He needed them here like a hole in the head.

Lance ignored Kevin and nearly lifted Cara out of her seat to give her a bear hug. "My God, you look great! It's good to see you, Cara."

"Same here, Lance."

Darius moved in and gave Cara a hug, too, his low, easy voice greeting her. "You have brightened my day, woman."

"Hi, Darius. How have you been?"

"I've got no complaints."

Cara beamed seeing the two and, without invitation, both Lance and Darius took a seat, cramming Cara and Kevin into the booth. Kevin sat back and listened as Cara and his friends caught up on their lives.

The interruption actually was more beneficial than he'd originally thought, since it had lifted Cara's mood. They'd gotten way off course with the discussion earlier and Kevin fully intended on charming his wife tonight. He'd been thinking about seeing her all day. And if nothing else, he could rely on a sinfully erotic chocolate dessert to get her in a risky frame of mind.

* * *

Cara had indulged herself fully, devouring obscene, hot-fudge cake while enjoying Kevin and his friends. She'd missed their friendship and remembered how much fun they'd all had in college. At the time, Kevin was the only one of the three men in a serious relationship. Now, the opposite was true. Lance had Kate, and Darius had Summer, while she and Kevin teetered on the edge of a divorce.

"They haven't changed much." Cara smiled, feeling melancholy on the drive back to her hotel.

"Those clowns? They'll never change." Kevin grinned.

When he stopped at a red light, he glanced at her, then leaned over to wipe a smudge of hot fudge from her bottom lip. "You're messy."

"Am not."

Kevin licked the hot fudge from his thumb, making Cara squirm a little in her seat. His gaze focused on her mouth, and erotic thoughts entered her head.

"Oh, no?" Kevin's voice went low and deep. "Then why do I have to clean you up?"

Puzzled, Cara squinted. "You don't have to—"

"Yeah, I do." He leaned in farther to cup her head in his hand and slanted his mouth over hers, his tongue doing a thorough swipe over her lips. Cara relished the liberties he took with her, enjoying every second of the kiss. When she began to kiss him back, savoring the moment, the car behind them honked.

"Darn it," Kevin said, moving away. He glanced

in the rearview mirror at the car behind them. "Hold your horses, buddy." Kevin straightened in his seat and drove out of the intersection.

Cara's chuckle had him turning her way.

"What's so funny?"

"You haven't changed your driving habits. Still arguing with everyone on the road."

His eyes twinkled. "Idiots. All of them." When he looked at Cara, a deep, rumbling laugh emerged.

"All of them but you, right?"

"You got that right, babe." His charming grin unnerved her.

Cara settled in her seat, still smoldering from that one red-light kiss and feeling light of heart at the same time. Kevin and chocolate had that effect on her.

Memories flooded her senses of all the silly, light-hearted moments they had shared during their courtship. Kevin had been entertaining and easy to be with. He'd been irresistible, too, and Cara found that tonight, all those traits that made up the man she'd loved had surfaced.

Kevin reached for her hand. "It's early and a beautiful night. Want to take a walk?"

Cara didn't hesitate. She'd enjoyed the evening and didn't want it to end. "I'd like that."

Kevin squeezed her hand and nodded. "I know just the place."

Cara leaned back in her seat, trusting Kevin to entertain her. He'd been doing a good job of it since she'd arrived back in Houston. Though their marriage was over, this short time together would help them heal from wounds inflicted years earlier. Maybe this was the salve they needed to repair their injuries so they could move on with their lives.

Whatever the reason for her carefree mood, Cara wouldn't analyze it too deeply. She was on vacation from life at the moment, a small black hole in time where she and her soon-to-be-ex husband could enjoy each other's company without repercussions.

She'd forget his blackmail for the time being, shoving his motives out of her head. In less than two weeks she'd be back in Dallas, planning her new studio design, doing what she loved doing.

Kevin stopped the car on a dirt road that overlooked Somerset Lake. Brilliant moonlit waters glistened with sapphire illumination. Kevin got out of the car and opened the door for her.

The air felt heavy and warm, typical for a summer Texas night. Crickets chirped on and off and, in the space of quiet, the gentlest rippling of waves could be heard.

Cara swallowed hard as she took in the view. This was the place they'd come with all their friends, to have picnics and bonfires during the summer. This was *their* place, the spot right beyond the picnic tables, where she and Kevin had first admitted their love for one another.

Cara took Kevin's offered hand and followed him down a dusky, bluebonnet-laden path that led to the water. She took each step with care. She hated trampling on the flowers.

"You're not going to hurt them, babe. They look delicate, but they're resilient."

Cara had heard that from Kevin before, in much the same way, but not about bluebonnets. He'd spoken those words about her when they'd had arguments about his workaholic tendencies.

You look delicate, but I know you're resilient.

Apparently, he hadn't thought she could be hurt. Yet even the most durable of flowers had a breaking point.

"Why take the chance?" she said softly. When Kevin glanced at her, she shrugged. "I don't want to destroy them."

Kevin let the comment go and Cara doubted he caught her true meaning.

"Remember this place?" he asked.

"How could I not? We came here almost every weekend in the summer."

"That was some summer, wasn't it?"

She knew he meant the summer when they'd fallen in love. They'd been inseparable. She nodded slowly and held his hand as they walked along the lakeshore.

"Tell me what happened after you left Somerset."

Cara took a long, slow breath. A cricket chirped a few times, before she was able to formulate the words. "I… It was hard, Kevin. The hardest time of my life."

Kevin remained silent. He gazed ahead, refusing to look into her eyes.

"When I decided to start Dancing Lights, my whole world opened up again."

Kevin's mouth twisted, though he tried very hard to conceal his angst.

Cara didn't want to spoil the evening by talking about a sore subject. "I'm sorry, but you asked."

They walked along the little cove and reached a clearing by another group of redwood picnic benches.

"Care to show me a thing or two about dancing? You know I have two left feet."

"Here? There's no music. And you *don't* have two left feet. As I recall, you have some pretty good moves."

Kevin grinned with mischief. He clamped his hands on her waist and pulled her against him. "As *I* recall, you liked all my moves."

Cara gasped, immersed in the gleam of his dark blue eyes.

"But I'm talking about dance moves, babe. I could use a refresher, since I'm inviting you to Lance and Kate's wedding reception at the club. I wouldn't want to embarrass you with my lackluster dance steps."

Cara blinked in surprise. She couldn't go to Lance's reception with Kevin. It was one thing to see him for a few casual dates privately, but being on his arm at a formal affair would give the wrong impression and make her dream things she had no right dreaming. "You won't have to. I can't go."

"How do you know? I haven't told you the date yet."

"Because," Cara said, stepping away from him to look at the calm waters for comfort. Weddings always made her sentimental and she already had enough to deal with. She didn't need a reminder of their utter failure. "It's just that I think—"

"Shh, you think too much," Kevin said softly, searching her eyes. "You're so beautiful in moonlight, Cara." He leaned in and kissed her tenderly on the lips.

Her insides melted at his gentle touch and she reached up on tiptoes to kiss him back, wrapping her arms around his neck. Maybe it was this place and the memories it evoked, or maybe she'd just been too long without any real tenderness in her life, but right now, she needed to be with Kevin, kissing him and feeling like a woman again.

It wasn't long before Kevin's kisses turned her into Silly Putty, except there was nothing silly about the intensity he displayed. He pulled her along, walking backward until he sat upon the edge of a picnic table. He fitted her between his legs and continued to nibble on her mouth until he drew his lips downward to the base of her throat.

Pinpricks of excitement flew up and down her body. She tingled everywhere, breathing in his sexy cologne. The musky scent she recognized from years before drove her further into oblivion.

It was easy for him to untie her rope belt and pull her blouse down. With a groan of appreciation, he murmured her name and her heart rate sped up.

Kevin unfastened her bra with adept fingers and he pulled the garment away from her. "Damn it, sweetheart," he murmured, the curse a soft and beautiful endearment.

Exposed from the waist up, the pushed-down sleeves of her blouse trapping her arms slightly, Cara could only watch as Kevin touched her breasts, caressing, weighing, cupping her with such tenderness, she wanted to cry.

He made eye contact as he flicked his thumbs over her nipples, toying with them and making her moan with pleasure.

"You still like me touching you," he whispered, his torturous fingers breaking her out in a sweat.

She bit her lip and nodded. She *loved* the way Kevin touched her. He'd been the only man who could turn her on so fast, so furiously. But Cara gave as good as she got and she never let Kevin have the last word. "Seems to me," she said, breathless, "you could put that mouth to better use."

Kevin chuckled, then clamped his hands around her trapped arms and brought her closer. Her breast grazed his mouth and he teased her with tiny tongue swipes until her knees nearly buckled.

"Better?" he asked in a whisper and she nodded enthusiastically.

He filled his mouth with her, suckling and blowing hot breath over her breast. Her nipple stood erect and a rush of sizzling heat invaded her body. Everything below her waist throbbed.

Kevin was in no better shape. His body was rigid, the bulge of his desire pressed against her clothes. Crazy thoughts entered her head of making love to Kevin right here, out in the open, beside the lake where they'd first revealed their love for each other.

Kevin's thoughts couldn't have been far behind. He kissed her soundly and stood up, his manhood grazing her between the legs. "I need more, baby."

Cara nodded and helped Kevin unzip her pants. He cosseted her close and slipped his hand inside. With nimble fingers, he pulled her panties aside and cupped her womanhood.

"Ohh." His touch sent her mind reeling. She'd been so long without this, without Kevin bringing her pleasure.

Alone at the lake in the darkness, the night lit only by moonlight, Cara succumbed to Kevin's ministrations. He slid his hand back and forth, his fingertips caressing her most sensitive skin. She rocked and swayed, and he kissed her while she moved over his hand.

"You feel so good, Cara," he whispered over her lips. He slipped one finger inside.

Cara's eyes closed. She surrendered to Kevin's will. Every single part of her body tingled as he stroked her, slipping his finger up and down until she moved in rhythm like the music of a sexy samba. When she arched her back, Kevin followed her, sliding his lips along her throat, creating sensations that burned like a branding iron.

Whimpers of pleasure tumbled from her lips and Cara's face twisted in ecstasy. "Oh, sweet heaven."

Kevin cupped her breast with one hand and stroked her unmercifully with the other. Again and again, until Cara's body rocked out of control.

"It's so good, baby. Remember?"

Cara remembered. Kevin had always been an unselfish lover. But her thoughts stopped there, because she was too far gone to answer him. Her pleasure heightened and heightened, Kevin drawing out every quiver, every earth-shattering morsel of ecstasy, relentless in his pursuit.

Her muscles contracted and squeezed, her body quaked, and Kevin stopped his assault, allowing her to enjoy this moment on her own terms. He knew, oh, yes, how he knew to bring her the utmost pleasure.

Her orgasm came in slow, torturous, drawn-out bursts. Cara relished each mind-blowing second of shuddering release. Then slowly, slowly she came back down to earth.

When she opened her eyes, Kevin was watching her, his gaze smoldering with lust. "That was—"

"Heaven," Cara whispered, not shy about her display.

Kevin shook his head. "The sexiest thing I've ever witnessed."

Cara glanced down at his obvious erection. "Are you…okay?"

"I could make love to you ten times on this picnic table and not be satisfied."

Cara squirmed, tempted by the erotic thought.

Kevin worked her zipper up and handed her back her bra. "But a deal's a deal."

Fully sated and feeling very lighthearted, Cara dressed. "A man of his word."

Kevin inhaled a sharp breath. She knew how much he'd held back, for her pleasure. "Would have been safer to teach me how to dance."

Cara couldn't contain her smile. "Safety is over-rated at times."

Five

"So, you'll come to Lance and Kate's reception with me?"

Cara turned to Kevin before entering her hotel room. He stood close, boxing her in by the door. Her face still glowed from the attention he'd paid to her at the lake, and the taste of her lips still lingered on his mouth.

"Are you trying to manipulate me?" she asked coyly.

Kevin winced and faked a stab wound to the heart. "You're killing me, Cara."

Cara nibbled on her lower lip with indecision. She'd had him at his boiling point. It had been all he could do not to make love to her on that picnic table tonight. Desire and lust combined made for a heavy aphrodisiac.

"Why do you want me to go?"

Kevin tilted his head and spoke in a serious tone. "Regardless of what has happened between us, Lance has always been your friend. I know he'd want you to be there."

"Why do you?" Cara asked, searching his eyes.

"You're awfully suspicious."

"Don't I have a right to be? After all, you're black-mailing me."

"It's not blackmail, Cara. We made a deal. And tonight, I asked you to celebrate the marriage of a good friend. It's as simple as that."

Kevin wanted her on his arm that night and he wanted to spend as much time with her as possible during these two weeks, but it surprised him how much it mattered to him.

Cara finally relented. "Okay. I'll go and share in the celebration. Lance is a good man."

Kevin nodded, glad that she'd changed her mind. "Good night, Cara." He leaned in and pressed his mouth to hers, relishing the soft, subtle nuances of her giving lips and baby-soft skin. "I had a good time tonight."

Cara closed her eyes briefly. An image of her panting out a rocking orgasm flashed in his head.

"Uh, Kevin. Maybe we shouldn't—"

Kevin leaned in and kissed her a second time, stopping her next thought. "I'll call you tomorrow."

She gazed into his eyes and shook her head as if

trying to figure him out before turning to enter her hotel room.

Kevin left her and drove to his penthouse. He stripped out of his clothes immediately and walked into an icy-cold shower. The brisk spray rained down, easing his stubborn lust. But sexy images of Cara stayed with him throughout. It wasn't easy to wash Cara from his system.

He wanted to make her pay for abandoning him. He wanted to charm her and bend her to his will. He'd succeeded somewhat, but Cara had always been bright. She was correct to be suspicious of him. The only trouble was that he, too, paid a price for his little plan.

He wanted her.

After he toweled off, he headed for his bar and poured himself two fingers of bourbon. Leaning against the black-granite counter, he lifted his glass in midair. "Here's to you, Cara. My wife for just a few more days."

After her lake encounter with Kevin, Cara warned herself she was playing with fire and vowed to keep her distance from her husband until Lance and Kate's reception. It was much safer that way. She needed to keep her perspective and remember why she'd come to Houston.

She'd maintained that resolve for exactly twelve hours, until Kevin knocked at her door midmorning, wearing a full Astros baseball getup. She glanced at him, puzzled, noting his red jersey and baseball cap with the Astros' official star logo. He waved box-seat tickets for the afternoon game in front of her and shot her a delicious grin.

When it dawned on her what he had in mind, she could hardly refuse his enticing offer. She was a huge Houston fan, going back to her high-school days. Going to a day game felt sinful and luxurious, and she felt that doubly with Kevin by her side.

Now, she sat in a box seat at Minute Maid Park, just behind home plate, eating a hot dog and slurping down a Diet Coke.

"Want another?" he asked, after inhaling two hot dogs in record time.

"Nope, but toss me that bag of peanuts and I'm good to go."

Kevin smiled and set the bag on her lap. "Have at it, babe."

They munched on peanuts, booed the bad calls, cheered the good ones and jumped from their seats when an Astro player made it on base. Kevin excused himself for a minute and when he returned, he plopped a red cap with a big white star on her head and handed her a jersey that matched his.

"Thank you!" After she put the jersey on over her blouse, she reached over and planted a big kiss on his cheek.

Kevin turned his head toward her and her kiss slid to his lips. He tasted of mustard and soda and sunshine and their kiss lasted far longer than expected. Kevin took her into his arms and, much like two teenagers in love, they lost themselves.

"Hey, get a room!"

The shout came from a few rows back and Kevin smiled as he broke off the kiss. "Not a bad idea."

"Oh!" Cara straightened in her seat, a full flush of heat rising up her neck. She refused to look Kevin's way for a few minutes but she did hear him chuckle several times.

The Astros won the game and, with their spirits buoyed, they strolled the ballpark hand-in-hand until the crowds diminished. Cara stood in the Grand Union lobby, the famous entrance to the ballpark that went back to the early beginnings of Houston. "Remember when they built the stadium?"

"Yeah, traffic was stopped up for months."

Cara glanced at him. "But you thought it was cool that they'd use Union Station as the entrance."

"Still do. It brings a lot of people to the downtown area. From a business standpoint, it was a great idea."

"Speaking of business, how did you manage to get away from the office today?"

When they were living as man and wife, Kevin would have rather cut off his right arm than take a day off from work.

"I'll make up for it tonight. Got a load of paperwork to sift through."

Cara figured as much. He'd never let his work go, not even for a day. There were times he wouldn't come to bed until two, the computer more of an enticement than she was. In the morning, she'd wake up to find him gone.

She remembered those lonely days and nights. Those memories stayed with her and marred the pleasant day she'd just had.

She remained quiet as Kevin took her back to the hotel, deciding it was a good idea not to invite him in. "I had fun today. Thank you for the invitation." Her voice stiff and formal, Cara made up for her lack of grace with a little smile.

Kevin didn't seem to notice the change in her. "Me, too. It's been ages since I went to a game."

"Because you're too busy?"

Kevin weighed her question, studying her. "I know how to delegate work now, Cara," he said, his tone none too gracious. "I haven't gone to a game because…hell, you're gonna make me say it?"

Stunned, Cara blinked. "Say what?"

Kevin shook his head and cursed. "Because it's what *we* did. Me and you."

"Oh." She wasn't sure she understood.

"I went a few times with the guys," he admitted. Then Kevin's voice went deep, and he tapped her baseball cap twice, planting it farther down on her forehead. "But they don't look as cute as you in a baseball cap."

Before she could react, Kevin leaned down and kissed her soundly on the lips, putting to shame the kiss they'd shared at the ballpark. After five minutes of making out hot and heavy at her door, Kevin backed away and caught his breath, his eyes devastatingly blue. "I'd better go. I'll call you tomorrow."

Cara slumped by the door, not knowing if she was glad he'd left or angry that, once again, his work took precedence over her.

What difference did it make, anyway?

Soon she'd be the *ex* Mrs. Kevin Novak, and what he did or didn't do with his time wouldn't matter.

She clung to that thought and took it to bed with her, trying not to wonder when Kevin would call her again.

Cara fumed for the next two days. Kevin didn't call. She knew she should be glad that she'd been given a reprieve from the relentless attention he paid her, yet she thought it all a waste of time. He'd forced her to stay in Houston for two weeks to obtain his signature. She'd put her life on hold for him. She'd made umpteen calls to her dance studio, dealing with problems and making important decisions from her hotel room instead of being where she was most needed.

Cara looked in the mirror and fidgeted with her unruly mop of hair, finger-combing strands back in place while she debated about going out for dinner or calling room service. Anger bubbled inside and she decided to take a brisk walk to cool off. She picked up her purse just as the hotel phone rang.

She stared at it for a long while, debating whether to pick up. Finally, she relented. "Hello?" she said, tapping her foot.

"Hi, Cara."

Cara winced when she heard Kevin on the other end. She wished she'd listened to her first instinct and not answered the phone. His voice sounded odd and distant, as if he were calling from a cave. "Where are you?"

"Home. Do you still make that killer chicken soup?"

"My grandma's recipe? Yes, why do you—" Then it dawned on her. Kevin didn't sound like himself. In fact, she'd never heard him sound so *off*. She put two and two together. "Are you sick?"

"You could say that," he whispered.

"How sick?"

"I've been in bed for two days and nights, going crazy."

Guilt washed over her and Cara was ashamed of how many unpleasant thoughts had entered her mind about Kevin. She had been certain that he'd been playing games and toying with her emotions, telling her he'd call and then deliberately avoiding her.

"Do you have a fever?"

"One hundred and two."

Oh, man. She softened immediately. "Have you eaten?"

Certainly a millionaire living in a penthouse would have someone to cook and clean for him.

"Toast, yesterday. Not much of an appetite. But I'm craving your grandmother's soup."

Cara inhaled sharply. She was hardly Kevin's nursemaid, but she was still his wife. And his pride wouldn't allow him to ask, unless he really needed her help. She remembered that Kevin hated being sick, never took a day off to heal and was the worst patient she'd ever seen. "I'll catch a cab and be right over."

"I sent a car for you. You can stop off and get the things you need. He should be there any minute."

Cara sighed. "Kevin, how'd you know I'd come?"

"I didn't," he said, his voice trailing off. Cara backed away from giving him grief—he really sounded ill. "But a man can hope, right?"

Kevin felt better already just knowing Cara was on her way. He didn't know what had hit him since he rarely got sick, but he'd been knocked for a loop after taking Cara to the Astros game. He'd spent the next two days in bed, hating every minute of it. His fever had spiked and he hadn't had a drop of energy. Today, he'd gotten up and worked from his home office until he couldn't move a muscle. He'd climbed back in bed, cursing, and the only thing he'd thought of besides his rotten luck was Cara.

In truth, since she'd come back to town she'd consumed his thoughts. His plan for payback was working exceptionally well. Maybe too well, because he'd spent the past two days dreaming of her and the dusky, molten look he put on her face every time they came together. Building up to their one night of lovemaking was killing him, but he enjoyed every torturous minute.

Tonight, he decided, he'd call a truce. He couldn't

take advantage when she'd come so willingly to help him recover, but he felt no guilt whatsoever for the little fib he'd told to get her here.

His fever had broken before he'd called her and he was feeling human again. But he hadn't lied about his craving. He wanted to see Cara in his kitchen, cooking her grandmother's hearty chicken soup. It was the best way to get her to his penthouse—he doubted she'd have come otherwise. But why the hell he'd pictured Cara in his kitchen in a little domestic scene instead of sprawled out across his silk sheets was a mystery to him.

Kevin took a shower, hoping to wipe out the last remnants of his fever and bring some color back to his face. He soaped up and the cool spray of water raining down invigorated him. He shampooed hair that he'd let go for two days and, once he'd turned the faucet off, he toweled dry and stepped out of the shower. This was the most activity he'd had in two days. Looking in the mirror, he let out a groan. "Shabby, Novak," he muttered, "and pale."

His beard served well to cover his sallow appearance, so he opted not to shave. After slipping on his briefs and a comfortable pair of jeans, he threw on a black shirt but didn't have the energy to button it. When the doorbell chimed, he walked the distance to the front door on legs that still felt like rubber.

He opened the door and found Cara holding a brown sack of groceries. "Hi, Kevin."

Cara's gaze immediately drifted to his bare chest, where his shirt spread open. His heartbeat sped up watching lust invade her pretty blue eyes. The flash of instant desire scorched him more than the fever he'd just fought. Then she blinked and redirected her gaze to his face, the moment gone. Soon, he'd put that look back on her face. Tonight, though, it was all he could muster to take the grocery bag from her arms. "My salvation. I'm glad you came, Cara."

"I, uh, sure. I'll make the soup and then let you rest. You really should be in bed."

"I've *been* in bed. It's boring. And lonely."

Cara arched her brow. "I'll find my way around. Point me toward the kitchen."

He placed his hand on the delicate curve of her back, wondering what she'd been up to today, dressed in a classy, sleeveless black-lace blouse and white slacks. Had he interrupted her plans tonight? "C'mon. I'll show you where it is."

Cara darted glances back and forth from one room to the other. Kevin liked his penthouse, having decorated it himself, but he imagined Cara didn't. Too much black and granite and hard angles for her liking—there was nothing here that spoke to a woman's feminine side.

"It's a nice place," she said politely. "Big. How many rooms?"

"Seven." He shrugged. "It's home for now."

When they reached the kitchen, Kevin set the bag on the polished-granite countertop. Cara took in the state-of-the-art stainless steel appliances and nodded. "Either you don't cook much, or you have an expert cleaning staff."

Kevin cracked a smile and it actually hurt his face. He hadn't smiled in two days. "Both. I know the place looks sterile. I eat out a lot or bring in food. You know I'm not a cook."

"Yeah, I remember. Boiling an egg is your specialty." She smiled wide. "I thought that might have changed."

He sat down on the counter stool across the island from Cara, content to watch her. "Some things have changed, but not my cooking abilities. I'm still pretty hopeless in the kitchen, but I make up for it in other ways."

She blinked, looking a little flustered, and rubbed her hands down her slacks. "Okay, well, I'll just get started."

She removed the groceries from the bag and started laying things out, opening and closing kitchen drawers until she had all the utensils she needed. "Are you going to sit there and watch me?"

He nodded. "Unless you need help."

God, he hoped she didn't. He'd sat down because his rubber legs needed the break. He'd felt better after his shower but, as the hour wore on, weakness consumed him again.

"Nope, this is a one-woman job." She smiled and went to work efficiently. "Just watch and learn."

Cara scooped up the carrots and potatoes she'd cut into small chunks and tossed them into the big soup pot. The chicken pieces were already cooking and she'd used caution with the spices. Normally, she'd spice up the soup to give it a sharp bite, but she had to stick to more bland ingredients for Kevin's sake.

He watched her intently, making small talk, asking her about the recipe, truly engaged in what she was doing. But each time Cara glanced at him, he appeared to slump lower on the stool. His voice droned in quiet tones and only his stubborn nature kept him in the kitchen instead of the bed, where he really needed to be.

"You're exhausted, sweetheart," she said softly. "The soup's going to need an hour of simmering. Let me get you into bed. I'll come get you when it's ready."

Kevin pursed his lips and stared at her with feigned irritation. Hell would freeze over before Kevin would ever admit defeat, but she knew he was grateful for the reprieve. "Only because you called me sweetheart."

"That was my strategy all along," she said, wiping her hands on a dish towel. She moved to his side of the island. "Can you get to your bedroom okay?"

He lowered his dark blond lashes. "Sure, but it'd be more fun if you helped me."

Cara couldn't tell if he was joking. He really did appear weak and his color had faded since she'd first arrived. She feared he'd overdone it. "Okay, I'll get you there."

Kevin stood and wrapped his arm around her shoulder. She followed his lead to the farthest room down the hallway. Double doors opened to a room that could only be described as a suite in itself. A black-manteled fireplace stood across from the massive bed. An enormous flat-screen television covered one wall and a room-size balcony ventured out from two French doors, overlooking the Houston skyline.

Cara refrained from commenting. Kevin had certainly come up in the world. Everything he owned spoke of great wealth. He had achieved his goals. He was a brilliant success. A part of her wanted to shed tears all over again, for the marriage that he'd sacrificed without realizing it. For the love that had taken the brunt of his success and for the shattering of vows spoken.

There was a moment of awkward silence when they'd reached his beautifully crafted bed. Would this be the place where they'd seal their divorce deal next week?

Cara heaved a sigh and ducked away from Kevin. "There you go," she said brightly. "I'd better go stir the soup. Get some rest, okay?"

Kevin removed his shirt and let it drop slowly. He stood by the bed in jeans and bare feet, his short hair disheveled and his face sporting stubble that made him look dangerous and sexy. Dear heaven. Cara's breath caught tight in her throat. Her husband was gorgeous, ripped with lean muscle and extremely appealing even in his weakened state.

She shook her head and backed out of the room. Images of Kevin opening the door earlier with droplets of water beaded on his fine chest hair invaded her thoughts. She'd wanted to lick each one and then run her hands over him, again and again. "Chase those thoughts from your head, Cara," she whispered as she reentered the kitchen. "And don't you dare fall for Kevin Novak again."

Six

Cara stood over the six-burner Viking range and stirred the soup. Every time she made this soup she thought of the sweet nature of her grandmother, who had taught Cara step-by-step how to prepare it. What set this soup apart from all others was the fresh crushed tomatoes she used and the cup of red wine that she put in during the last twenty minutes of cooking. It was her grandmother's secret ingredient and her signature meal.

She hadn't made this soup once since she and Kevin had broken up. But now, images of standing beside Grandma Flo in her kitchen, helping toss in ingredients, came to mind and lingered in a pleasing way. The aroma of oregano, basil, fresh tomatoes and onion drifted throughout the kitchen and brought her back to a happy time in her childhood.

She had Kevin to thank for that. Not that she wanted to see him sick, but she missed cooking for someone else, deriving great satisfaction in it. "There you go," she said, giving the soup one last stir before allowing it to simmer.

Cara looked about the kitchen, wondering what to do next. She'd already cleaned up the mess she'd made chopping up the ingredients. On impulse, she walked to Kevin's room and peeked inside the double doors that she'd left ajar earlier.

He slept.

That was a good sign. What wasn't a good sign was her unexpected physical attraction to him, seeing him sprawled out on the bed, nearly naked but for the jeans he wore. She had an uncanny urge to both nurture him and make crazy love to him.

Quickly, Cara stepped away and mentally scolded herself. "Don't go there," she whispered. Then curiosity got the better of her and she perused the rooms in the penthouse, looking for signs of…what? Another woman? Something that would clue her in as to what he'd done with the past four years of his life.

Sourly she admitted that Kevin wouldn't have been celibate for four years. She wondered how many relationships he'd had. How many women had he brought up here to admire the view?

She entered his office and noticed a soft, buttery-brown sofa, the only piece of furniture that looked welcoming. His mahogany desk was littered with files and papers. She walked behind the desk to look out at the Houston skyline and pictured Kevin twirling around in his chair to take a breather and look out the window. "Nice."

Cara wandered over to a sturdy wall unit and lifted up a few picture frames sitting on the shelf, noting that every scene depicted Kevin with one or more of his friends—Lance and Kevin on the golf course, and Darius, Mitch, Lance and Kevin on the tennis court. She glanced at a photo of Kevin with Kate and Lance, the happy threesome smiling into the camera.

Cara picked up a picture of Kevin standing beside his parents at his University of Texas graduation. Still in cap and gown, Kevin's face displayed confidence and determination. She saw the resolute gleam in his eyes—nothing would stop him from achieving his goals. Had she been so blindsided by love that she hadn't noticed that quality in him before? Or had she thought she wouldn't fall victim to his dogged persistence and drive? Cara had been at his graduation and at one point had stood beside him and his parents for a photo. But that picture, she presumed, was long gone, tossed out when she'd left, which he considered abandonment and she considered survival.

Regret and nostalgia brought a whisper of a sigh to her lips. She recalled how they'd celebrated his graduation that night.

In bed.

And making plans for their future.

Now, she wondered who'd be making future plans with Kevin once he was single again. Bemused, Cara's curiosity escalated. She entered the other two bedrooms in the penthouse and noticed, with a good deal of relief, there were no pictures of Kevin with a woman. She dared to peek inside the walk-in closets, loathing the nosy-body she'd become but too curious to keep herself from snooping.

Cara walked back into the kitchen and stirred the soup again. Thankfully, it was ready. She closed her eyes and the flavorful aroma hit her anew, but she couldn't shake the feeling that she'd learned far more about herself than Kevin on her little escapade through his house.

The elation she felt seeing no signs of another woman anywhere in his home caused her great concern. She nibbled on her lip and made up her mind to get out as quickly as she could.

"Something smells good in here."

Cara whirled around. Kevin stood at the doorway, barefoot in those same soft jeans. Thankfully, as he made his way into the room, he pulled a T-shirt on over his head, covering the chest she itched to touch.

"The soup's ready. I was just about to come get you."

"What, no dinner in bed?" He wiggled his eyebrows in that charming way he had.

"I see you've got your sense of humor back," she bantered. "How're you feeling?"

He stopped his approach to take assessment. "Rested. The best sleep I've had in two days."

"Must be the powers of the soup," she said, taking out a bowl from the dark maple cabinet.

Kevin scratched his head. "The powers of something."

They stared at each other across the kitchen, his deep-blue gaze penetrating her until she thought she'd bubble over, like the soup she'd just prepared.

Cara made herself really busy, slicing French bread she'd bought at a bakery down the street. She poured Kevin a bowl of soup and set a thick slice of bread on his plate.

"I should go," she said.

Kevin's gaze never left hers. He walked over to the cabinet and took down a second bowl. "Do you have a hot date tonight?"

An unfeminine chuckle erupted from her chest. "Yeah, with my book."

"Then stay. Have a bowl of soup with me. I could use the company."

Dumbfounded, Cara watched Kevin's efficient movements around the kitchen. Before she knew it, he'd duplicated his own meal for her.

He took both of the plates to the living room and set them down on a cocktail table. "You'll never guess what's on TV right now."

Cara groaned. She knew Kevin had her. She followed him into the living room. "James Bond marathon."

Kevin worked the remote and Bond's classic opening music played as an image of 007 filled the screen.

"Oh, man, and I really wanted to finish that book tonight."

Kevin smiled and sat down on the sofa, stiff leather squeaking as he got comfortable.

She was a sucker for Bond. They both were. So when Kevin patted the seat directly next to him, Cara didn't hesitate, the temptation too great. She sat down beside him and together they watched the movie and enjoyed her grandmother's delicious, hot soup.

Somewhere between *Dr. No* and *Never Say Never Again,* Kevin felt the grip of illness dissipate. He'd woken up past midnight on his sofa with a more than healthy erection. The flat screen droned in the background, long since forgotten. Cara was sprawled on top of him, her head on his shoulder, her silky blond hair tickling his chin, her soft breathing giving testimony to her slumber.

Kevin let go a silent groan of pain. Cara's breasts crushed his chest, but it was her softly feminine, erotic scent that had his mind reeling with possibilities. For now, all he could do was stroke her hair, weaving tendrils through his fingers. Her blouse had drifted up her back, exposing skin that dipped below the waistband of her white slacks.

Kevin stretched his fingers out, debating whether

to give in to impulse and run his hand over her back and dip under her waistband. Man, oh, man, how he wanted to, but she'd been a good sport about coming over here and making soup so he couldn't very well wake her now for his own selfish reasons.

Could he?

Kevin asked himself, why not? He'd had a reason and purpose to have her stay in Houston for two weeks. She owed him and he meant to make her pay for leaving him high and dry. Having her lying atop him tempted him beyond belief. She'd only be his wife another week, so why not derive as much pleasure as possible from the situation now?

Kevin stroked her back lightly and she stirred, letting go a little moan.

Kevin's erection stiffened. Yet he couldn't bring himself to disturb her peace. Holding her, he closed his eyes again, enjoying the feel of her in his arms. Wouldn't be too long before he'd lose the legal right to do so.

Less than a minute later Cara moved, and Kevin opened his eyes to find her casting him a sleep-hazy look. "Hi, babe."

She blinked, disoriented, and lifted her body somewhat to stare into his eyes. Kevin noted the exact moment when Cara's eyes widened with dawning knowledge of where she was and how aroused she'd made him. "Oh."

"I've recovered," he said, before lifting the corners of his mouth. "But now I have another problem."

Cara pushed against his chest and made a move to get up. "What time is it?"

Kevin wrapped his arms around her, gently bringing her back down. "After midnight."

She looked around the room, spotting a tuxedo-clad Pierce Brosnan racing for his life on the flat screen. "I fell asleep."

"*We* fell asleep."

She stared into his eyes. "How are you?"

"Except for the obvious," he said, his gaze dropping down to her spectacular cleavage, "I'm feeling great."

She stared at him and silence ensued as she took stock of her position and the strain of his jeans against the apex of her legs. "You're turned on."

"Big-time."

She nibbled on her lower lip, clearly panicked. The pulsing sensation where they joined wasn't one-sided. Heat and pressure built and Cara couldn't deny she was just as turned on. "I should go."

"Stay, Cara." Kevin put his hand behind her neck and pulled her head down. They looked into each other's eyes before Kevin nipped at her lips. Once, twice, then he wrapped his arms around her more tightly and those nibbles became full-fledged, hot, hungry kisses.

Cara whimpered in her throat, eager for more and fully aroused. Kevin dipped his tongue into her mouth and swept through, tasting her with long, openmouthed motions. As the kisses went deeper, she moved on him, rubbing her body over his erection until he thought he'd die of agony.

Kevin lifted her enough to bring his mouth to her breast. He suckled her through the lace of her blouse, moistening her until the material became nearly sheer. Her nipple strained, tight. Kevin flicked the tip with his thumb and simultaneously, they both pulled her blouse up and over her head. Kevin didn't take time to undo her bra, he simply reached inside and released her breasts from their enclosure.

Cara kissed him hard on the lips and allowed him free rein to do whatever he wanted. He took his time, cupping, weighing, adoring each breast, licking the tips and wetting each perfect globe until Cara's breathing became frenzied.

She lifted up partway and pushed his T-shirt off over his head. She dropped her mouth on him immediately, kissing his chest, her hands roaming freely. "Ah, Cara," he murmured, his pleasure heightening.

She circled his flat nipples and nipped at the tips, her fingers weaving into his scattered chest hair. She pulled at him and he smiled at her prowess, while his erection strained even harder against his jeans.

He ran his hands in her hair, enjoying every second Cara made love to him. It was better than he remembered, having her hands caress him, having her mouth drive him crazy.

Revenge can be sweet, he thought, and wondered if his plan was working, or if Cara simply derived sexual pleasure from him. Either way, he wouldn't question it now.

Kevin took Cara's hand and set it on his waistband, directly over the zipper that was ready to combust. "Touch me," he whispered. "Like you used to."

Cara closed her eyes and inhaled sharply. Then, after a second of thought, she slid slightly to the side to unsnap his jeans. Kevin held his breath. He ached for her touch, for Cara to ease his need. The top of his waistband opened and, with two nimble fingers, she moved the zipper down slowly.

Cool air hit him yet his body flamed. Her touch was light and tentative as she stroked him initially. He lifted up, slanting his lips over hers, deepening their mounting desire.

"This is dangerous," she whispered between kisses.

"You've never shied away from danger, babe."

"It's better to be safe."

"Didn't you once say safety is overrated?"

Cara laughed and the sound of her lightheartedness turned the tide. Kevin laughed, too, his body no less hard-pressed for her, but they'd reached a playful plateau that they might have called their trademark, once upon a time.

"We always had fun together," he added.

"I know, but I didn't come here for fun."

"Why did you come?"

"Soup, remember?"

"No, I don't remember. Anything that happened more than ten minutes ago is a complete blur."

Cara punched him lightly on the shoulder and Kevin reacted by taking hold of her arm and tugging her down. He tasted her lips again and again, the playfulness forgotten as heat and passion consumed them again.

Kevin relished every second Cara touched him, her soft hand against his shaft stroking him in her subtle then bold ways, creating sizzling hot tension. He wanted nothing more than to ease his lust inside her. To feel her soft perfect body welcome him. Man, oh, man, he remembered how it was to be with Cara. He'd never forgotten. No woman had ever compared. But he couldn't make love to her tonight. Not yet. Kevin sat up abruptly before he lost all control.

"Are you feeling weak again?" she asked, seriously concerned.

"Just a dose of Cara fever," he said with a quick smile.

Her expression softened and Kevin rose before he gave in to his desire to make love to her.

He reached down to grab her hand. "It's late. I'll drive you home."

They dressed quickly, both silent in their thoughts. But when he escorted Cara to her hotel room, she turned to him, puzzled. "Kevin, I don't understand any of this."

She looked sex tousled and beautifully confused. "That makes two of us."

The trouble was, Kevin knew his plan the way a general knew his battle strategy, but that didn't make it any less confusing to him, either. They stared at each other for a long moment, searching one another for the truth and coming up short.

"Thanks for coming to my rescue tonight," he said finally. "The soup was great." Then he added, "You haven't lost your touch."

Kevin turned from Cara and forced himself to walk away without looking back.

Cara was at her wit's end, wanting Kevin so terribly that the tension caused her a sleepless night. Sensibly, she knew she and Kevin were doomed as a couple, so making love to him could only hurt her. Her rational side understood that. But her heart and her body were a different matter. She wanted to have sex with her husband—was that so wrong? She had asked that of herself last night and then again this morning. She craved Kevin. He knew how to make her skin prickle and how to satisfy her innermost desires. But the sad fact remained that, once she got what she wanted, their marriage would be over.

When her cell phone rang, Cara looked at the number and hesitated before answering. "Hi, Kevin."

"You cured me last night."

"I'm...glad."

"How about letting me make it up to you. Dinner, tomorrow night? I promise to be better company. I'll even shave."

Cara laughed. She rubbed the slight beard-burns on her face where his stubble had bruised her last night. Memories rushed forth. She shook her head and knew she should make up an excuse and refuse him.

It's for the best, Cara.

Cara opened her mouth to say no, and surprised herself. "I'd love to."

She slammed her eyes shut. Why did she find Kevin so irresistible? Had he changed? Could she trust him? None of it mattered, anyway. In less than a week she'd be gone, with her signed divorce papers in hand.

After making arrangements with him, she hung up the phone, at odds with herself. When her cell phone rang a second time, she answered it quickly, happy to receive Alicia's call.

"Hi, Cara. It's Alicia."

"Alicia, I'm so glad you called."

"Are we still on for lunch and shopping this afternoon?"

"I'm looking forward to it." Cara needed a girl's day out to clear her mind.

"I'm in town, so I'll pick you up and we'll head to Somerset. Can you be ready in half an hour?"

"Yes." So ready, she thought. "I'll be waiting for you downstairs."

After she hung up the phone, Cara dressed in brown slacks and a sleeveless crème top. She slipped her feet into comfy, chocolate-brown Jimmy Choos and pulled her curly hair back into a tortoiseshell clip. She grabbed her matching handbag and exited the hotel room.

Alicia drove up just as Cara exited the Four Seasons. The doorman wished her a good day and off she went, ready to put Kevin out of her mind for the next few hours.

Cara took in the sights as the bustling downtown soon gave way to quiet residential roads. Somerset, in the heart of Maverick County, was a small, beautifully constructed town northeast of Houston. Cara had once loved living there in a modest home with Kevin. There were times in Dallas when she would be reminded of their house—she'd see a fabric similar in design to her kitchen curtains or smell fresh mint and recall the stone pathway that led to their front door, laden with the herb. She would sigh, wondering how her life had changed so much. Sentimental feelings would rush in, but Cara had always quickly shooed them away.

Now, as Alicia drove on, Cara looked to a digital sign set atop a tall post just outside the front gates of Maverick High School, announcing in flashing yellow letters the first dance of the new semester. "I hear those Friday-night dances were something wild. Lance and Mitch were always going on and on about them. I bet they stopped just short of telling me how much trouble they'd really gotten into back then."

Alicia shrugged. "I wouldn't know. I didn't go to many dances."

"No?"

With a shake of her head, Alicia replied, "No, I, uh, didn't care to…"

"Dance? Now, Alicia, I bet you can move."

"I like to dance," Alicia said carefully, "but Alex

didn't want me to go to the dances. He, uh, thought people looked down on us." Alicia turned to her, her dark eyes almost apologetic. "Alex has a lot of pride."

Cara remembered how protective Alejandro Montoya was of his little sister, just from bits and pieces she'd heard of Kevin's conversations with his friends. Alicia was timid and Alex had done his best to shield her. Cara still couldn't believe that Alex would have had anything to do with the fire at Brody Oil, though he may have been resentful of the men who had more than he had while growing up. He had come from a different social standing, working at the Texas Cattleman's Club as the groundskeeper, but now he was just as wealthy and powerful as Kevin and his friends. Alex may hate the Brodys, but Cara refused to believe he was a criminal.

"You two are very close."

"Yes, and I have to keep reminding him, I'm all grown up now."

"Sometimes men can't see what's right in front of them," Cara acknowledged.

Alicia beamed with amusement. "So true."

They dined at a little outdoor restaurant on Somerset's main street. Wrought-iron chairs and umbrella-covered mosaic-stone tables gave a Spanish ambiance. After glancing at the menu, Cara noted the fare was mostly Southwestern, which suited her just fine. She was in the mood for hometown spice.

She loved eating outdoors on warm days and

didn't get too much chance to do so in Dallas. Usually, she ate her lunch in the office at the dance studio, going over accounts or viewing video of her students' progress.

"This is really nice," Cara said.

"It's new. I thought you might like it."

They sat in silence for a minute looking at the menu and when the waiter walked up, offering the daily specials, Cara and Alicia both decided on spicy Southwestern chicken salad with chipotle, and strawberry margaritas.

The margaritas arrived first. Cara lifted her glass in a toast. "To friends," she said with a smile.

"To friends," Alicia repeated, and they touched together their full margarita glasses before taking a sip.

Cara told Alicia all about her dance studios, explaining about how her background in gymnastics and dance had given her the idea when she and Kevin had split up. She admitted she'd had to do something with her life. She'd been brokenhearted and depressed. Pouring herself into her work and seeing the progress she'd made in just a few short years had come to mean so much to her.

"And now I'm back for a short time."

Alicia cast her a curious look. Cara had never really explained why she'd come back and Alicia had been too polite to inquire, but she assumed her friend was puzzled. If the roles were reversed, Cara would be, too. "I've been spending some time with Kevin."

She couldn't bring herself to confess that the reason she'd been seeing Kevin was his blackmail. Admitting so wouldn't shed a positive light on either of them. The entire subject brought bitterness to her mouth. She sipped her margarita, sweetening up the sour subject. "We're mending fences, sort of."

"Are you two dating?"

"Well," Cara said, taking a deep breath, "I guess we are. We've gone on a few casual dates."

Alicia observed her carefully and Cara wanted to confide in her friend. She needed someone to talk to. Her mother was out of the question, and none of her friends in Dallas would understand her dating Kevin now when she'd been so adamant about getting on with her life. She added, "Actually, we're going out to dinner tomorrow night. And he's taking me to Lance's wedding reception."

"Sounds very hopeful," Alicia said.

The entrees were delivered to the table, releasing Cara from commenting further. They both dug into the salads. "So, what got you interested in working for the museum?" Cara asked. Alicia had mentioned she was the curator of the Somerset Museum of Natural History.

"I love history." Alicia shrugged with a little smile. "It's a small museum, but I enjoy getting up in the morning and going to work. There's so much history in this area."

Cara noted a gleam in Alicia's dark eyes when she spoke of her work. "It's a fulfilling job."

Alicia nodded. "Yes, I feel fortunate."

Cara felt fortunate, too, at the moment. Alicia's sweet nature reminded her of all the good things in her life.

An image of Kevin popped into her head. They were getting closer each day. Was that one of the good things in her life?

Cara concentrated on shopping the rest of the afternoon. She and Alicia walked the long streets, entering various shops, an antique bookstore, a pottery store filled with hand-painted vases and plates, and an art gallery. As they strolled along sharing anecdotes, Cara remembered why she'd been so fond of Alicia. She was easy to be with and their conversation flowed naturally. Their last stop was Rebecca Huntington's lingerie boutique, Sweet Nothings.

"Wait until you see the gorgeous lingerie in here," Alicia said.

The minute Cara entered Somerset's newest shop she saw for herself what Alicia had meant. Lace, satin and silk lingerie in a variety of pastels was displayed throughout the shop. Cara took all of it in, noting the exquisite fabrics presented on satin hangers. Mirrored wall shelves showcased exotic perfumes. A sitting area with sofa and chairs surrounded a marble table set with delicate coffee cups and teapots for a little respite between shopping sprees. "How lovely," Cara said.

A woman with stunning red hair that was pulled

into a knot at the back of her head approached. With green eyes as warm as her manner, she greeted them. "Hello and welcome to Sweet Nothings." She looked at Alicia with a slight slant of her head. "You're Alejandro Montoya's sister, aren't you?"

"Yes, Alex is my brother. I'm Alicia. I've come into your shop a few times, but wasn't sure you recognized me. You're Rebecca Huntington, aren't you?"

Everyone at the Texas Cattleman's Club knew the Huntington name, of course. Her father, Sebastian Huntington, was one of the oldest members of the club and he was well-known but not well liked, from what Cara recalled.

Rebecca's eyes lost their glow for a second, then she nodded. "Yes. I was sorry to hear about your mother's death. Carmen was a lovely woman."

Emotion flitted through Alicia's gaze and Cara sensed a history between the two women, and not a good one.

"Is there anything I might show you?" Rebecca said, looking from Cara to Alicia. "Or would you like to browse?"

"Browsing, first," Cara said. "You have a lovely shop. I want to see *everything*."

Rebecca cast her a wide smile. "Thank you. Just let me know if you need any help."

Rebecca walked behind the counter to resume her duties, and Cara and Alicia ventured farther into the shop.

"Look at this," Alicia said, strolling to a rounder.

Her attitude warned that she didn't want to discuss her past relationship with Rebecca. She pulled out a hanger holding a skimpy, pink baby-doll two-piece set striped with black lace. She held it up for Cara to see.

"Oh, that would look great on you, with your olive skin."

Alicia let go a chuckle. "And where would I wear this? Or more exactly, for whom?"

"There's no one special in your life, Alicia?" Cara asked, keeping her voice low.

"No," she said. "There are days when I wonder if I'll ever have someone to wear such exquisite things for."

"How about for yourself? Pamper yourself a little."

Alicia glanced at the nightie one last time before quickly setting it back on its rounder. "Someday, maybe." But the longing in her voice belied her fast action. She turned her attention to Cara. "Maybe you should pick up something for your date with Kevin."

Cara smiled and glanced around the store, her gaze stopping on a rack that held one-of-a-kind black-lace nighties. Cara wanted to blow Kevin's mind with a naughty number that would create a lifelong memory for them both. "I intend to, and you're gonna help me find just the right one. Come look at these over here."

Alicia followed her to the rack. Cara held up a garment that appealed to her and ran her hand inside to demonstrate how the fine, delicate, lacy threads would expose more skin than they covered. "What do you think?"

"Makes a statement," Alicia said with twinkling eyes.

Cara grinned. It was perfect. "I think so, too."

Alicia let go a deep sigh. "You're glowing." She looked at Cara with a tilt of her head, her voice filled with yearning. "Must be nice to be so much in love."

Love?

Had Cara fallen back in love with Kevin?

Cara's heart surged. Warmth spread through her body and the realization struck that she *was* in love with Kevin Novak. All over again. Maybe she'd never stopped loving him. And the night she'd wear this lingerie would be her last night with Kevin before they finalized a divorce that had been four years in the making.

Only now, she wasn't certain she wanted it at all.

Seven

Kevin glanced at his watch for the twentieth time today. In just three hours, he'd be picking Cara up for their date. Anticipation coursed through his body, making him impatient and eager.

He peered down at the completed files on his desk. Working like a madman today, he'd managed to get through most everything in record time and hold a team meeting for his latest apartment complex project on the outskirts of Houston. He had a few notes to make about the project before turning them in to legal.

He was just finishing up his last thoughts when Darius and Lance walked in, unannounced. Kevin glanced past them to the opened door and his secretary, Marin, who sat at her desk. "Can't get decent help these days. She lets just anybody walk into my office."

"I heard that," Marin called out. "You're lucky to have me."

"Yeah, you're lucky to have her," Darius said with a wide grin.

"We came to deliver you from all this," Lance said, sweeping his right arm over Kevin's paper-laden desk. "It's happy hour, starting right now."

Kevin twisted his mouth, stood up and walked to the door. "Kidding," he said unnecessarily to his secretary. She'd been advised to never hold Lance or Darius in the outer office unless he was in a meeting. He closed the door and looked at his friends. "Can't. Not tonight."

"Why not?" Darius asked.

"I've got a date in a few hours."

"With Cara?"

Kevin folded his arms over his middle. "That's right."

Darius shook his head. "I know what you're up to. I recognize all the signs. You're trying to get back at Cara for hurting you. But trust me, it's only gonna come back to bite you in the ass."

"It's something I need to do," Kevin said in his own defense. "What makes you such an expert?"

"I did the same thing with Summer. I wanted revenge for what she did to me seven years ago, but I hurt myself in the process by denying my love for her. I almost lost her, Kevin."

"My situation's different."

"If you're that angry and hurt, it's only because you're still in love with her and won't admit it."

Lance agreed with Darius. "I think you should listen to him, Kev. You'll see it more clearly over a good drink."

"Yeah, well, maybe I'm changing my mind about having drinks with you two."

Lance scrubbed his chin.

Both men grabbed him by the elbow, one on each side, and bulldozed him out of his office. "Maybe if we'd have pulled you out of your office more, back in the day, you two would still be together. On your way to making us uncles," Darius added.

Kevin yanked his arms free and regained his composure just before reaching his secretary's desk. "We're closing up early. Go on home and have a good night," he said, ignoring Lance's and Darius's smug smiles.

"Thanks, Mr. Novak."

They rode the elevator down. "Five years ago, I'd have punched both of you out for trying that stunt."

Darius threw his head back and laughed heartily. "You would've tried, Novak. But not succeeded."

"Five years ago," Lance began, "you never would've stopped working, not even for a drink with friends."

"Meaning?"

Lance cocked his head and shrugged his broad shoulders. "Meaning, you're making progress. Though you're a slow learner."

Kevin shook his head. "You guys don't let up."

"C'mon," Lance said, stepping off the elevator. "The bar is calling. We won't make you late for your date with Cara."

"Better not." What Kevin wouldn't tell them was that his plan had already worked. Cara was falling for him again. He saw it in the soft way she looked at him now and in the sweet tone of her voice when they spoke on the phone. "The last thing I want to do is tick her off."

By eight-fifteen, Cara was pacing the floor of her hotel room. At eight-thirty, she glanced at the phone on the nightstand, then pulled out her cell phone and gave it a sour look. Kevin had been due to pick her up half an hour ago. He hadn't called. Cara vacillated about whether to call him or not. But rising anger won out. She slammed her phone shut and tossed it back into her purse.

"He knows how to reach me," she muttered.

Cara's mind rewound to all those days he'd come home later than she'd expected, all those dinners she'd worked on meticulously going untouched. The lonely nights she'd waited up for him. And later, the lonely nights when she'd gone to bed before he'd come home. She'd begun to think it was her. After all, all the other young married women she knew had husbands who came home like clockwork. They ate their dinners together. They spent their weekends doing fun things. She'd found herself longing for Kevin, when it was obvious he hadn't longed for her.

He'd never needed her company, not like that. Not like most newlyweds, who couldn't get enough of each other. She'd begun to feel inadequate as a wife, like she couldn't keep her husband interested. Her feelings had escalated when she'd wanted to have a baby and Kevin had kept putting it off. "There's time for that. We're young yet."

She'd been a sucker then, forgiving him after each excuse, until finally after years of hearing him out, his excuses had fallen on deaf ears. At least she was grateful they hadn't had children. She didn't want to raise a child in a broken home. Because when the pain had gotten too strong, Cara had had no option but to leave, and salvage what was left of her heart.

She wondered what excuse he'd come up with now. And then lightning struck.

"I'm not sticking around to find out."

Cara wasn't the understanding, innocent young wife she once had been. She grabbed her purse and took a quick look at herself in the mirror. Dressed in her little black dress, her blond curls resting on her shoulders, she gave herself an approving nod before walking out the door.

With each step she took, her anger rose. She rode the elevator down to the lobby and headed straight for the concierge desk. She found a middle-aged man with a kind face standing behind the counter.

"I'd like a cab. Where can I find a nice place to listen to music and have a drink?"

The concierge, whose name tag revealed his name was George, smiled. "Well, a cab might not be necessary. The Fairfield Room is available to our guests tonight and the band is scheduled to go on in a few minutes."

"Perfect," Cara said. She could have a drink or two and not worry about finding her way back to the hotel. "Just point me in the right direction."

"I'll do better than that," he said, coming around the counter. "I'll walk you there myself."

Kevin knocked on Cara's door at precisely eight forty-five. He was late picking her up, but it couldn't be helped. After having one drink with Lance and Darius, he'd gotten a call from the night watchman at the apartment complex project. The apartment structure had been vandalized. Teddy Burford had been roughed up a bit and knocked unconscious for a few seconds.

Kevin had given the elderly night-guard the job personally. He was a war veteran who'd been qualified for the job and he had sensed the old guy needed to feel useful in his later years. Kevin stayed with Teddy while he gave the police his story. Nothing was stolen and, from Teddy's description of the culprits, it appeared to have been a teenage prank. Teddy had startled three boys. They'd panicked and one of the boys had shoved him hard. He'd hit his head against the wall and blacked out for a few moments.

Kevin had waited with Teddy until his daughter had picked him up to take him to the emergency room for observation. Then he'd finally glanced at his watch. When he'd realized he'd be late for his date with Cara, he'd called her immediately. She hadn't answered her phone.

Now he stood outside her door, knocking more loudly the second time. "Cara, it's Kevin."

No answer.

He let go a vivid curse and knocked one more time before leaving. He dialed her cell phone number again on his way to the elevator and it went straight to voice mail. She'd turned off her phone.

In the lobby, Kevin spoke with two bellmen, then three women behind the registration desk. One of the employees pointed out the concierge.

Kevin nodded and headed his way. "Excuse me, but I'm looking for my wife, Mrs. Novak. Blond, about so high—" he gestured to her five-foot-eight height "—and beautiful."

George looked him over carefully, then nodded. "I just walked your wife over to the Fairfield Room. It's on the third floor just off the—"

"Thanks." Kevin took off before the concierge finished giving him directions. He'd planned on being with Cara tonight and nothing was going to stop him. Even though he might have to grovel a bit, he'd make her understand why he'd been late.

Kevin followed the sounds of live music, a soft, sultry ballad leading him easily enough to the Fairfield Room. He stood in the double-door entrance to a room with elegant swag draperies, Venetian chandeliers that sparkled like diamonds and a dark wood, parquet dance floor. People huddled around the long bar. Kevin leaned casually against the doorjamb, arms folded, in search of his wife.

When he spotted her, he lifted away slightly to get a better look at Cara in the arms of a stranger, slow-dancing and making conversation.

She looked beautiful in her little black dress and long, glittering earrings, showing enough leg to make a grown man cry.

Kevin tried to temper his frustration, yet the voice in his head wouldn't let it go.

What did you expect?

She's young and beautiful and once you sign those papers, she'll be free to date other men.

Get used to it, buddy.

When the man dancing with Cara brought her up closer, Kevin's frustration transformed into something that made him stride into the room with deliberate steps. His gaze pinned solely on Cara, he walked up to her and set a hand on her arm. She whirled around, her eyes wide.

"Sorry I'm late, babe."

Her mouth dropped open. "Kevin."

She glanced at the man she'd been dancing with and smiled apologetically.

He gave her a quizzical look, then spoke to Kevin. "We're in the middle of a dance."

"I'm aware of that." Kevin couldn't fault the guy for his attempt at chivalry. "But you're dancing with my wife." He cocked the man a smile. "I can take over now."

The man stared at Kevin, then darted a glance at Cara's ringless left finger before dropping his arms from her.

"Soon to be divorced," she added in explanation. The man nodded and lingered. A tic worked at Kevin's jaw.

"Nice meeting you, Cara."

"Same here, Dylan. Sorry about the interruption."

Kevin's patience ebbed. "If you'll excuse us, I need to speak with my wife."

"Sure thing." Dylan eyed Cara once more before walking off the dance floor.

"That wasn't pretty, Kevin." Cara's eyes darkened.

"Maybe not, but it's justified. I'm apologizing for being late."

"Apology declined." Cara marched off the dance floor.

Kevin rolled his eyes and had a good mind not to follow her, but damn it, she'd hear his explanation and then she could decide to be angry or not.

She walked to a table and picked up her purse, tucking it under her arm. "You ruined my evening, Kevin. And you ruined a perfectly nice dance I was enjoying."

"With *that* guy?" Kevin pointed in the direction of the dance floor.

Cara ignored his question. "As I recall, it was you who wanted me to be in town for these weeks, pending our divorce. The least you could do is *show up* when you say you will."

Kevin took a deep breath. "Let's sit down and I'll explain."

"Kevin, don't you see? I don't want your explanations. I heard all of your excuses years ago."

"Okay, if you won't sit down, then dance with me."

"Kevin," she said, exasperated. She ran a hand through her hair and looked away.

He stroked her cheek and she turned to face him. He smiled and said softly, "I'm sorry. I called you as soon as I could."

"I was always second best."

He heard the pain in her voice.

It was important to him that she understood what had happened tonight. She'd always accused him of not putting her first, when that's exactly what he'd done. She'd left him for ill-conceived reasons and he wouldn't let her go to bed tonight thinking she'd been right all those years ago and right tonight as well.

The band played a mellow tune. He took her purse from her and set it down on the chair. "One dance. I'll tell you what happened tonight. I'll tell you about Teddy Burford. Then you can decide what happens next."

Cara's pretty blue eyes gave away her curiosity. "Who's Teddy Burford?"

"Dance with me, and I'll tell you."

"Blackmailing me again?" She whispered the question with a slight tilt of her head and the sweetest curve of her lips.

Kevin's resolve bumped up a notch. He stared at her soft pink lips. "Seems to be the only way with you."

"Not true," she said as she started toward the dance floor. "But I do enjoy dancing."

He watched the sexy twitch of her hips as she moved without him on the dance floor. Without another second of hesitation, he took her into his arms, bringing her up close, her body flush with his. "Ah, Cara. You feel good." He ran his hands up and down her sides, from shoulder to hip.

"Uh-huh." She took his hands and planted them firmly on her hips. She wrapped her arms around his neck and leaned back. "So what happened tonight?"

Kevin explained how he'd first met Teddy Burford when they'd been renovating the Community Senior Center. Teddy had sat among bingo-playing women, looking miserable. He'd lost his wife the year before and was living with his daughter. Though she hadn't complained, Teddy had felt as though he was intruding on her family life.

"I'd meet him for lunch and he'd tell me his war stories. He served two tours of duty in 'Nam. Earned a few medals, too. I kept thinking it was a shame that he wasted his days at the senior center. He'd told me he'd been looking for work, but he wasn't having any luck. You know, he wanted some financial independence. Anyone would want that."

"But he was too old?"

"Only in years. Not in heart. So when the night watchman job came up at the apartment complex, I told him to apply. I didn't want him to think I was giving him the job, but I knew I would. He's a tough old guy with military experience. He knows his stuff."

"Sounds to me, you might have given him the job, regardless," she mused.

"Lucky for me, he was qualified. And he appreciated the work."

"I like him already," Cara said.

"I was having a drink with Lance and Darius tonight when he called. He sounded pretty shaken up."

Kevin went on to explain about the vandals and Teddy's injuries. "Really, Cara, the old guy is my friend. I didn't go there for any other reason but to make sure he was okay. He was distraught, not about having been knocked out, but because he didn't protect the property. He thought he'd failed me and I assured him he did his job and then some. I stayed with him until his daughter picked him up. By that time, I was late calling you. I know I should have called you sooner, but—"

Cara shook her head. "I get it, Kevin. You did the right thing. But even you have to understand why I'd think the worst. You've left me standing alone a hundred times in the past, so why should I have thought any differently tonight?"

Kevin inhaled the fresh citrus scent of her hair and closed his eyes. "You were never second-best, Cara."

Kevin felt the exact moment Cara surrendered. Her shoulders loosened, her body relaxed and she put her head on his shoulder. "Just dance with me, Kevin."

He tightened his hold on her, satisfied that she'd understood and forgiven him. They didn't have much time left together and he wanted to make the most of every minute.

Two hours later, the band called it quits. Cara stood on the dance floor facing Kevin, her body sizzling. They'd had drinks and danced through the night. Cara had a sneaking feeling that Kevin had paid off the band to play only slow, sultry tunes. The music, sweet to her ears, and swaying to each song in Kevin's strong arms was a heady mix she couldn't deny.

Kevin's lips constantly brushed her forehead, his warm breath caressed her throat and his hands roamed to places on her body that were just this side of decent. She moved against him and taught him to seduce the music. And in turn, he'd very nearly seduced her.

She ached for him. Deep down. Not only had she forgiven him but his friendship with a down-and-out, lonely war veteran endeared him to her even more.

"It's getting late." Everyone on the dance floor had dispersed. The band began packing up their gear.

Kevin nodded. "The night didn't turn out as I'd planned. It was even better. Did you have a good time?"

Cara closed her eyes briefly and sighed. "Yes. I love dancing." She loved being with him. They'd talked and laughed, and then got hot and bothered in each other's arms. "Thank you."

"We'd better leave before they kick us out," he said.

A uniformed clean-up crew had entered and were removing the tablecloths from the tables.

"Did you know Pavoratti once sang in this very room?"

Kevin shook his head as they walked to their table. He handed over her purse. "Didn't know that."

"George told me on the way up here."

"Ah, George, the concierge. I think he was smitten with you."

"No, just a nice man."

"Cara, there are no *nice* men. Not when it comes to a beautiful woman. I thought I'd have to fight off that Dylan character just to get a dance with you."

They walked toward the elevator. "You used the wife card, instead."

Kevin let go a chuckle. "Worked like a charm."

"Technically, I'm not your wife. Or I won't be in a few days."

Kevin's tone changed instantly. "Would you rather I'd socked the guy in the jaw?"

Cara laughed. "You wouldn't."

One brow lifted and his eyes narrowed. "I would."

Cara walked on. Kevin wrapped his hand around

hers as they headed to the elevator. "I can make it to my room from here."

"I'll walk you." His jaw firm, his tone determined, she wouldn't argue.

They stepped into the elevator and the second the doors closed Kevin backed her up against the wall. "I've been waiting all night to do this."

One hand flattened against the elevator wall while the other hand wound around to the back of her head, bringing her face close to his. His mouth swooped down and he crushed his lips to hers.

Pent-up tension uncurled in the pit of her stomach. She welcomed the release, craving him with fiery need. His lips sought hers again and again and she matched each kiss with equal ferocity. The sharp taste of hard alcohol mingled with his breath. Her heart pounded and goose bumps rose up her arms.

He dropped his head, bringing his lips to her throat, nibbling, nipping. She curled her fingers in his short, thick hair and allowed him access. He kissed the swells of her breasts, then brought his hands around to caress each one through the material of her dress. His touch made her toes curl. Her nipples stood at full attention. He slid his fingers over the tips, and heat surged through her body.

"Kevin," she cooed, his name slipping from her lips.

The elevator continued to climb and he continued his assault, his kisses frenzied now. Cara huffed out quick breaths, wrapped up in the thrilling moment.

Kevin hiked up the hem of her dress and stroked her along her inner thigh. Rapid-fire sensations shot up her leg, making every cell in her body alert and aware. She moaned from the sheer pleasure, Kevin's hands roaming all over her, his kisses hot and wet and determined.

His erection pulsed against her.

Oh, no, she thought. We can't make love in the elevator. Can we?

The elevator dinged. She froze and looked at the digital display above the doors. She'd reached her floor.

Kevin backed away from her and composed himself.

The doors opened. Luckily, no one was on the other side. Both of them looked disheveled, hair mussed, clothes awry as if…as if they'd had sex in the elevator.

Cara quickly stepped out and looked at Kevin.

His back against the elevator wall, he cast her a crooked smile.

He looked adorable, like a mischievous schoolboy who'd gotten away with ditching class.

"Just four more days, baby."

Heat crawled up her neck. Cara nodded, unable to say a word, but picturing the night they'd finally make love. Kevin hit a button and the doors closed, leaving Cara alone on the hotel floor, hot, bothered and angry with herself for having made this deal with Kevin in the first place.

Four more days before they'd satisfy their desire.

And four more days before Cara was a free woman.

She didn't know which of the two worried her the most.

Eight

"All right, Marissa. I'll see you in a few days." Cara hung up the phone after averting a disaster with two of her most talented dance instructors. Both had threatened to quit and Cara spent the entire morning consoling each one, listening to their complaints about the other and asking them to hold on until she could talk with them in person.

Felicia and Marissa were as temperamental as they come. When Cara was in Dallas, she managed to keep the peace between them. Quite frankly, she was tired of being their intermediary and babysitter. When she returned, she'd lay down the law. If they wanted to continue working at Dancing Lights, they'd have to get along. Period. Cara would hate to lose either one of them, but she'd learned that professionalism was not only admirable but necessary in her employees. She'd learned a good deal about owning a business in the past few years. But she'd always vowed never to allow her business to dominate her personal life.

Her thoughts turned to Kevin. *He* was her personal life right now. For the next four days, anyway. She'd had a great time with him last night. Even though the evening had begun badly, he had managed to turn the night around to become something she would long remember. If there had been any doubt before, being with him last night had convinced her that she'd fallen for him again.

"I love you, Kevin," she whispered in the quiet of her hotel room. She could hardly believe her own revelation. Cara closed her eyes, refusing tears.

Grateful that he was out of town today, Cara could spend the rest of the day trying to sort out her feelings. She'd go online to get some work done, shop for a wedding gift for Lance and Kate, and spend the evening alone with her thoughts.

She needed the time to think things through. She'd get the divorce she'd come to Houston for, but was that what she really wanted? Was she guilty of the same thing she'd accused Kevin of doing, putting business before her personal life? Should she try to work things out with her husband? He hadn't given her any indication of what he wanted for the future. Cara had one day to mull over her situation before

Kevin would knock on her door to take her to Lance and Kate's wedding reception. One day to figure out what she wanted for the rest of her life.

At precisely six-thirty the next evening, Kevin stood at Cara's door wearing a three-piece tuxedo in James Bond fashion. No, she amended—he looked better than 007, and Cara had to purse her lips tight to keep her mouth from dropping open. In black from head to toe, except for the silver-gray tie tucked into his vest, Cara had never seen a more handsome man.

He's my husband.

And I'm standing here drooling.

"I missed you yesterday," were the first words he spoke.

Cara had a hard time keeping her ego from floating off into space.

"I had a contractual meeting in Austin that had been planned months ago or I would have cancelled in a heartbeat."

"I understand." He really had no obligation to see her every day, yet he'd called her three times yesterday when he'd had free time.

"You look beautiful. Red is my favorite color on you." His gaze stayed on her glossy-red lips for a long moment, then drifted down to her off-the-shoulder dress, then farther down to her red heels.

"I bet your toenails are red, too."

Cara kicked off one shoe and wiggled her toes. "You guessed right. Candy-cane red."

"Ah, Cara." He grabbed her hips and brought her close, then bent his head to lay a mind-boggling kiss on her lips. Staying close, his mouth just a breath away, he whispered, "Don't invite me in."

Cara blinked.

"Lance would never forgive me if I showed up late. But he's gonna owe me one, big-time."

Cara chuckled and took his arm. "Then maybe we'd better go."

"Yeah, I was afraid you'd say that."

Twenty minutes later, they pulled up to the Texas Cattleman's Club. A valet opened the door to the Jag and helped Cara out. Kevin handed the valet his keys and was beside her instantly, putting a solid hand on her lower back. He guided her inside and they entered the formal dining room.

Two tall, white columns draped with deep-red rose arrangements stood in invitation at each side of the entrance. White tablecloths and flowered center-pieces in rich earth tones of red, amber and wine decorated each table. Twinkling lights illuminated the arched cathedral window and a dozen round pillar candles lit the carved travertine-stone fireplace mantel. Soft music from a four-piece orchestra played in the background. "Wow, it's stunning."

Kevin glanced around the room, then turned to her. "You make it so."

Her heart did a little flip. "Thank you," she whispered. Kevin had been so complimentary lately and so attentive that she could barely relate him to the man she'd left four years ago, or the man who'd blackmailed her into this two-week charade.

He escorted her farther into the room and she set her gift on a table. "What did you get them?" he asked.

"Personalized wineglasses and a wine tour."

"A wine tour?"

"A bottle of wine delivered each month of their first year of marriage from different regions of France and Italy."

Kevin nodded. "Very original. I'm sure they'll love it."

"Hmm, I hope so. It's hard choosing a gift when you've been out of the loop as long as I have." With a tilt of her head, she looked into Kevin's eyes. "I bet you chose a perfect gift for them."

Kevin shrugged. "I made a sizable donation in their name to their favorite charity."

Cara rocked back on her heels, overwhelmed at Kevin's sensitivity. "That's…very generous."

"I think they'll appreciate it."

A butler served them a glass of merlot and Kevin made a private toast. "To you, Cara. I hope all your dreams come true."

"And to you, Kevin," she said, offering a sentiment of her own. "I hope you find happiness."

They touched glasses gently and looked into each other's eyes as they took a sip.

Kevin remarked, "I'm pretty happy now."

So was she.

Cara's stomach clenched. Blood drained from her

face. Could she give all of this up? Could she divorce Kevin and not wonder if she'd made the worst mistake of her life? Was being with Kevin her real dream? He'd courted her for days now yet he hadn't said one word to lead her to think he wanted to reconcile.

"Anything wrong?" he asked.

"What could be wrong?" Cara answered quickly, pasting a smile on her face.

A tic worked in Kevin's jaw. That same tic that had always come out when they'd argued. He lowered his voice and his tone grew serious. "Yeah, what could be wrong?"

Justin Dupree walked up with a young, leggy blond woman. Cara recognized her immediately as Mila Jankovich, a supermodel she'd seen on a dozen magazines lately. Justin had classic good looks, a handsome profile and dynamic blue eyes, and the two together made an eye-catching couple. Introductions were made and more wine was poured as they conversed.

Mila seemed infatuated with Justin, being years his junior, Cara presumed. And though she'd always thought Justin a nice guy, he had a reputation with women. No father in his right mind would like to see Justin Dupree courting his daughter.

The orchestra quieted and an announcement was made when Kate and Lance entered the room. The small crowd of friends and family applauded.

Kate beamed with joy and Lance had never looked happier. Cara's heart sank even further. She remembered her own wedding and the brightness that had filled her when she and Kevin had spoken their vows. She'd had hopes of a happy future, with a new husband and children someday. None of that had happened for her. Yet, here she was, standing beside Kevin, unsure of their relationship.

Should she tell him she loved him?

Or should she take him at his word, that he wanted to part as friends?

Friends?

She didn't want him as a friend. Not anymore. She wanted more. She'd seen the changes in Kevin and believed that he was a different man than the one who'd hurt her so terribly.

Could she trust in that?

Kevin held Cara in his arms on the dance floor, the orchestra strings creating a romantic mood. He breathed in her exotic scent and threaded his fingers into her blond curls. He had trouble holding on to his bitter need for revenge when he had her in his arms. Soft and feminine and the most beautiful woman in the room, Cara made him forget all the pain she'd caused him. Kevin had never had a woman run out on him before. He'd never been left holding the bag, racked by humiliation, his pride shredded to pieces. He remembered those drunken days after she'd first left, the ache of desolation mixing with anger and frustration. He remembered having to tell his parents and friends the truth. He'd hated their pity and sympathy. He'd felt like a failure in his personal life, when he'd been nothing but successful in his professional life.

Those feelings had stayed with him for four years. His resentment was fueled even more by the reason she'd come back for a divorce—to get a bank loan. He'd seduced her for the past eleven days with one goal in mind, and he wasn't a man to deviate from a plan once it was constructed. But perhaps he'd laid out his plan too well because he was softening to her.

"Are you okay?" she asked, her blond brows furrowing.

"I'm fine." He gave her a reassuring smile.

Darius tapped him on the shoulder. "Mind if I cut in?"

Yeah, he minded, but Cara had already released him. "Darius, I'd love to dance with you."

Kevin relented, turning Cara over to Darius. He took up his glass of wine and found it lacking in alcohol content. He headed to the bar in search of a stronger drink, needing a moment to get a grip, to back off from feelings he wanted no part of. Lance came up beside him and leaned one arm against the bar, facing him.

"Whiskey, straight up," Kevin told the bartender. "And bring the groom one, too."

Lance laughed. "Cara's getting to you, isn't she?"

"Nice party, Lance." Kevin refused to take the bait.

"Glad you're enjoying yourself. Cara seems to be, too."

"She's having a nice enough time."

"You haven't let her out of your sight for two hours."

Kevin scratched the back of his neck. "Are you keeping track?"

The bartender slid two drinks their way. Lance smirked before he took a sip of his drink. "Hell, I saw the look you shot Darius when he interrupted your dance. If looks could kill…"

"She's only here a few more days."

"Are you still working on your brilliant plan to get back at her?"

Kevin winced. He lifted his glass to his lips. "Maybe."

"Man, don't be stupid."

"Shut up, Lance."

"Am I hitting too close to home? Are you having doubts? If you are, then I'd say you're making progress."

"You have no idea what you're talking about."

"I know you were hurt, Kev. I know you thought she abandoned you. But did you ever consider her side? Maybe both of you were right and both of you were wrong."

Kevin sucked in oxygen. "I'm so glad I came to your wedding reception. Does Kate know what a nosy-body she married?"

"She knows I love my friends."

"Two more whiskeys," Kevin said to the bartender, then turned to Lance. "Do me a favor, don't love me so much."

"Funny, Kev. You're a real comedian."

Kevin nodded. "Whether you think so or not, I know what I'm doing."

Lance sipped his second whiskey and put a hand on Kevin's shoulder. "That, my friend, remains to be seen."

When Kevin returned to the table, Darius and Summer approached, along with Justin, Mila and Mitch Brody. They all sat down, and Summer and Cara struck up a conversation.

"What gave you the idea to develop a chain of dance studios?" Summer asked Cara.

Cara's eyes sparkled. "Well, I'd always loved to dance. I studied several forms of dance as a young girl. Ballet, of course, but swing, too, and some ballroom and I…well, I—" She glanced at Kevin, then shrugged and sipped her drink.

"With all the dance competitions on television now, I imagine it's very sought after in the real world," Summer said.

Cara nodded, her smile wide. "There's a good-size market out there now. People want to feel good about themselves. There's nothing more freeing to me than moving with the music."

"You do it well," Darius added. He looked to Summer. "She gave me some pointers when we danced."

Cara chuckled. "Oh, no. I'm not taking credit for that. Darius has enough rhythm for a three-piece jazz band. He could very well be on my staff as an instructor."

"Right," Darius said with a shake of his head. "I'd probably scare off your clients."

Summer laid a hand on his arm. "Darius is a man of many talents."

"You keep saying that," Justin chimed in with a twinkle in his blue eyes, "but no one else sees it."

Darius feigned an angry look. "Careful, pretty boy."

Kevin listened as his friends bantered back and forth, for the most part keeping quiet. Cara shot him curious looks from time to time while she engaged in conversation. He noted the strong, confident woman she'd become. She'd always been intelligent and clever, but Cara had grown in other ways and, more and more, he liked what he saw in her. And as she spoke with Summer about her social work and the Texas Cattleman's Club shelter, Helping Hands, the two discussed how to best serve the community. It was clear Cara had made a new friend.

But Cara wouldn't have time to develop that friendship. It would all end soon. After they consummated their deal, he'd sign the divorce papers and let her go, his revenge complete.

And by letting her go, he'd be free, too.

To move on with his life.

Yet Lance's words kept reverberating in his head.

Don't be stupid, Kevin.

Am I hitting too close to home?

Are you having doubts?

Damn it, yes. He had doubts. He had feelings for

Cara that he couldn't deny. The more he tried to push them out of his mind, the stronger they'd become.

Thankfully, Mitch Brody interrupted his train of thought. "How about a game of tennis tomorrow after work?"

"Yeah, sure." He'd make the time. Maybe knocking a ball around would knock some sense into his head.

Twenty minutes later, Cara slipped away from the party to use the ladies' room. She needed a breather from Kevin and the thoughts of reconciliation that kept entering her head. Being on his arm tonight, meeting up with old friends, more and more she felt like she could slide right into the role as wife to Kevin. He'd changed from the type-A personality businessman he'd been, driven to succeed no matter the cost to his personal life. He'd made his millions and, with nothing more to prove, he seemed to have figured out how to keep an equal balance between business and pleasure.

It felt right being here with him and feeling a part of the Somerset community again. A swirl of excitement coursed through her system. Caught up in the festivities and the romance of Kate and Lance's wedding reception, Cara felt like she belonged.

She entered the ladies' room lobby. "Cara!"

Cara faced Alicia Montoya in the large, gilded vanity mirror. Alicia swirled around with lipstick in midair to face her directly.

"Alicia, hi! It's good to see you."

Alicia set her tube of lipstick down and they embraced. "What a nice surprise."

"I'm here with Kevin. Remember I told you about Lance and Kate's wedding reception?"

"Yes, I know. Alex and I were having dinner in the café and we could hear you all having a great time."

"We are." Then Cara lowered her voice. "Especially me. It's been a really wonderful night."

Alicia leaned in. "Wonderful enough to use your new Sweet Nothing purchase?"

Cara chuckled. "Who knows what the night might bring?" She wouldn't explain that she'd wear her new lingerie the night she and Kevin made love, in a few days. Not before. She really wanted to knock his socks off and make a lasting memory.

Alicia bubbled with excitement. "I may have to make a trip back to that store soon. I just met the most dreamy man here at TCC and he asked me out."

"Oh, Alicia. That's great. Who is he?"

Alicia's face took on a glow and her dark brows lifted. "His name is Rick Jones. We had a brief conversation outside while I was waiting for Alex. I would have remembered if I'd seen him before. He's not a man a woman could forget. Not with those amazing blue eyes."

"Well, you'll have to spill all the details after your date. I'm dying to hear how it all works out."

"No more than me, Cara. I haven't had a date in a while. And, well, Rick is charming and handsome. He's attending the wedding reception."

"Oh, really?" Cara tried to figure out which of the partygoers could be Rick Jones, but she came up short. Though the reception was relatively small, Cara didn't know all of Kate and Lance's friends.

"I've been floating all night, driving Alex crazy with my good mood."

Cara took her hand and couldn't stop the grin that pulled at her mouth. "Good for you. For being happy, that is, not for driving Alex crazy."

Cara couldn't blame a man for being attracted to Alicia's sweet demeanor and beautiful looks. Cara had always admired her light olive skin tone and dazzling brown eyes. Tonight, she looked stunning in a simple, brown, off-the-shoulder sweater and pencil skirt, her dark hair swept back in curls. "Whoever this Rick Jones is, he's a lucky guy."

Alicia hugged her again. "Thanks, Cara. I'd better go before Alex thinks I deserted him."

"Okay. Enjoy the rest of your evening. We'll talk soon."

"Yes, we will. Have a good time tonight with Kevin." Alicia wiggled her fingers in a farewell wave and dashed out of the ladies' room.

Cara returned to the reception minutes later, surprised to find the orchestra had ceased playing, replaced by piped-in rock music. Alcohol flowed in abundance, the dance floor was in full swing and the small crowd filled the room with laughter and shouts to the bride and groom. She found Kevin swinging the young supermodel around on the dance floor, the lanky blonde laughing heartily and sipping her drink.

Cara's heart sank seeing Kevin with another woman, seeming to enjoy the attention she bestowed him. Cara searched the reception for Justin Dupree but couldn't find him anywhere.

When the music ended, Kevin headed her way. "Hey, I thought you'd never come back."

Cara granted him a quick smile, concealing the jealousy she felt seeing Kevin with Mila. He was by Cara's side again now, giving her his full attention. "I ran into a friend in the ladies' room. What happened to the orchestra?"

Kevin grinned. "Lance made a deal with Kate. A few hours of sedate orchestra music, then we let our hair down."

"Wow. Now it looks like a party."

"Yeah, an open bar and heavy rock can do that to a perfectly good wedding reception." Kevin glanced at Mitch Brody. "I think they're ready for the toasts. C'mon," he said, taking her arm. "I want you next to me when I roast Lance."

"Over a fire pit?"

A wicked smirk crossed his features and Kevin's eyes gleamed. "Yeah, something like that."

But after Mitch's toast to his brother, amid whistles and hoots from the boisterous crowd, a stern-looking man entered the room and spoke directly to Lance.

Cara watched Lance argue with the man, shaking

his head until Kate put her hand on Lance's arm. Lance spoke briefly with Kate and then rose to speak with their guests. "Apparently, we're having too much fun in here for someone at the club. Complaints have been lodged from the room next door about the noise level and we've been asked to leave."

The entire room groaned in unison.

"I know, I know," Lance said, holding his apparent anger in check.

Kate rose and spoke to her guests. "This has been an amazing party, and Lance and I want to thank all of you for coming. I can't tell you how much it means to both of us to have our dearest friends here to celebrate our marriage."

"Yes," Lance said. "Thank you all for coming, but Kate and I don't want the party to end. We're inviting all of you back to our place. And I promise you, we can make all the noise we want there!"

The crowd in the room applauded.

Cara turned to Kevin. "Can they do that? Break up the party because of noise?"

Kevin shrugged. "TCC has rigid rules and apparently whoever complained made a big stink about it. Lance is furious, but he's keeping his cool for Kate's sake. So, what do you say? Want to go to the after party with me?"

"I wouldn't miss it," Cara said, grinning.

The party guests followed Kate and Lance out the front entrance of the club. Kevin noticed Sebastian Huntington speaking with Cornelius Gentry under a streetlamp. Gentry, a wiry little man known to be Huntington's foreman, glanced over to the group. Both men wore smug expressions on their faces.

Immediately, Kevin's suspicions were aroused. Huntington, a snob in the worst way, hated the "new money" millionaires at the club. He didn't think they were good enough to rub noses with the elite of Houston and he never failed to make his feelings well known.

Kevin tightened his hold on Cara, squeezing her hand gently as they walked with the group toward the valet station to wait for his car.

Cara glanced up at him and smiled sweetly. Her smile made him forget his suspicions and he concentrated on how beautiful she looked tonight. He bent his head and kissed her lightly on the lips.

"What was that for?" she whispered.

A swell of possessiveness filled his heart. He looked into her soft blue eyes and couldn't come up with a witty reply. He opened his mouth to say something, but emotions overwhelmed him and sensations swept through his system as he realized his time with Cara was coming to an end.

"You son of a bitch!"

Kevin whirled around to find Lance marching toward Alex Montoya just outside the doors of the TCC. With each determined step he took, his eyes filled with more rage.

"You did this! You broke up my wedding reception!"

Alicia stood beside her brother, her eyes wide, her expression terrified.

Montoya stiffened and stared at Lance with hard eyes and tight lips. "What the hell are you talking about, Brody?" Alex took note of the guests standing behind Lance. Immediately, he shielded his sister by taking a step in front of her. Patience and understanding were not virtues in either man when they faced each other. It was bad enough that Lance believed Montoya had set fire to his refinery, but now Lance was accusing him of shutting down his wedding reception.

"You complained about the noise at my reception and had us all booted out of there!"

Alex's face flamed with indignation. "Now, why would I do that? I don't give a damn about your pathetic little wedding reception."

They stood nose-to-nose now, each man refusing to back off.

Kate watched the scene unfold, fear entering her eyes. "Oh, no."

"This is low, even for you." Lance glared at Alex.

"Watch it, Brody." Alex kept tight control of his temper. "Don't go making accusations you can't prove."

Alex turned around to take Alicia's arm. "Let's get out of here."

"Not so fast, Montoya. I'm not through with you!"

Slowly, Alex turned back around, his expression grim. He released his sister's arm. "You're not *through* with me?"

The situation had gone from bad to worse. Cara bit her lip and Kate appeared panicked. Lance and Alex were heading for trouble.

Kevin strode purposefully toward the two men. He faced them like a referee breaking up two linebackers ready to brawl. "Come on, Lance. Kate's upset. Let's not add to it."

Lance darted a glance at him. "Stay out of it, Kevin."

"Yeah, stay out of it, Novak." Montoya eyed him with disdain. "If the groom's got a bone to pick, I'm ready."

Lance gritted his teeth. "Damn right, I have a bone to pick."

Kevin scratched his head, wondering if he should let them have it out once and for all. They'd been rivals since high school and this would be the culmination of years of hatred and resentment. But one glance at Cara with those hope-filled blue eyes and Kevin knew what he had to do.

He stepped between them, facing Lance. "C'mon, man. Let's get out of here. Kate's waiting for you."

Lance inhaled sharply and peered around Kevin to cast Montoya a hard look. He took a long second to stare. Kevin held his breath. Finally, Lance relented. "This isn't over."

"Don't ever toss accusations at me again, Brody," Montoya warned with stern indignation. "But for the record, I had nothing to do with breaking up your party."

With that, he grabbed Alicia's arm and guided her back into the club.

"Bastard," Lance muttered.

Kate ran over to him. "Lance, are you crazy?"

Lance took one look at Kate's concerned face and threw his head back and laughed, finding humor in the situation. He reached for her, wrapped his arms around her waist and pulled her close. "Yeah, I'm crazy. About you. You deserve a beautiful wedding reception."

"And I got one. Tonight was wonderful. I enjoyed every single minute of it. Now, let's be good hosts. Our friends are waiting."

Lance glanced at the group who had witnessed his outburst. "The party's still on. At our house."

Satisfied, Kate kissed him lightly, then turned to Kevin. She mouthed a silent thank-you to him and he nodded.

Cara strode over and slipped her hand under his arm. "My hero."

Kevin glanced into her pretty eyes.

"You averted a disaster," she said.

"Heroes do that." He grinned, making light of the situation, yet couldn't shake his gut feeling that there was more to all this than met the eye.

Nine

The after party continued into the wee hours of the night. Cara and Kevin found a cozy corner of the living room and stayed cuddled together, kissing like two high-school teenagers who couldn't get enough of each other. When the party wound down, just the four of them remained. "I think we should give the newlyweds some privacy now."

Kevin glanced around, just noticing that they were the last of the guests. "Yeah, I bet they want to get to bed." He shot Cara a sizzling look, lowering his voice and leaning in. "I want to get you to bed, too."

His hot kiss erupted tingles on her arms. It had been like that all night—steamy kisses and smoldering glances and enough innuendo to bring her fantasies to life.

Fantasies of loving Kevin wholly and completely.

It had been nearly two weeks of torture. Two weeks of wondering, of being tempted beyond belief and two weeks of needing to quench the thirst she had for her husband.

Lance walked up with a crystal whiskey decanter in hand. "Ready for another?" he asked Kevin.

Kevin rose and took Cara's hand. "No, thanks. I think we're going to let you two get to bed."

Lance laughed, swaying a little. He grabbed Kate and kissed her smack on the lips. "Good idea."

"I think he's partied a little too hard tonight," Kate said, patting his arm lovingly.

Lance swayed a bit more and Kate wrapped her arms around his waist to steady him.

"Just…happy," Lance said, slurring his words slightly and casting Kate a crooked, silly smile.

"I can get him to the bedroom for you, Kate. It'll be like old times back at UT," Kevin offered.

"Nah," Lance said. "Don't need your services tonight, Kev. My wife knows how to take care of me." He wiggled his brows in villainous style.

Kate chuckled. "Well, I'm learning."

"You're a lucky man." Kevin slapped Lance on the back. Lance disengaged from Kate and smiled at him. "Kate, will you walk Kevin to the door?" Lance turned to Cara and offered his arm. "Cara?"

She slipped her arm through his and he tottered a

bit before straightening up. He waited until Kate and Kevin were steps ahead of them, then looked at Cara through lowered lashes. "Kevin's a good guy," he leaned in to whisper, his words running together. "Damn hardheaded though…I warned him to be careful…not to hurt you."

"How will he hurt me?" Cara asked, confused and wondering if she should pay attention to anything he said while intoxicated.

"I think he already has." Lance mumbled a curse, then shook his head as if shaking off cobwebs. "Never mind. Forget I said anything." He placed her hand in his and smiled warmly, then walked her to the front door.

That night, the last thing Cara could do was forget Lance's comments. She replayed his parting words over and over in her head, trying to make sense of them. He may have had too much to drink, but Lance wasn't so intoxicated that he didn't know what he was saying. She heard his true concern in the sobering way he whispered in her ear. What bothered her the most wasn't that she stood to get hurt by Kevin, but that Lance had knowledge of it. What was going on? What had Kevin said to Lance to make him believe she'd get hurt?

Or had Lance simply been way off in his assessment of the situation? Cara tossed on those thoughts before falling asleep that night.

In the morning, with sunshine pouring into her window and all things looking bright, she rose early, worked out to a Pilates exercise program on the flat screen and felt too happy to worry about anything. She'd spend the afternoon with Kevin today. They'd made those arrangements during the reception and, after a spellbinding good-night kiss, he'd reminded her that they'd have a day of fun in the sun. "We're going to play all day," he'd said to her.

A thrill ran up her spine. Kevin was proving to her again and again that he wasn't the same man she'd set out to divorce. He'd learned how to delegate. He'd learned how to have fun. He'd learned that there was more to life than work. Cara smiled as she showered and pulled on a breezy, flowered sundress.

When Alicia Montoya called, Cara couldn't refuse to meet her for coffee. Clearly upset, Alicia needed a friend. Half an hour later, they sat on tufted sofa chairs drinking espresso at a local coffee shop near Cara's hotel.

"Thanks for meeting me on such short notice," Alicia said, her pretty face forlorn. Dressed in black, as if in mourning, she wore her hair pulled tightly back, held by a clasp. Light pink lipstick brought color to her olive skin tones.

Alicia played with the rim of her coffee mug, searching for the right words. "This is…hard."

"I know," Cara said, compassion filling her heart. Alicia wanted so much to be accepted. It couldn't be easy being Alejandro Montoya's sister. Alicia had been on cloud nine last night when they'd last spoken. She'd been so happy that she'd met Rick Jones and he'd asked her out. Cara still didn't know who Rick was, but judging by the look on Alicia's face last night, he'd made her very happy. Then there had been the blowup outside of the club and poor Alicia had looked panic stricken. "I'm glad you called me."

"Are you? I think I'm putting you in the middle."

Cara reached for her arm. "No, I'm not in the middle of anything. You're my friend."

Alicia lowered her stiff shoulders and let go a sigh. "Oh, Cara. I can't tell you what that means to me."

"It means a lot to me, too."

"It's just that everyone thinks the worst of my brother."

"I can't pretend I don't know that. Alex and Lance go way back and none of it is pretty."

"Your husband doesn't like him either."

"Kevin thinks Alex blocked one of his projects. It's business more than a personal thing."

Alicia nodded her understanding, her expression somber. "Alex didn't break up the reception last night. He wouldn't do that."

"Are you certain?"

"Yes. I'm sure. I was with him all night, except for the time I met you in the ladies' room. He never complained about the reception. In fact, he didn't know about it until I mentioned it to him."

"But you said you'd heard the music playing."

"Alex barely noticed it and it certainly didn't

bother us. He may think Lance a rival, but he's not that petty. I just know in my heart Alex would never do something like that."

No, Cara thought. If only Alicia knew what bigger crimes the Brody brothers accused him of perpetrating, she'd be devastated. "Alicia, I believe you. But Lance and Alex are going to have to find a way to work out their differences on their own."

"My brother isn't perfect. He's stubborn and prideful, but he's a good man. It hurt to see him being accused last night in front of so many people. It's a good thing Kevin intervened."

"Yes, I agree. Lance looked ready for a fight."

"And Alex never backs down from one."

Cara smiled at her friend with sadness in her heart. "Not a good combination, I'm afraid." She didn't have any answers but she knew Alicia didn't expect any. She only needed a friend to talk to.

"I'm glad we spoke."

"Me, too. I hope it helped a little."

"It did." Alicia sipped her espresso, which up until this point had gone untouched. "Oh, this is good."

Cara sipped her decaf. "So what are you doing the rest of the day?"

A smile broke out on her face. "Well, I think they're having a sale at Sweet Nothings today."

"You're going back for that pink baby-doll lingerie!"

"I think so. Just in case, mind you. It's nice to know there's hope of wearing it one day."

Cara's laugh displayed her great delight. "That a girl."

"What about you? Do you have plans for the rest of the day?"

Cara nodded with thoughts of Kevin's deep-blue eyes on her as he'd bid her good-night. "I have plans with Kevin later today."

Alicia took her hand and gazed directly into her eyes. "I hope it works out for you and Kevin, Cara. You deserve to be happy."

Cara couldn't agree more. She wanted to be happy again. "Thank you. And remember, I'm here if you need me."

At precisely 1:00 p.m., Kevin picked Cara up in front of her hotel. He opened the car door for her, took her tote bag and tossed it into the trunk. "What's in the bag?"

"Everything necessary for fun in the sun," she quipped. "Bathing suit, sunscreen, oils and lotions."

Kevin shot her a heated glance from the driver's seat. He looked simply edible in tan trousers and a black polo shirt sitting behind the wheel of his powerful sports car. "Sounds perfect."

He gunned the car and they took off toward Somerset. "Are we going to the club?" she asked.

"No way. I have something better in mind." He swiveled his head to gaze at her once again. "You look beautiful, Cara."

So do you, she didn't add. Her heart sang. "Thanks."

Kevin reached over to take her hand as he drove on, his fingers wrapping around hers with gentle possession. Cara closed her eyes briefly. Electricity flowed between them. She felt it and knew that what they had was more than simple physical attraction.

Kevin pulled up in front of a large, lovely cottage-like home on the outskirts of Somerset. Cobblestone and a white picket fence marked the entry, the garden robust with colorful pansies in full bloom and sculpted greenery.

Cara stared at the home, then questioned Kevin with a curious look.

"It's a rental I own. Vacant at the moment and ours for the day."

"How convenient," she teased.

"Isn't it though?"

Kevin opened the car door for her and lifted her tote bag from the trunk easily, laying it onto her shoulder. With a hand to her back, he guided her down the cobblestone path to the front door. Fidgeting with a set of keys, he finally came up with the one that fit in the lock. "Here it is."

"Good, because breaking and entering won't look good on my record."

Kevin kissed her smack on the lips. "Sassy today."

"Always."

"That's what I love about you."

The minute the words were out, she knew Kevin wished he hadn't spoken them. He turned away from her quickly and fumbled with the key. After a few seconds, he managed to get the door open. "Sticky lock," he explained with a little hitch in his throat.

Cara remained silent.

He guided her into the house, which had a country feel to it. From what she could see, the entry hall led to a massive living space, complete with a ceiling-to-floor stone fireplace, wood beams above and large windows on either side of an oak-framed set of French doors.

"Very nice. How long has it been empty?"

"A month. The previous tenants moved to Europe. The new tenants move in next week. It's been cleaned and polished to a shine."

"I can see that." Cara stared at the shiny wood floors beneath her feet and imagined dancing on them. "The rooms are big, but it still feels cozy to me."

"Looks even better with furniture."

Kevin tugged on the tote bag hanging from her shoulder. "C'mon. I want to show you the grounds."

Kevin opened the French doors wide and led her out to a large stone patio. Three sets of love seats wrapped around an in-ground fire pit. Kevin took her hand and led her down a small staircase to the private garden below, infused with bright color.

"Beautiful," Cara murmured.

A swimming pool the size of a small lake came into view beyond a low outcropping of dark green hedges.

Kevin gestured to a mini-replica of the cottage serving as the pool house. "Two pitchers of margaritas are waiting for us in there, one strawberry."

Cara peered into his eyes. "You thought of everything."

Kevin grinned. "That remains to be seen."

Cara walked along the path to the black-bottom pool. Kicking her sandals off, she dipped her toes in. "You did think of everything. It's the perfect temperature for me."

"Well, then, let's take a dip."

"But where's your stuff?" she asked, noting that he hadn't brought a beach bag for himself.

"Don't need anything." He sat down in the center of a slatted lounge chair and took off his shoes.

He didn't need anything?

Cara's heart raced.

Next, he stood and removed his shirt, pulling the polo over his head in one fluid move. Texas sunshine streamed down on his bare chest. Ripped with muscle and bronzed as a golden statue, Kevin took her breath away. When he unzipped his trousers, she took a deep gulp of oxygen, unable to avert her gaze. "Kevin?"

He pulled down his trousers and stepped out of them, his swim trunks appearing underneath.

"What's taking you so long?" He gestured with a nod of his head. "The pool house has a dressing area."

"R-right," she said, taking hold of her senses. "I'll be back in a sec." Just before she entered the dressing room, she heard a splash from Kevin's dive into the pool.

After donning her two-piece, strawberry-red bathing suit, she grabbed two plush white towels and hugged them to her chest. Feeling foolishly self-conscious at the amount of skin showing, Cara glanced in the mirror and wondered what had possessed her to buy this skimpy suit.

She'd never worn it in public before. And granted, being poolside with her husband wasn't exactly like being on the sands of Waikiki in the middle of summer, yet she still felt terribly exposed.

"Cara, you coming?" Kevin's boyish tone brought a smile to her lips. "I'm getting lonely out here."

She glanced at the refrigerator in the small kitchenette on the way out. "You want a margarita?" she called.

"Later, babe."

Cara nibbled on her lip and exited the pool house just as Kevin glided out of the water, his head lifting and his gaze zeroing in on her. Water sloshed off his shoulders as he rose to stand in the pool. He swiped back his short hair and smiled, reaching for her. "Drop the towels, Cara."

She let them fall from her hands near the edge of the pool. "Don't pull me in."

He secured her hand in his. "I won't. Take your time, babe. I could stand here all day and look at you."

Heat crawled up her neck from the soft tone of his voice and the captivating way his gaze stayed on her. Slowly, she lowered her body down to sit on the edge of the pool. Putting her feet in, she wiggled her toes. "Feels good."

Kevin ran his hands along her thighs, moistening her legs with pool water. "Yeah, it does."

"I don't just jump into things anymore," she explained.

"You used to." Kevin's deliberate touch along her thighs made her bones melt.

"I've changed." She was more mature, more thoughtful about things. She'd learned a valuable lesson being married to Kevin. She hadn't really known him when they'd married. His drive and ambition had caught her off guard. She vowed not to let her emotions dictate her future anymore. Every single decision she'd made since leaving Somerset had been done with great thought and deliberation.

"I have, too."

Cara stared at Kevin. He had changed. He'd proven that over the past two weeks. But she didn't know if she could trust in that. Or in him anymore.

But she did love him.

That fact couldn't be denied.

Kevin parted her legs and grabbed her around the waist. "Whenever you're ready."

She nodded. She was ready to take a chance. She wrapped her legs around his waist and her arms around his neck. He lowered her gently into the water, swirling her around and around, slowly, their eyes never parting.

Buoyant and floating, Cara felt a wave of peace and happiness she hadn't experienced in a long time. She reached out to touch his face, the stubble of his day-old beard grazing her fingers. Then she leaned in and kissed him softly on the mouth.

Kevin stopped and cast her a long, penetrating look, his eyes searching hers intently. Tingles ran up and down her body. Her throat dry, powerful emotions swept over her.

"Cara?"

Cara pressed her fingers to his lips. "Shh, don't say anything, sweetheart."

She couldn't bear to hear what he had to say. She didn't want the mood to turn serious or change in any way. It had been so long since she'd felt such serenity. She wanted to live in the moment and not analyze every word Kevin spoke or scrutinize every gesture he made. "Fun in the sun, remember?" She kissed him again.

Pleased, he groaned deep and waded through the water with her in his arms until they reached the wall of the pool. Resting his back on the tile, he tugged her closer, her breasts rising above the water to press against his chest.

Kevin kissed her fiercely, his mouth traveling over her face, her chin, her throat and shoulders, nipping at her skin and creating impossible tingles that spun her mind in ten different directions.

"Did I tell you how much I like your bathing suit?"

Cara kissed his shoulder. "You neglected to say that earlier."

He cupped her rear end, his fingers spread over her cheeks. "I do. I like it a lot. What there is of it."

"Oh, yeah?" She wiggled out of his arms and dived into the water, swimming a few laps from width to width. Things were heating up too fast between her and Kevin. As much as she wanted him, she had an impending need to protect herself.

When she came up out of the water after her swim, she faced Kevin from across the shallow end of the pool. "I'm ready for a margarita."

"I'll get them," he said without hesitation and she watched him lift himself out of the water and head to the pool house.

Kevin poured Cara a strawberry margarita, then rimmed his glass with salt and poured himself one from the other pitcher. Putting the pitchers back in the refrigerator, he lifted out two covered plates—lunch. He'd had a chef from his favorite restaurant prepare gourmet sandwiches and salad, and had them delivered here, refusing the chef's offer to serve the meal. Kevin wanted to be completely alone with Cara today.

They had two days left together.

He winced, thinking his days were numbered in regard to her. Soon, he'd be a free man, his plan accomplished and revenge complete.

He hadn't expected to regret his decision, though. He'd become accustomed to having Cara by his side again. Yet it was her decision to come to Somerset for a divorce. She hadn't wanted reconciliation and if he hadn't blackmailed her into seeing him these past two weeks, she would have been long gone, signed divorce papers in hand. He couldn't get over that. She'd rejected him not once but twice in his life.

His ego had taken a pounding and his pride was at stake. On many levels, he wished he hadn't come up with his brilliant scheme for payback. Because he, too, had suffered the consequences of spending time with Cara and wanting her with a need so great, he'd had trouble keeping to his plan, again and again.

Kevin set the dishes on a tray along with the margaritas and hesitated before bringing them outside.

Why not give in to his needs now? Why not seduce her today and be done with it? They'd been leading up to this point since the moment she'd agreed to his plan. Why wait? Why extend the torturous need they had for each other?

Kevin debated that notion as he picked up the tray and carried it outside. He found Cara in a chaise lounge, sliding sunscreen oil onto her legs. He stopped to take in the scene, watching her finish coating her legs with the golden liquid. Once she was done with her legs, she spread the oil onto her torso, working it in and then farther up, onto her chest. She grazed over the swells of her breasts with the oil and slid her fingers slightly underneath her swimsuit top, making sure to cover every inch of exposed skin.

"You should have let me do that," Kevin said, making light of the extremely sexy scene he'd just witnessed.

"You were taking too long, buster. A girl's got to protect herself, you know?"

Kevin set the tray down on a glass table between her lounge and his. He gazed at her very appealing chest for a few lingering seconds. "Hungry?"

"Famished," she said. "Swimming gives me an appetite."

He liked that about Cara. She wasn't one to not eat when hungry. Usually, she scarfed up her food with enthusiasm.

He handed her the margarita. "To…us."

She gazed at him, puzzled. He picked up his glass and touched it to hers. "To us," she finally replied with a small smile.

They conversed while eating lunch and sipping margaritas in the sunshine. Cara told stories of her dance students, some of whom had gone on to real careers in dance and other lonely souls who'd pay the fee just to have some one-on-one attention from a pretty dance instructor. Kevin enjoyed listening to her—the animation in her voice and her broad gestures spoke of her love and commitment to her business. When she'd first arrived, he'd resented hearing of her success, but now he felt proud of what she'd accomplished.

"You know," she said in a thoughtful tone, "I think Somerset might need a dance studio."

Kevin stopped chewing for a second. He gazed into Cara's bright eyes. Finally swallowing, he asked, "Here?"

"Why not? I like it here. I could expand my horizons in this direction as well as any."

Kevin didn't reply. It was one thing being divorced from Cara while she was miles away, but having her come back here as a single woman? He didn't know if he was ready for that. Visions of bumping into her while she was on a date with another man, or seeing her with his friends, didn't sit well with him. A dozen emotions swirled in his gut. He felt sick to his stomach at the prospect.

When his silence became obvious, Cara asked, "Kevin, would you have a problem with that?"

Hell, yeah. "No, not at all," he lied, hoping the idea was just a passing fancy.

Cara watched him carefully, then lowered her lashes. "It's just a thought." She sipped her margarita and shrugged. He couldn't help but feel he'd disappointed her somehow, though.

Shoving the notion from his head, he was determined to enjoy the day with Cara without worry. They went on to more amiable topics of discussion as they finished their lunch.

Cara sighed and leaned back in her chaise lounge, lifting her face to the sun. "This is really nice, Kevin. I'm glad you invited me here."

"Don't get too comfortable, baby. You still have to do me."

Cara lifted partly up from the lounge and peered at him. "What?"

He pointed to the sunscreen oil. Then grinned.

Cara shook her head, a wide smile erupting on her face. "Funny, Kevin."

"Well?"

"Okay, lie back." Kevin obeyed without hesitation. Cara poured oil onto her hands and straddled his legs.

He looked up into her pretty sky-blue eyes, barely able to contain his lust. When she touched him, her hands splaying across his chest, he groaned inwardly. She massaged the oil in, her fingertips light, gliding over his skin. He watched her as she leaned forward, intent on her task, her beautiful cleavage in full view and practically begging for his touch. It took every ounce of his willpower not to pull her down on top of him and show her what she did to him.

Once she'd massaged his arms and shoulders, he took the bottle out of her hand. "I think you've done enough."

"You don't sound grateful," she said, her teasing tone too much to take.

"Oh, I'm very grateful," he said, wrapping his arms around her neck and pulling her close. "You know, it's very private here. No one can see what we're doing."

Her eyes went wide with surprise. With that, he pulled her closer and crushed his lips to hers, absorbing every inch of her. But it wasn't nearly enough. He parted her lips and drove his tongue into her mouth, tasting the sweetness of strawberries and her unabashed passion.

In just a few seconds, Kevin had Cara sprawled atop him, his erection straining the confines of his swim trunks. She fit him perfectly and made him crazy with want. He untied her top easily, one little slice of material keeping him from heaven. Her breasts spilled out and Kevin caressed them, holding their weight in his hands, flicking his thumb over both tips until they pebbled into beautiful erect buds.

His gaze trained on hers, he took one perfect globe into his mouth. Cara's eyes slowly closed and a beautiful expression flowed over her features.

He suckled her until both buds were moistened and glowed in the warming sunshine.

Kevin wrapped his hands around her bottom and positioned her onto his erection until she felt the full force of his desire. "I can't wait to have you."

Cara moaned and kissed him fiercely, her breasts crushing his chest. In another second, they'd both be beyond reason. But Kevin held back. This wasn't in his plan. He wanted a full night with Cara, under his own terms. He had it all set in his mind.

Yet he wouldn't deny them both this moment of pleasure. He dipped his hand under her swimsuit and touched her sweetly sensitive spot. "Feel good?" he whispered.

Beyond words, Cara nodded, her lids half-closed. Kevin stroked her carefully with deliberate movements, laying his fingers along the soft folds of her sex.

Wrapping his other hand around her curly blond locks, he pulled her head down to his and kissed her over and over again, her body rocking back and forth, finding a sensual rhythm.

"Oh, Kevin," Cara whimpered, as he continued to glide his fingers over her folds. Kevin watched as tension built quickly, her body rocking forcefully, an expression of sheer lust crossing her beautiful face.

His heart ached witnessing her sheer abandon as her breathing escalated and her body tightened. He stroked her harder, deeper and longer. She arched up and her release came in powerful short bursts of exquisite movements. Watching her orgasm stole his breath.

And made him rethink his plan.

Once spent, a satisfied sigh escaped her throat and she laid her head on his chest. He massaged her lower back, holding her loosely in his arms. "Damn."

"Yeah, damn," she repeated.

Thoughts of making love to Cara on the lounge chair entered his head. Hell, he was ready and Cara wasn't denying him. But once they made love, he'd have to make good on his deal to deliver signed divorce papers.

She wants out of our marriage.

This is the price she's willing to pay.

And I'm paying for it, too, a little annoying voice inside his head reminded him.

"You know what we both need?"

Cara chuckled, the sound emanating from deep in her throat. "Oh, yeah. I know."

Kevin laid one last kiss onto her lips. "Good, then come with me."

Kevin lifted her up and in one sweeping movement, he jumped into the pool, taking Cara with him.

Ten

Cara lay in bed the next morning with thoughts of Kevin intruding on her sleep. Visions of their day together raced through her mind.

Fun in the sun.

Yes, Kevin had seen to that. And much more. Her body still sated from the incredible climax he'd provided her, Cara relived every exquisite moment of his unselfish sexual advance. She was completely, one hundred percent in love with him and had come close to telling him ten times yesterday by the pool.

But Kevin had never spoken of the future to her. He'd never once let on that he wanted reconciliation. He'd held back his own desire yesterday in order to keep his blackmail deal with her.

Why?

Had nothing changed between them over these past two weeks?

Lance's comments about Kevin hurting her were never far from her mind. What had he meant? She couldn't help but think Lance, even in his intoxicated state—or maybe because of it—had set out to warn her about Kevin.

And then at the pool, when she had mentioned her plan to open a dance studio in Somerset, Kevin's nonreaction had stung her pride. He hadn't said much about it, until she had pressed him for an answer. He'd given her a halfhearted reply. It had been clear that Kevin didn't like the idea.

In fact, for a few seconds, his whole demeanor had changed. She hadn't dwelled on his reaction yesterday—they'd been too wrapped up in each other for her to have entertained clear thoughts. But now, in the clarity of morning, she faced facts.

"He doesn't want me in Somerset," Cara muttered, her heart hurting with that realization.

Cara mustered her courage. Instead of deliberating about it all day, driving herself crazy, she made up her mind to find out the truth.

Or at least find out what Lance's comments had meant.

With that notion in mind, Cara rose from bed and showered. She dried her hair and put on a bright canary-yellow sundress, slipped her feet into sandals, then grabbed her cell phone from her purse and dialed Lance's number.

An hour later, she faced Lance Brody in his high-rise executive office at Brody Oil and Gas. "Thanks for seeing me on short notice," Cara said, taking one of two seats facing his desk.

"My pleasure," he said, sitting casually on the edge of his desk, just a few feet from her. "Would you like a cup of coffee, breakfast, anything?" Lance leaned over his desk, with a finger on the intercom button, ready to accommodate her.

"No thanks, Lance."

He straightened and smiled. "Okay." His dark eyes searching, he wore an earnest expression. "I was a little surprised that you asked to see me. What's up?"

Cara straightened the folds of her dress, then looked deep into his eyes. "It's about Kevin."

"O-kay," Lance said slowly, looking a little confused.

"The other night at your house, you said something to me that I didn't understand."

Lance tossed his head back with self-deprecating laughter. "I probably said a lot of things that didn't make sense that night."

"You made a point of taking me aside and warning me about Kevin. You said he was hard-headed. That he would hurt me."

Lance averted his gaze. He found the floor inter-esting, then the wall. "Did I?"

"Do you remember saying that to me?"

Lance shot her a direct look. "No, I don't remember saying that."

"But you do know what that means, don't you?"

Lance rose, walked behind his desk, then faced her again.

"Cara," he said, taking a deep breath. He rubbed the back of his neck. "If I said something to upset you that night, I apologize."

Cara shook her head and stood. "The only thing that's upsetting me is not knowing what you meant. You know what's going on with Kevin. Now, are you going to tell me the truth?"

Lance stared at her for a few long seconds. She could almost see the debate going on in his head. He *knew* something. She pinned him with a penetrating gaze, refusing to back down—even if it meant hearing something about Kevin that she didn't want to hear.

"He's one of my best friends," Lance said.

Cara stood her ground, patiently. She wouldn't let Lance off the hook. She continued to stare.

"Okay," he said with reluctance. "Have a seat. It's probably better this way. You two need to talk this through. I'll tell you what I know."

Cara glanced at the clock radio on the hotel's night table. Kevin would be here any second. It would be their last night together and she planned on making it memorable.

She'd had to pull the words out of Lance's mouth earlier today. Poor man. He'd tried hard not to hurt her, but it hadn't taken too many words to make Cara see the whole picture. She'd always been great with putting puzzle pieces together, making them fit. And once she'd gotten the corners of Lance's knowledge assembled, she'd put the entire puzzle together very quickly.

She knew Kevin's plan and was through playing his game. It was high time she took control of the situation. Tonight, she'd play her own game and sadly, no one would come out the winner.

Furious with her soon-to-be ex, Cara hadn't had time to feel the tremendous hurt she knew would follow. Right now, fury fueled her to give Kevin a dose of his own medicine.

"You deserve it, *sweetheart.*"

When the knock sounded on her hotel door, Cara assumed the guise both mentally and physically. She tossed her arms into her silk robe and walked over to the door.

Taking a deep breath first, steadying her nerves, she opened the door.

Kevin stood in the doorway, wearing a very expensive dark Italian suit. Groomed to perfection, there was no denying his sexual appeal and charisma. Cara's heart lurched, but she ignored the pangs.

His expression dropped, seeing her in her robe. "Hi. Am I early?"

Cara shook her head. "No, you're right on time."

Kevin's brows furrowed, puzzled. "I'll tell the limo driver to wait. Dinner's not until eight. I have a great night planned—"

Cara dropped the robe, letting it puddle at her feet. She took great satisfaction seeing Kevin's deep-blue eyes widen with appreciation. She allowed him a few seconds of shock, seeing her dressed in the one-piece formfitting black-lace unitard. Strategically placed lace was meant to tease and tempt, exposed skin in erogenous zones that would make Catwoman blush.

Cara grabbed Kevin by his sleek silk tie and yanked him inside the room. Extending her leg past him in a fluid lift, she kicked the door shut and pinned him against it. "No date, no dinner. It's time, Kevin. For us."

Cara wrapped her arms around his neck and crushed her mouth to his, leaving the taste of wild cherry on his lips.

She backed away and stared at him. Thoroughly confused, Kevin glanced around the hotel room. Two dozen pillar candles lit the room and flavored the air with a sweet vanilla scent. Rose petals decorated her king-size bed, the sheets turned down provocatively. Chocolate-covered strawberries and a champagne bottle chilling in a silver bucket stood on a tray by the window table.

Kevin leaned back, thumping his head against the wall. "Cara, what is all this?"

She smiled. "You talk too much, baby." She loosened his tie and lifted it over his head. "The time for talking is over. Make love to me. It's what we both want."

Kevin blinked, then stared into her eyes. Cara

kept the ruse up—she wouldn't deny herself this night. As long as she was in control, she'd be fine. She unbuttoned his shirt and ran her hands along his hard, perfect chest. "C'mon, babe. I thought you'd be as hot for this as I am."

Cara nipped at his lower lip, then rimmed his mouth with her tongue. Kevin groaned and slipped his tongue into her mouth, taking her on a wild erotic ride with just that one frenzied kiss.

"Mmm, Kevin," she said, licking her lips, pulling away from him just a bit. "I can't wait for you to be inside me."

Kevin groaned deeper and pulled her close, so that every juncture of their bodies touched. Exquisite tingles ran up and down her length, his manhood already evident. "Damn it, Cara. Keep talking that way, and we won't make it over to that bed."

She tossed her head back, a throaty laugh escaping. "Since when did we *ever* need a bed?"

Cara nipped at his lips again. Kevin heaved a breath and pulled off his shirt. Immediately, Cara touched him again, running her palms over his skin, pressing her tongue to his erect nipples.

Kevin lifted her easily and started for the bed. "I'm older now. I like creature comforts."

Cara shook her head, gazing into his eyes. "Oh, that's a shame. I wanted to dance for you."

Kevin stopped in midstride. He peered down at her with inquisitive eyes, his voice filled with keen interest. "Dance for me?"

She nodded innocently.

"What do you want me to do?"

"Just lie down on the bed and watch."

Kevin sucked oxygen into his chest. "Okay."

He set her down. Cara put her iPod in the dock on the nightstand and hit Play, selecting a specific song. When she turned around, Kevin was bathed in candlelight, lying on his back on the bed, his head propped up on her pillow.

"You are a beautiful woman, Cara Novak," Kevin said in a humble tone.

Cara closed her eyes and felt the music fill her. Then she began to move, swaying her body, her hips gyrating sensually. Everything she had inside, everything she felt for Kevin, the love she'd never declared, came out in the dance.

She gave Kevin this gift, this exposing of her innermost being, so that he would never forget her. So that he would look upon this time with her and know that no other woman could provide what she had given to him.

She danced, flowing to the music, lost in her own movements, giving to Kevin what she'd never given another man.

Cara didn't have a vengeful bone in her body, yet this she felt compelled to do. For her own sense of justice. He'd hurt her beyond belief and she hoped this gift would be his undoing. She danced and danced, her eyes half-lidded, her body in seamless motion with the music and her spirit free.

When the song ended, Cara opened her eyes fully, facing Kevin. The awed expression on his face nearly caved her resolve. "Cara," he said, opening his mouth to speak. He couldn't find the words and Cara knew at that moment what Kevin felt was genuine and true.

She smiled and for a few seconds she forgot his deceit.

"I'm not through."

She chose a different song. It was smooth and sensual, filled with lyrics about suspicions. She moved slowly, erotically, peeling herself out of her lacy one-piece. She stepped out of the garment and stood before Kevin, naked. "Touch me, Kevin. I want to remember your hands on me."

"Cara," Kevin said, his voice little more than a croak. He came to her on his knees and helped her onto the bed. On her knees, too, they faced each other. Kevin kissed her, then touched his fingers to her lips. He moved his hand down her throat and kissed her there, then lower. He cupped her breasts in his hands, circling them and making Cara's nerves go absolutely raw.

She closed her eyes and hung on to him, relishing the feel of his hands caressing her. He skimmed his hands down her torso, teasing, tempting, then cupped her womanhood gently, his fingers lingering just enough to make her head swim.

Next, he touched her thighs as far as he could

reach and wound his hands around her legs to the back. Her skin prickled in anticipation and when he touched the rounds of her buttocks, she let go a pleasured moan.

Kevin took hold of her head then, his restraint nearly spent. He crushed his lips to hers, again and again. "You're killing me slowly, babe."

Tension wound in her belly. She needed Kevin. She needed to make this memory, before she bid him goodbye for good. Taking the reins, she shoved at his chest, pushing him down on the bed. He went willingly with a big smile on his face.

She undid his belt and pulled it free of the loops. Next she took off his shoes and socks, tossing them aside before removing his slacks. He lay naked before her now, his thick erection a temptation all in itself. Cara cupped him, wrapping her hand around his silken shaft. She stroked him several times, eliciting curses from deep in his throat. "Babe?"

"I know what I'm doing, Kevin."

"Ah…uh, no doubt, but—"

Cara replaced her hand with her mouth, taking Kevin inside and silencing any complaints he may have had. He lay back quietly while she made love to him that way.

Tension built quickly from there. Their breathing heaved hard and they moved with a need that could only be satisfied one way. Scalding heat and sticky moisture fused their bodies. Cara wanted this. She'd dreamed of this. And she wouldn't be denied.

She rose atop Kevin, straddling his legs, and peered deep into his eyes. He seemed to understand her need. He reached for her hips and she lowered down on him, taking him inside her. Sensations ripped through her system, pleasure and desire, need and want, fulfillment and appreciation. Cara cried out. Kevin groaned as if in pain. She looked into his eyes, joined with him now, complete. Vivid memories of earth-shattering sex and dire love crossed between them.

"Oh, yes, Cara."

"I know, babe."

She moved down farther and he let go a grunt of satisfaction. She rose up and then took him in even deeper. Her skin prickled. Her body tightened around him. Her nipples budded to round peaks.

They peered at each other amid candlelight and rose petals. But none of that mattered anymore. Their sheer joining was enough to warrant erotic images and romantic atmosphere. It was all that either of them needed.

With Kevin's guidance, Cara moved on him, riding him up and down, each time taking him deeper, fuller, faster until Cara's body grew tight with climactic tension. Hot currents shocked her nerve endings and she rose up.

"Let go, baby," Kevin whispered, his voice strained.

She slammed down on him, as small rockets of sensation whipped through her. She moved back and forth, her body tight, her nerves sensitized. Her release exploded hard and fast and shook her to her core.

She reveled in the sensation a moment, before Kevin reached for her, bringing her down onto his hot body. "That was amazing," he said, between kisses.

"Now it's your turn," Cara said, kissing him fiercely.

"Oh, yeah."

Kevin rolled her onto her back and placed little kisses along her face, jaw, chin and throat. He cupped her breast and paid a good deal of attention to the erect bud with his tongue.

His thick erection still unfulfilled, Cara squirmed under him. "Hurry, baby. I need you inside me again."

"Just making sure you're ready."

"I'm always ready."

Kevin kissed her one last time, before spreading her legs and entering her, driving deep in one thrust. "I love that about you."

Cara felt as if she'd come home. Being with Kevin, making love, sharing intimacies, all seemed so right. There were so many things Kevin said he loved about her…yet he didn't love her at all. Sadness filled her heart again, knowing that this was all a vengeful little game. Only tonight, she'd made up the rules.

Soon, it would all be over.

Cara pushed those thoughts away and focused on the pleasure Kevin brought her. She vowed to make him remember this night and nothing would stop her.

Kevin sustained slow, fulfilling thrusts long enough to arouse Cara to the peak of orgasm again. He moved on her as if committing her to memory, every powerful drive of his body deliberate and controlled. "Cara, I've missed you."

Cara blocked that from her mind. She refused to believe him and passed it off as ramblings from a sexually aroused lover. Instead she focused on the wonderful little explosions occurring in her body.

When Kevin arched, his face given to release, Cara rose up, those tiny explosions waiting, building. Kevin called out her name, driving one last force into her body and Cara let go. The orgasm rocked them both, each lifting, releasing, the complete, agonizing pleasure of their bodies aligning and bursting as one.

Kevin came down on Cara gently, taking her in his arms. He kissed her passionately, murmuring, "I knew it would be like this."

Cara smiled sadly. The truth was the truth. "Me, too."

Cara woke up to an empty bed. The room bathed in candlelight, she squinted and focused her eyes as she sat straight up in bed. Kevin stood across the room, his slacks on, his feet bare, pouring two flutes of champagne. "Nice nap?" he asked, turning to her.

"Mmm." They'd exhausted each other, making love again, christening several corners of the room both in standing and sitting positions. After, they'd both fallen into a deep, if short, slumber.

"It's time for champagne, babe."

Cara looked at the digital clock on the nightstand, then rose and pulled on her robe. She tightened the belt with a tug and approached him. "To toast our divorce?"

Kevin visibly winced.

Cara gathered her fury. "Or maybe you'd like to extract another ten or twenty minutes out of my soul?"

"Cara, what's wrong?" He attempted to hand the flute to her, but she wouldn't take it. She refused to take anything from Kevin, ever again.

Cara walked over to the nightstand and opened the drawer. "I think I've met all the terms of your blackmail, Kevin." She pulled out the divorce papers. "Now it's time for you to sign on the dotted line."

A tic worked in Kevin's jaw. He eyed her carefully and set down the champagne flutes.

"It's almost midnight. My two weeks are over." Cara rolled her eyes dramatically. "Thank God."

Kevin's face flushed with color. He strode over to her and grabbed both of her arms. "What's gotten into you?"

"Besides you?"

Kevin flinched as though he'd been slapped.

"I want my divorce, Kevin. I've earned it." Cara's voice wobbled as she mustered her courage. She refused to cry, to let Kevin see his victory.

He'd wanted to hurt her and he had. She'd taken the bait, hook, line and sinker. She'd fallen in love with him, but she wouldn't give him the satisfaction of knowing that he'd won his little game.

"I don't believe you."

Oh, how she hated him.

"Why? Why don't you believe me? Because I played along and let you manipulate me the entire time I was here? Did you think I'd fall head over heels in love with you again?"

Cara walked away from him, picked up a glass of champagne and downed it in one giant gulp. She turned her back on him. "Sign them and leave, Kevin."

"You're angry, Cara. Damn it, so was I. When you left me. I couldn't believe you walked out on our marriage. Was it so easy for you? You just picked up and started a new life in Dallas."

She whirled around. "That's not what this is about, Kevin. Not at all. I thought you'd changed, but you've proven that you haven't. You're still out for blood, to win at all costs, no matter who gets hurt. You had to have your revenge, didn't you? You had to break me. You had to—"

"Who told you that?" Kevin approached her, his gaze piercing. "Where did you hear that?"

"Don't deny it. I know it's true."

Kevin sucked oxygen in and shook his head. "Damn it, Cara. Damn it all."

Cara downed the second glass of champagne, then turned her back on him once and for all. Her heart ached just looking at him, thinking of the passion they'd just shared. Not once had he apologized. Not once had he offered any sign of hope. Not once had he confessed to wanting reconciliation. The ache went deep, slicing through her gut. Her body shook painfully and tears welled in her eyes. "Sign the papers, Kevin. Then get out."

"Fine," he said. She didn't dare look at him. She didn't dare turn around. She waited, with her back to him, listening as he picked up his clothes and slammed the door shut behind him.

Then Cara fell apart. Tears streamed down her face and she sobbed in painful shudders. She felt as if she'd been broken in half. Her head ached and her heart plummeted to deep depths of despair.

Her marriage was over. She made her way to the bed and lowered down, shaking and seeking the bed frame for support. Braving a glance at the nightstand to see the signed evidence of her broken vows, she blinked. "What?"

Catching her breath, she got up and gave the nightstand a better look. With a quick tug, she opened the drawer and myriad thoughts flooded her head.

The divorce papers were gone.

Kevin slammed his penthouse door and tossed his jacket aside. Ten bouquets set about the room scented the air with sweetness. Candles stood at the ready in every corner of the penthouse, waiting to be lit. Decadent finger desserts arranged on the dining-room table added to the ambience, as champagne chilled in the wine closet. The seduction scene he'd planned mocked him with sickening clarity.

Cara had beaten him in his own game. She'd been cunning and clever and sexier than any woman he'd ever known. She'd fooled him and he hadn't seen it coming.

Yet he'd accomplished his goals and hated himself for it. Everything they'd built upon during the past two weeks had been wiped out in just a few minutes tonight. Kevin had thought he knew what he wanted. Apparently, he'd been wrong. Unmindful of the time, he picked up his cell phone and dialed Darius, waking him.

"Hey, man, do you know what time it is?"

"Yeah, sorry. Listen, I need to know if you spoke with Cara today."

"No, I didn't speak with Cara. Aren't your two weeks up yet?"

"As of about an hour ago, yeah. My time's up. Gotta run."

Next, he dialed Lance's number. "Did you see Cara today?"

Lance hesitated before answering. "Yeah, Cara came to see me today. She knew something was up with you and she asked me for honesty."

"What did you tell her?"

"I didn't have to tell her too much. She's an intelligent woman. She figured out what you were doing. You should have seen the look on her face."

"Mad as hell, I assume?"

"No, that would have been easier to take. More like complete devastation. She looked defeated and hurt. She's in love with you."

Kevin squeezed his eyes shut. He'd seen the devastation on her face tonight, heard it in her quivering voice. He'd wanted to go to her and tell her truths he'd only just realized, but she'd been too angry and too hurt. She wouldn't have listened to him. She wouldn't have believed him. He'd needed to regroup and figure some things out. "I blew it with her. And don't tell me, 'I told you so.'"

Lance sighed into the receiver. "Did you sign the divorce papers?"

"No. It's the first time I've ever reneged on a deal. But I couldn't sign them. I took them with me."

"Do you love her, Kev?"

"Yeah, I just realized it tonight. I've never stopped loving her. But telling her wouldn't have meant anything to her. Not after the hell I put her through."

"Now what?"

"Now I'm going to have to blackmail her one more time, to get her to listen to me."

"Oh, man. Good luck."

The divorce papers are signed. You just have to come pick them up.

Cara fumed as she drove her rental car to the address Kevin had given her. He'd called this morning, offering a limo service to take her to the destination. But Cara had refused. She didn't want anything to do with Kevin Novak, his limo or his life. From now on, she could only count on herself.

"Why is everything with you so difficult, Kevin?" she muttered as she drove into Somerset. "Couldn't you have just signed the papers last night? No, you have to do everything on your own terms. You always have to be in control."

Cara cursed as she sped along, looking at the address Kevin had given her. She had just enough time to pick up her divorce papers and get to the airport. Her flight left in two hours.

She pulled into a newly built mini-mall in an upscale location of Somerset and double-checked the address. She was in the right place. She parked the car and took a deep breath, then got out and strode into a building still under construction.

She found herself standing in the center of a large, empty shell of a space, sawdust on the floor and windows yet to be installed. Kevin came out of the shadows to face her. For what it was worth, he looked as awful as she felt, his eyes red, his face troubled. Wearing the same clothes he'd worn last night, he appeared rumpled.

"Hello, Cara."

Cara drew a steadying breath. "Did you bring the papers?"

He nodded and gestured toward a workbench in the corner of the room. She glanced over and recognized the pages sitting atop the wooden slats.

"They're signed."

"Thank you," she said stiffly, then headed over to retrieve them.

"Wait," Kevin said abruptly and she stopped.

He approached her, his gaze never leaving her face. Cara backed up a few steps. "There's nothing more to say, Kevin."

He pierced her with a sincere look. "How about, I love you. I've never stopped loving you, Cara. But I didn't realize it until last night. I've been a fool and I apologize a hundred times over for how much I've hurt you."

Cara shook her head, unwilling to forgive and forget so easily. "How can I believe you? How can I possibly trust you? You deliberately set out to hurt me. And you succeeded."

Kevin took a few steps closer, his gaze intense. "I'm not going to justify my actions. They were wrong, both then and now. I'd been fooling myself all these years. I let my pride and ego get in the way. We should have talked this out, years ago."

"I'll admit, I probably shouldn't have run away like I did. I was distraught. I didn't know how to get through to you," Cara confessed, finally owning up to her part in their breakup. "And when you didn't come after me, I thought you didn't care anymore."

"Cara, I should have come after you. God knows, I loved you very much. Everything I did was for you. I had something to prove and now I know, I made mistakes along the way. But you have to believe me when I say I'm crazy about you."

Cara let a smile slip out and Kevin smiled, too. "I love you, Cara. And I'll spend the rest of my life proving it to you."

"We're officially divorced now. Unless you lied to me and you didn't sign those papers over there."

"I signed them, to prove how much I love you. If you really want to leave me and Somerset, you can take them and go. But…if there's a chance for us, I want to offer it to you." He made a sweeping gesture with his arm. "This place can be your dance studio, Cara. You can open up Dancing Lights right here in Somerset. I'll build you a house and we'll fill it with children. I want all of that with you. And I'll prove to you every day and night how much you mean to me."

Cara's heart lurched. She could picture a new dance studio here. The place was perfect. More important, she could picture making a home with Kevin…a fresh start. And *children*. Oh, God, he was offering her the sun, the moon and the stars. She wanted to trust him, to believe him.

"I love you, Cara. Do you love me?"

Cara peered into his hopeful, gorgeous blue eyes. "Yes, of course I love you," she said softly. "I've never stopped loving you."

Kevin took her hand in his and squeezed it gently. "Give us a second chance, sweetheart."

Cara smiled. She found the truth in his eyes, the faith

she had in him restored. She walked over to the workbench and peered down at the signed divorce papers.

"It's up to you, Cara."

Kevin had given her an out. He'd given up control and let the decision rest solely in her hands. He'd let her go if that was what she wanted. But he *loved* her. And she loved him right back.

She picked up the divorce papers. "I don't really have a choice." She ripped them in two, letting the pieces fall to the ground. "I love you too much."

Kevin strode over to her and wrapped her into his arms. His strength and love enveloped her and she knew she'd made the right decision.

They began to sway together.

"Hmm, I hear music," Cara said with a satisfied smile as sweet, joyous music played in her head.

"I hear it every time I hold you." Kevin tightened his arms around her as they rocked gently back and forth. "I can feel the love, sweetheart."

Reminded of their wedding night and the Elton John song that had become their signature, Cara kissed him softly on the lips. "Me, too."

"Promise me one thing, Cara."

"Anything."

"You'll dance for me every night."

"I promise."

And they continued to move to the rhythm of love that played solely in their hearts.

* * * * *

THE OILMAN'S
BABY BARGAIN

BY
MICHELLE CELMER

Dear Reader,

Welcome to book four of THE MILLIONAIRE'S
CLUB series – the story of oilman Mitch Brody and
Alexis Cavanaugh!

As far as I'm concerned, the only thing sexier than a
man who knows exactly what he wants is a man who
thinks he does, then realises he's wrong. That sums
up Mitch. He has it all worked out. At least he thinks
he does, then Alexis comes along and turns all of his
perfectly engineered plans upside down.

Alexis is a woman on a mission. She knows what she
wants, and she's willing to go to any lengths to get it.
Until she realises that what she wants may not be worth
the price she has to pay.

These two put me through so many emotional twists
and turns I nearly wound up with whiplash! But in the
end it was more than worth it.

I hope you enjoy their story as much as I did!

Michelle Celmer

Bestselling author **Michelle Celmer** lives in southeastern Michigan with her husband, their three children, two dogs and two cats. When she's not writing or busy being a mum, you can find her in the garden or curled up with a romance. And if you twist her arm really hard you can usually persuade her into a day of power shopping.

Michelle loves to hear from readers. Visit her website at www.michellecelmer.com, or write to her at PO Box 300, Clawson, MI 48017, USA.

The Millionaire's Club

August 2010
Taming the Texas Tycoon
Katherine Garbera
&
One Night with the Wealthy Rancher
Brenda Jackson

September 2010
Texan's Wedding-Night Wager
Charlene Sands
&
The Oilman's Baby Bargain
Michelle Celmer

October 2010
The Maverick's Virgin Mistress
Jennifer Lewis
&
Lone Star Seduction
Day Leclaire

One

June

Alexis Cavanaugh was in love with the wrong brother.

She gazed across the candlelit table at the man she had spent the better part of the past week in D.C. with, only half listening as he spoke fervently about Brody Oil and Gas, the company he co-owned with his brother Lance. The brother she was *supposed* to be marrying.

Not that she had expected to fall in love with Lance. The marriage was little more than a business deal cooked up by the Brody brothers and her father, Bruce Cavanaugh, senior senator from her home state of Texas. But hadn't she always done what her father asked of her? Didn't he, as he'd always claimed, know what was best? A marriage to Lance would provide her the financial security and station in society that she'd earned—although other than possess the Cavanaugh name, she wasn't sure what she'd ever done to deserve it.

Not that she didn't find Lance appealing. He was tall and dark and devastatingly attractive—not to mention built like a tank—with a charm that drew people to him. A gentle giant. But he wasn't as refined a man as she was accustomed to. He seemed more comfortable among the roughnecks at the refinery than the shareholders. Mitch, on the other hand, had seemed perfectly at ease with the elite of D.C. They had attended half a dozen parties and fundraisers together—Mitch on his brother's behalf, of course—and he could schmooze with the best of them. He was clearly the brains behind Brody Oil and Gas.

And the brother she clearly was falling for.

So many men treated her like a brainless, witless showpiece. Better seen and not heard. But Mitch listened to her. He *heard* her, and seemed genuinely interested in what she had to say.

She realized suddenly that he was meeting her gaze across the table, a grin on his ridiculously handsome face. A face that had become quite familiar over the past few days. She had memorized every line and curve, the slope of his nose, the sensual shape of his chocolate-brown eyes, the fullness of his lips and sharp set of his jaw. She knew every expression and nuance. And the smile he wore now was an amused one.

"What?" she asked.

"You haven't heard a word I've said, have you?"

He was right. He'd been talking about his business, which obviously meant more to him than anything else, and she had completely zoned out. In her own defense, it was tough to watch those full lips move and not become entranced, not be lulled by the deep tenor of his voice. But that was no excuse to be rude. She was usually an exceptional listener.

"I'm sorry," she apologized.

"I'm the one who should be apologizing. I'm obviously boring you to death. I forget that not everyone is as passionate as I am about the oil business."

"I enjoy hearing you talk about it. I guess I'm just a little tired. It's been a very busy week."

"It has," Mitch agreed, with a smile that was just this side of seductive. "My brother has no idea what he's missing."

Did he feel the same connection, the same longing for her that she had for him? Or was he simply being polite? Was he just naturally flirtatious, like his brother?

"It's late. I should get you back to the hotel."

Just for a moment, she let herself believe that he

couldn't wait to get her back to her room so he could make passionate love to her. The idea both thrilled and terrified her. She had always hoped her first time would be special, and she knew without a doubt that with Mitch, it would be.

But that wasn't going to happen because she was marrying his brother. And shouldn't she save something as precious as her virginity for her spouse? Even if it wasn't a real marriage?

He summoned the waiter and paid the exorbitantly high bill without batting an eyelash. What did she expect when he took her to the most exclusive restaurant in D.C.? Money was obviously of no concern.

He helped her up from her seat and walked her to the door. She took pleasure in the way every head in the room swiveled in his direction. Men watched with envy as their female companions swooned, eyes filled with silent longing.

Sorry, girls, he's all mine. At least until she became officially engaged to Lance. If only she could capture this time and make it last forever. Make a life with Mitch instead of Lance.

The limo was already waiting for them as they stepped out into the hot and muggy evening air, but the soft leather felt cool as she slipped inside. "The Watergate Hotel," Mitch told the driver.

She hoped they would talk more on the way there, but his cell phone rang. He checked the display and told her, "Sorry, but I have to take this."

Though he said nothing specific, it was clear by his tone that the conversation had something to do with the fire at the refinery. She'd heard from her father that the investigation pointed to arson, and though there were no solid suspects, rumors were spreading that Lance's rival, Alejandro Montoya, might be responsible. She couldn't understand why anyone would put so many lives in danger, but having grown up around politics, she'd learned that some people were capable of terrible things.

Mitch disconnected just as the limo pulled up to the hotel. Usually they parted ways in the lobby, as their rooms were in different wings, but tonight Mitch offered to accompany her to her door.

He was just being polite, she told herself. But why now? Why was tonight any different than the last?

The air seemed to sizzle with electricity as they rode the elevator up to the penthouse. More than usual she felt acutely aware of his presence beside her. Or maybe it was just her imagination.

When the doors slid open, he touched her waist to lead her out. His hand felt huge, and warmth seeped through the silk of her sundress, making the skin beneath tingle. She couldn't recall him touching her this way before, and she was sure she would have noticed. When they reached her door, he took the key from her and opened it. She stepped inside and he leaned against the jamb.

"I had a nice time tonight, Lexi," he said. There was heat in his eyes as they searched her face, then drifted lower, to the front of her dress, where, thanks to her very expensive and uncomfortable push-up bra, her breasts swelled over and begged to be noticed. He did notice, and he obviously liked what he saw.

She had never been one to play the seductress, but tonight she was feeling the part. Would it hurt her, for the first time in her boring and proper life, to do something scandalous and wicked? Something just for herself? Who, besides the two of them, would ever know? After years of chastity, hadn't she earned one night of unbridled passion and ecstasy?

She knew without a doubt he would give her exactly that.

"I had a nice time, too," she said, gazing up at him through the fringe of her lashes, wearing what she hoped was a seductive smile. Maybe it was the wine, or the candlelit dinner, but she could feel her inhibitions melting away. "Would you like to come inside for a nightcap?"

Without hesitation he stepped into the room, closing the door behind him. She opened her mouth to ask him what he wanted to drink, but before she could make a sound his arms were around her, drawing her against him. Her nipples tingled almost painfully as they pressed against the wall of his chest and her knees went weak with excitement. Then he lowered his head and kissed her. Her lips parted with a surprised gasp, and he dipped in for a taste.

She expected him to plunder and dominate the way the men did in her favorite romance novels. Instead, his lips were soft and gentle, his touch tender. In spite of having wanted this with all of her heart, she was so stunned she was actually kissing her future brother-in-law that she stood stiff in his arms.

He must have interpreted her reaction as a rejection, because he released her and pulled away. "I'm sorry," he said. "But I've been fantasizing about doing that all night. All *week*."

So had she, and she wasn't going to blow it. She wasn't going to let her fear of the unknown ruin this chance for a night with the man of her dreams.

She grinned her most wicked smile and slid her hands up his chest, wrapping them around his neck. "Then why did you stop?"

This time when he kissed her, he didn't stop. And when he took her to bed, he proved to be everything she had imagined.

And more.

Last night had been the most amazing, terrifying and wonderful night of Lexi's life. She'd had no idea two people could connect—could be in perfect sync—the way she and Mitch had been. She had tried to hide the fact that she was a virgin, but of course he'd figured it out. She'd worried that he might be angry or put off, but the opposite had been true. He'd been so sweet and gentle with her. What could have been a painful, awkward experience had been more beautiful than she had ever imagined possible.

The instant she woke the next morning, cradled in a cocoon of warm silk sheets that still held the scent of Mitch's aftershave, she knew without a doubt that she wouldn't be marrying Lance. She wanted Mitch. And she was sure that if she pleaded her case to her father, he would see that the other Brody brother would be a much better match. As far as he was concerned, it was only the Brody name that was important.

Before she even opened her eyes she smiled to herself and began to imagine what life would be like married to Mitch. How happy she would be because they would love each other. She imagined what their children would look like. They would have a son who would be tall and fit with Mitch's dark hair, olive tones and striking features, and a girl, pretty and graceful with Lexi's creamy complexion and blond hair.

They would have a ceremony in the garden at her father's Houston estate, then honeymoon somewhere warm and exotic. Maybe Cabo San Lucas, or the Bahamas. And if Mitch was agreeable, they could try to conceive while they were there. What better time to get pregnant than on her honeymoon? She had always wanted to be a mother, to have at least three or four children.

Lexi heard movement in the room and realized Mitch was already up. She peered at the clock on the bedside table, surprised to find that it was barely 7:00 a.m.

"Are you awake?" Mitch asked.

She rolled to face him, ready to smile and say, *why don't you climb back in bed and find out,* but he was already showered and dressed, and when she saw the look on his face, her heart sank. Then she realized, of course he would look distressed. He was about to steal his brother's fiancée. Maybe he thought she loved Lance.

She sat up, holding the sheet against her bare breasts. "Good morning."

"We need to talk," he said.

She nodded, barely able to contain her excitement. Here it comes. He was going to tell her he loved her, and beg her to marry him instead of Lance. Of course she would say yes. Then he would undress, and climb back into bed, and she would spend the rest of the morning showing him just how much she loved him. Then everything would be perfect, just like the happily-ever-afters in the romance novels.

His expression somber, he said, "I don't suppose I have to tell you that we've made a drastic mistake."

Wait, what?

A *mistake?*

She had to replay the words several times in her mind, convinced she must have misunderstood.

"No one can ever know that this happened," he continued, his tone grim. "Especially my brother."

He might as well have reached into her chest and ripped out her heart, because that was the way it felt. The fierce, hollow ache was nearly unbearable.

For years she had endured her father's criticism and indifference. No matter what she did to please him, however closely she played by his rules, it was never enough to win his love. Now, once again, she had been rejected by a man whose affection she desperately craved.

Maybe there was something wrong with her, something that made her unlovable.

"Lance is flying in this afternoon to officially propose," Mitch told her. "You have to pretend that everything is fine, and nothing has changed."

How could she act as though everything was fine when she was falling apart? And how could she have been so stupid? Why didn't she see that it was just sex to him? Maybe it was some sort of warped sibling rivalry. Maybe Mitch seduced all of his brother's girlfriends.

Humiliation burned her from the inside out, but she would die before she let Mitch know.

She lifted her nose at him and pasted on a look of boredom. "I don't have to pretend everything is fine,

Mitch. As far as I'm concerned, things are great. You definitely served your purpose."

He frowned. "What purpose was that?"

She racked her brain, grasping for the worst, most awful thing she could possibly say to hurt him as much as he'd hurt her. "A cheap thrill, to cheat my arranged husband out of my virginity. And who better to do it with than his brother. Although I'm sorry to say, I expected better. Your performance wasn't exactly earth-shattering."

Mitch's expression went from one of confusion to ice-cold hatred. She waited for him to shout and berate her, the way her father often did when he was displeased with her. But all he said was, "I should have expected as much from a spoiled and pampered heiress."

No words could have stung more or cut deeper.

He grabbed his wallet from the bedside table. "Meet me downstairs in the lounge at noon," he said, then turned and left without another word.

She sat there for several minutes, feeling sick with grief, but then she began to feel something else. She began to feel angry. How dare he play with her emotions that way. How dare he make love to her and take from her the most precious gift she had to offer—her innocence—then ruthlessly reject her.

Well, she would show him. She would marry his brother and she would make Lance love her. She would be the best wife, the best mother—everything Lance could ever want in a mate.

Mitch would see how happy they were, see how perfect she could be, and he would regret letting her go for the rest of his life.

Two

Mitchell Brody had never been one to compromise, but when it came to Brody Oil and Gas, he would do just about anything to ensure its continued growth and success. Even if that meant marrying a spoiled, heartless, manipulative heiress who had a block of ice where her heart belonged.

Bruce Cavanaugh glared at Mitch from behind his massive desk—the desk he boasted once belonged to JFK—in his Houston office, where he sat like a king addressing a lowly peasant. Everything in the room, from the rich furnishings to his many accolades framed and hung on the walls, was designed to intimidate. Mitch would happily tell the overbearing son of a bitch to go to hell, but unfortunately, he and Lance needed his senatorial support. Even more so since the fire at the refinery. If they planned to keep profits up, they needed to expand.

"Your brother has humiliated my family," he told Mitch.

"I know he has, sir. Once more, I would like to express our deepest apologies."

"Rejecting my Lexi for a lowly secretary," he scoffed, as if Kate's profession somehow made her unworthy. Mitch wondered how the senator would feel if he knew that while she was supposed to be planning a wedding with Lance, his precious daughter Lexi had been seducing Mitch instead.

"He was in love with Kate," Mitch said, which seemed to carry little or no weight.

The senator just glared and said, "I don't think we have anything left to discuss, Mr. Brody."

Mitch had never had to grovel in his life, but there was a first time for everything. His brother had damn well better appreciate this. "I'd like you to consider a compromise, sir."

The senator narrowed his eyes. "What kind of compromise?"

"We still need your support, Senator Cavanaugh, and I'm assuming you still want the best for your daughter."

"Your point is?"

"The Brody name can provide that."

"What are you suggesting?"

He had to force the words out. "A marriage between Alexis and me."

He looked wary, but also intrigued, leaning back in his seat and folding his arms over his chest. "Explain."

In other words, kiss the old man's ass, make this worth his while. "I think this arrangement will be in everyone's best interests, Senator. Married to me, Alexis will be set for life financially, and remain in the upper echelon of Texas society."

"And in return?" the senator asked.

"With your senatorial support, my brother and I will expand Brody Oil and Gas and take it to heights our father never dreamed possible."

"I'm sure you can imagine how humiliated my Lexi was when your first arrangement fell through. If I do say yes, what assurances do I have that you won't fall in love with *your* secretary and decide to marry her, instead?"

It annoyed Mitch the way he referred to her as "my Lexi," as though she were a possession, or a commodity. If he really cared about his daughter, would he expect her to settle for an arranged, loveless marriage? Wouldn't he want her to be happy? Or maybe in his mind, wealth and security equaled happiness.

Whatever the man's motivation, it wasn't Mitch's

problem. Besides, as far as he was concerned, Lexi was getting exactly what she deserved. He should have realized that the woman under the sweet and demure exterior was in reality a viper. Not unlike his mother, who made his father fall in love with her, gave birth to his sons and then abandoned them.

Lexi had played with his emotions and used him. Now he was going to return the favor.

"In the first place," Mitch told him, "my secretary is sixty-eight and married with grandchildren. Second, I am not a frivolous man when it comes to my emotions. I'm prepared to do anything for the sake of my business. I also have a plan to counteract any humiliation my brother's rejection caused. When all is said and done, Lance will be the one who comes out looking like a fool."

"How will you manage that?"

"With all due respect, sir, I would prefer to discuss it with Lexi first, to be sure that she's okay with it."

Senator Cavanaugh silently considered that for several moments, then he nodded. "I'm inclined to say yes, but under one condition. I won't force Lexi to marry you. She must be agreeable to the match, or the deal is off."

Mitch winced. That could definitely be a problem. She obviously despised Mitch. He was going to have to get creative, make her an offer she couldn't refuse. Perhaps a credit card with no limit and all the department store accounts she could dream of. He would give her everything her spoiled and greedy little heart desired. That is, if she *had* a heart.

"Agreed," Mitch said. He rose from his chair and offered the senator his hand. The man's grip was firm and binding.

"One more thing," the senator said, as Mitch turned to leave. "If you hurt my daughter in any way, shape or form, I will crush you and your brother. Understand?"

Mitch nodded, then turned and walked to the door, hoping he hadn't just made the biggest mistake of his life.

Lexi stood in her private bathroom at her father's Houston estate feeling as though she might be sick. She'd been feeling that way every morning lately. Which was what had motivated her to finally take a home pregnancy test. That, and two missed periods. And sure enough, when the little wand was ripe, up popped that little pink plus sign.

She groaned, and dropped her head in her hands. She had always been the perfect, dutiful daughter. The *one* time in her life she'd had the guts to say to hell with what her father wanted and have some fun, this was what happened.

Didn't that just figure?

There was a soft rap on the door and her personal assistant, Tara—the one who had been kind enough to fetch the pregnancy test in the first place—poked her head in. "Well?"

Unable to make herself say the words, Lexi held the results up so Tara could see for herself. "I am so completely screwed."

Tara crossed the room and wrapped Lexi up in a hug. "We'll get through this," she promised. "Everything will be okay."

Lexi rested her head on Tara's shoulder and let herself be comforted for a minute. Tara was the closest thing she had to a best friend. Lexi's father was particular about who Lexi was allowed to befriend. As far as he was concerned, no one was good enough for his little girl. As a result, people believed she was a snob.

And what would they think if she had a baby out of wedlock? Her father would be absolutely mortified. He talked for years about how someday she would marry and give him grandsons to spoil, but this was not part of his carefully laid plan.

"If my father finds out, he'll kill me," she said.

Tara held her at arm's length. "You have options."

Lexi knew exactly what she meant, and shook her head. "Termination isn't an option."

"So, you'll have it?"

"If I do, my father will disown me." Of that she had little doubt. Perception meant everything to him. He would probably accuse her of doing it on purpose, to sabotage his reputation. He would accuse her of not loving or respecting him after everything he had done for her. How many times had she been tempted to ask, *what have you done for me?* Other than shelter her, control her life and treat her more like political leverage than a daughter.

But she would never have the courage to say the words. Despite everything, he was still her father. Without him, she had no one.

"What do *you* want, Lexi?" Tara asked.

That was part of the problem. She didn't know what she wanted. If her father did disown her, cut her off financially, would it be fair to the child to raise it in poverty and shame? But the idea of a stranger raising her own flesh and blood made her heart ache.

This is Mitch's child, too, she reminded herself. Shouldn't he be part of the decision?

As if reading her mind, Tara asked, "What about the father?"

He may have been the biological father, but Mitch had made his feelings unequivocally clear. Their night together had been a mistake, and no one could ever know. "The father wants nothing to do with me."

"Curious," Tara said, looking thoughtful. "Mitchell Brody always struck me as the responsible type."

Lexi's mouth dropped open in surprise. She hadn't told anyone about the night she'd spent with her former fiancé's brother. It would have been too humiliating. How did Tara…?

"I would have to be an imbecile not to have figured it out," Tara told her. "For a week, you talked of nothing else. It was Mitch this and Mitch that. Mitch took me to the Smithsonian and Mitch took me to the most exclusive French restaurant in all of D.C. Mitch and I sat talking for hours. It was obvious you had feelings for him. A woman doesn't hold on to her virginity for twenty-four years, then give it up to a stranger."

That week had been one of the best in her life. She had learned that there was more to Mitch than his serious, and sometimes intimidating exterior. He could be sweet and fun. She'd allowed him to seduce her, and look at the mess it had gotten her into.

"On the other hand," Tara said, "if he was really *that* responsible, he would have used protection."

"He did! That's why I was so hesitant to believe I could be pregnant in the first place."

"Did you use a condom *every* time?"

"Of course we—" She frowned.

Tara mirrored her expression. "What?"

Lexi shook her head. "No, that couldn't be it."

"You had unprotected sex?"

"Only for a minute. It was the middle of the night, and we woke up and he started to…" Her cheeks blushed a brilliant shade of pink. She'd never spoken about anything so personal to anyone in her life. Not even her physician. "But he put a condom on before he…you know…finished."

Tara looked pained. "Sperm can be released before ejaculation. And it only takes one. They teach this stuff in health class, Lex."

But she hadn't had health class. She had been homeschooled by tutors, to spare her the improper influence of other children. And not a single one of those tutors, not even her science instructor, had ever said a word about sex education. Her father would have had a fit. Everything she knew about sex, she'd learned from the romance novels she used to sneak into the house. Lately, she had come to realize that those books offered a somewhat slanted view of what love and relationships truly entailed.

"So, this is my fault," she said. If she hadn't been so naive, she would have known better.

"It's no one's fault. Besides, it sounds like you two had one heck of a night together. Maybe, if there's a chance—"

Lexi shook her head. "There's no chance. He wasn't the man I thought he was."

"Well, he still has rights."

"I know," she said, feeling more confused than she ever had in her life. "I don't know what to do."

"Maybe what you need is some time away to think this through. You've been telling me for months that you'd like to take a vacation. Didn't you mention a trip to Cabo San Lucas?"

The place where she had hoped to spend her honeymoon in marital bliss with Mitch? She couldn't bear the thought of it.

"Too hot," she told Tara.

"Okay, how about an Alaskan cruise?"

She blanched. "As if I'm not nauseous enough."

"I didn't think about that." Tara gnawed her lower lip for a moment, then she brightened. "I know! What about that villa in the Greek Isles that Senator Richardson mentioned? That would be perfect."

Actually, that was an excellent idea. She wanted quiet and seclusion, and no one in Greece was likely to know, or even care, who her father happened to be. But there was still a problem. "What if my father won't allow it?"

"Tell him the humiliation of Lance's rejection is just too much to bear, and you need some time alone."

It was the humiliation of Mitch's rejection that was really killing her, but still, it wasn't a bad idea.

"Make him feel guilty for putting you in this position," Tara said. "It is ultimately his fault that you're going through all this."

Tara had a point. If her father hadn't insisted she marry Lance, Lexi never would have met Mitch. So, in a roundabout way he was responsible, although she doubted he would agree. He would lay the blame solely on her. As always. No matter how hard she tried, she never seemed to do anything right. And though she had never been one to play the pity card, if the circumstance demanded it…

She smiled at her friend, thankful she had someone so supportive to lean on at a time like this, even if she was getting paid handsomely to do so. "How soon can you make the reservation?"

Three

As soon as he left the senator's office, Mitch called his brother.

Lance answered on the first ring. "What did he say?"

"He agreed."

Lance released a breath.

"You're sure you're ready to deal with the backlash?" Mitch asked. "This isn't going to look great for you."

"After the way I humiliated her, I would say I probably deserve it. I'm just sorry that you have to go through this."

"Sorry for what? You were going to make the same sacrifice."

"But I didn't. I went with my heart."

"I'm sure Lexi and I will eventually grow fond of one another," he lied. It was probably more likely they would live completely separate lives. If they didn't kill each other first.

"I just feel guilty as hell making you do this. Now that I know what it feels like to be with someone I love and trust, I want the same for you. I want you to be happy."

"When our company is thriving and we're leaving our competitors in the dust, I will be. Besides, you know I don't believe in love. Life doesn't work that way. Not for me, anyhow." Nor did he want it to. It was tough to betray a man who refused to leave himself vulnerable. No woman would hurt him the way his mother had.

His brother could see right through him. "Not all women abandon their families," he said. "And when Mom did, I'm sure she had her reasons."

Of course she did. Their father was a bastard, emotionally, and at times physically, abusive. But if she loved Mitch and Lance, why leave them behind to suffer in her place? Why not take them with her?

He had no doubt that Lexi was self-centered and spoiled enough to do the same. If she did agree to marry him, he would insist they remain childless. It would be cruel to bring a baby into a loveless shell of a marriage. Sometimes he wished his parents would have spared him the burden of ever being born.

"There is a catch," Mitch told him. "Alexis has to willingly accept my proposal."

Lance let out a low whistle. "Maybe it was my imagination, but there didn't seem to be any love lost between the two of you when I broke the engagement."

Lance had no idea. "He also warned me that if I hurt her, he'll crush us."

Lance chuckled. "The old goat doesn't pull any punches, does he?"

"You're not concerned?"

"Why should I be? I have total faith in you."

Mitch hoped that faith wasn't misplaced. He'd already let his brother down once, betraying him by sleeping with his soon-to-be fiancée. Although it wasn't as if Lance loved Lexi, or thought of the marriage as anything more than a business arrangement. Mitch, on the other hand, had honestly believed there had been a connection between Lexi and him. If he had known that Lance loved Kate the night that he slept with Lexi, he might have asked Lexi to marry him, instead. But she had only been using him.

Ironic that he would be stuck marrying her regardless.

"You can still back out," Lance said.

No, he couldn't. This marriage was imperative. "I've already made my decision. I'm going to call her right now and set up a meeting."

"Suppose you ask, and she says no."

A very likely scenario. But every woman had a weakness. He would find hers and use it to his advantage. "I'll just have to make her an offer she can't refuse."

Though she hadn't yet sought her father's approval, Lexi laid out her clothes for the maid to pack. Her plane departed the day after tomorrow and nothing short of the apocalypse would stop her from being on it. The way she figured it, an emotional meltdown during supper and tearful pleading should bend him to her will.

Her cell phone rang and she checked the display. It was a Houston number that she didn't recognize. Curious, she answered.

"Lexi, it's Mitchell Brody."

Her heart plummeted to her toes at the sound of his voice. "Hello, Mr. Brody," she said in her coolest tone.

"I was wondering if we can arrange a meeting. This afternoon, if possible."

A meeting? What could they possibly have to say to each other?

Fear slithered down her spine. He couldn't know about the baby, could he? Only Tara knew, and she swore not to breathe a word to anyone.

She was being paranoid. Of course he didn't know. Anything he could possibly have to say to her at this point was irrelevant.

"I'm afraid I don't have time," she told him. "I'm packing for a trip. Perhaps we could schedule a meeting in a few weeks, after I return." Maybe by then she would know what she planned to do.

"I'm afraid this can't wait," he said. "It's urgent that I speak with you today. I can be there in twenty minutes."

Though he was the last man on earth that she wanted to see right now, her curiosity had been piqued. Maybe he wanted to beg her forgiveness, tell her that calling their night together a mistake had been a gross error in judgment.

Maybe he was coming to tell her that he loved her. She could at least hear him out, let him grovel a little before she told him to go to hell.

"Fine," she said.

"I'll see you in twenty minutes."

Mitch was at her door in fifteen. When the bell rang, she waved the butler away and answered it herself.

She'd almost forgotten how beautiful he was, how tall and dark and imposing. How delicious he smelled. Some small part of her ached to be close to him, to touch him again, to vault herself into his arms. Probably thanks to the pregnancy hormones that had been wreaking havoc with her emotions the past few weeks.

The easy smile Mitch usually wore was absent. His jaw was set and his expression serious. In fact, he looked almost…nervous. She didn't think men like Mitch ever got nervous.

"Thank you for agreeing to see me," he said.

She folded her arms across her chest. "What was so important that it couldn't wait?"

"Is there somewhere we can speak privately?"

She nodded, and he followed her across the foyer to the study. When they were inside, she shut the door. "Well?"

"First, I want to apologize again for my brother's behavior."

"Don't bother. He did me a favor. We would have been miserable together." She paused, then asked, "How is Lance?"

"Great. Very happy."

"I'm glad. But that isn't what you came here to talk about."

"No, it isn't," he said, looking troubled. "As you probably know, Lance and I are still in need of your father's support."

"Good luck with that." Her father had been furious with the Brody brothers, and still was, as far as she could tell.

"I had a meeting with him today."

Her eyes widened. "He actually agreed to meet with you?"

"I can be very persuasive."

He didn't have to tell her that. Had he not been so persuasive, she wouldn't be in her current dilemma.

"The senator and I have reached an…understanding."

Why did she get the feeling that she wasn't going to like this?

"What kind of understanding?"

"Your father has promised his support if you marry me, instead."

Marry him? After what had happened with Lance, would her father honestly force her to marry the other Brody brother? And why hadn't he said anything to her? Why hadn't he warned her?

"Another business arrangement?" she asked, and Mitch nodded. "Do I have a choice in the matter?"

"In fact, you do. The stipulation was that I have to convince you to marry me."

Her mouth fell open. "He actually *said* that?"

"Essentially, yes."

She could see that the prospect of having to beg Lexi to marry him made Mitch uncomfortable. As it should, after the way he'd used her. Score one for good ol' Dad. And she knew exactly why the senator had agreed to this arrangement. He'd mentioned more than once that he believed Mitch possessed presidential-size political potential. Social status meant everything to him and he would love nothing more than to see his precious daughter serve as first lady to the nation.

Whether or not Mitch was the least bit interested in a political career, Lexi didn't have a clue, and the idea of spending the rest of her life married to someone so coldhearted and manipulative—too much like her father—turned her already questionable stomach.

Yet she couldn't deny that this could be the answer to all of her problems. Marrying Mitch would give her child legitimacy. Although people—her father in particular—might get suspicious when she gave birth to a full-term-size baby two months early. But she could figure that out later.

The real question was, could she stand to be married to Mitch for the rest of her life?

Even if she did decide to marry him, she wouldn't let Mitch off the hook too easily. She was going to make him work for it.

"After the way your brother humiliated me, what makes you believe I would even consider marrying you?" she asked.

"Because I have a plan that will leave my brother looking like the humiliated one."

She narrowed her eyes at him, unable to resist taking the bait. "How will you manage that?"

"It will be leaked that you and I have been secretly seeing each other, and that I seduced you away from my brother that week in D.C. People will be led to believe that you were planning to break the engagement, only Lance did it first, before you had the chance."

"And what will make them believe that? What if they think it's just gossip?"

"My brother and I will have a very public argument to drive the point home."

Reputation was everything to men like Lance and

Mitch, so she couldn't help but feel the slightest bit touched. "Lance would do that for me?"

"We'll do anything for the sake of our business."

So, they weren't doing this for her. They were doing it for their business. Her vindication was just a convenient side effect. She should have known.

Ironically, their so-called plan wasn't that far from the truth. Mitch *had* seduced her, and for a short time she had seriously considered choosing him over his brother.

"Does Lance know what happened?" she asked.

"You mean that night at the hotel?"

She nodded.

"Of course not. As far as he's concerned, this is a total fabrication."

And she could see from Mitch's demeanor that he intended to keep it that way. That would be tough when news of the baby broke. Lance was eventually going to find out.

The truth was, she cared little about her humiliation, and what people might think of her. For the baby's sake, however, she would be a fool to turn down Mitch's offer. A marriage to him would grant the kind of life that the baby deserved.

"My answer is yes," she said. "I'll marry you."

He looked surprised that she would acquiesce so easily. "We should do it soon. I was thinking a small civil ceremony at the courthouse."

The sooner—and the simpler—the better as far

as she was concerned. So much for the extravagant and blissful white wedding she had always dreamed of. "Fine."

"And we should plan a honeymoon. To make it look more authentic."

She thought of the nonrefundable trip she had just booked. "I'm leaving for a seven-day trip to Greece the day after tomorrow. Would that be authentic enough for you?"

He nodded. "That would be perfect."

"I'll have my assistant book you a seat."

"And I'll have mine make the wedding arrangements."

"All right."

"While we're away, I'll arrange to have your things moved into my townhouse."

She hadn't given any thought to the fact that he would expect her to live with him. But of course he would. Married couples lived together. Although the idea of living under his roof made her feel vulnerable. Would he try to run her life, controlling her every move the way her father had? Would she be moving from one prison to another?

And if so, what choice did she have?

Mitch must have read her expression. "You'll have your own room," he assured her. "You'll want for nothing."

Unfortunately, that wasn't true. She wanted something he wasn't capable of giving. She wanted to be loved. She wanted someone to respect and appreciate her for who she was deep down inside. And while he did seem to appreciate what she was doing for him, the love and respect part seemed impossible. Maybe she wasn't worthy. Maybe that was the price she paid for wealth and security. Or maybe the sad truth was, she just wasn't all that lovable.

"You won't regret this," Mitch assured her, which she found terribly ironic, seeing as how she was beginning to regret it already.

"Are you ready for this?" Lance asked Mitch the following evening. They sat across from one another at a linen-draped table in the elaborately decorated dining room of the Texas Cattleman's Club. It was the most public place they could think of for the desired result. If all went as planned, word of what was about to transpire would burn up the town like flaming tumbleweed in the dry season.

"I'm ready," Mitch said.

It was a little hard to believe that this time tomorrow he would be married and on his way to Greece. Twenty-nine was too damned young to be a husband, to be tied down. Not that he or Lexi were thinking of this as a real marriage. It was a business arrangement. One that would no doubt cost him dearly. Both emotionally and financially. That was evident from the astronomically priced wedding ring she'd chosen. Her expensive taste apparently knew no bounds.

A grin kicked up one corner of Lance's mouth. "I'll go easy on you, little brother."

"Don't bother. Whatever you can dish out, I can take." God knows that there were many times he'd gotten a lot worse from their old man. "We have to make this look real, Lance."

"Don't worry, I will," he said, and just like that, the grin faded. Lance assumed a look of pure disgust, and said in a voice loud enough for the entire room to hear, "You son of a bitch."

A hush fell over the room and all heads turned in their direction. No turning back now, Mitch thought.

He held up both hands in a defensive gesture and said in a pleading voice, "Let me explain."

Lance stood so fast his chair flipped backward onto the floor, narrowly missing the table behind theirs. He grabbed his half-full highball glass, rose to his feet and with a flick of his wrist flung the contents into Mitch's face. As the alcohol burned Mitch's eyes and soaked through the front of his shirt, he couldn't help but think, *what a terrible waste of the club's finest whiskey.*

Gasps of surprise filled the silence as Lance stormed from the dining room. Mitch grabbed a linen napkin from the table and wiped his face. With all eyes on him now—most of them friends, neighbors or business associates—he jumped up from his chair and followed his brother to the crowded main lobby, calling, "Lance, wait! I can explain!"

He caught up with him just outside the dining room door. To anyone watching, Lance appeared enraged. "*Explain?* What sort of man seduces his brother's fiancée?"

Mitch heard gasps from the crowd.

"We didn't mean for it to happen," he said, finding it ironic that if Lance had discovered the truth, Mitch probably would have been saying the same thing. Although it would have been a lie. Lexi had admitted to using him to rob her husband of her virginity. Seems the joke was on both of them.

"As far as I'm concerned, you and Lexi deserve each other," Lance spat, and turned to leave. Just as they had choreographed, Mitch grabbed his arm.

The fist came at him so swiftly that, had he not expected it, he wouldn't have had time to duck. As it was, Mitch could only stand there defenseless as Lance's fist connected squarely with his jaw. The blow knocked him backward several feet. He lost his balance and ended up on his ass on the unforgiving marble floor.

Lance shot him one last seething look, then shouldered his way out the door. Mitch's behind ached something special, his jaw stung like a mother and his pride had taken a hit, but the reaction from the patrons told him it had all been worth it. A steady buzz of voices hummed through the lobby and at least half a dozen people were jabbering excitedly into their cell phones. He gave it an hour before the entire population of Maverick County heard the news.

Mitch swiped a hand across the corner of his mouth and came back with a smear of blood. Two employees appeared at either side to help him to his feet, and the hostess handed him a napkin to stop the bleeding.

"I'm all right," he mumbled, shrugging away from their help as though humiliated and distraught. From outside, he heard the squeal of tires and knew Lance was peeling out of the lot, putting the finishing touches on their little charade. And what a show it had been.

He just hoped it was worth it.

Four

With only Tara, Lance, and Mitch's best friend Justin Dupree to serve as witnesses—her father had been called to D.C. on so-called urgent business—Lexi and Mitch said their "I do's" before a county judge the following morning, then drove directly to the airport to catch the first leg of their flight to Greece.

Lexi sat beside her new husband in first class, eyes closed, willing her stomach to settle. Either her hormones were wreaking havoc on her nerves, or her morning sickness had taken a severe turn for the worse. If it was the latter, to hell with having three or four children. This kid could count on being an only child. Up until now, she'd suffered only occasional, mild nausea. Today, she had vomited three times. Once at home, right after she crawled out of bed, once in the ladies' room of the courthouse, and again in the airport bathroom just before their flight boarded. She was beginning to think this trip was a bad idea.

Even worse than marrying Mitch Brody.

"Are you all right?" Mitch said softly.

Far from it. She swallowed back the bile rising in her throat and opened her eyes, grimacing once again when she saw the angry-looking bruise that spanned the left side of his jaw and the nasty gash at the corner of his mouth.

"I'm fine," she lied.

There was concern etched on his face. He folded the newspaper he'd been reading—the financial section, of course—and set it in his lap. "No offense, but you're looking a little green."

How nice of him to notice. "And you're looking black and blue."

He reached up and rubbed a palm across his jaw, wincing slightly.

"I can't believe he hit you. Couldn't he just have pretended to punch you?"

Mitch shrugged, as if it was no big deal. "I told you, it had to look convincing."

Apparently it had. According to Tara, the entire town was buzzing with gossip, and every chance Tara got, she helped out by fanning the flames. In no time, everyone would be convinced that Mitch and Lexi had been having a secret affair. News of the baby would only cement the rumors.

Even though Lexi knew Mitch and Lance had ultimately done it for their business, she couldn't help but feel honored that they had gone to such lengths in part to salvage her honor.

And she thought chivalry was dead.

Despite his casual attitude, it must have been humiliating for Mitch. Or maybe he was one of those men who honestly didn't give a damn what anyone thought.

"I could ring the flight attendant for an ice pack," she offered.

"I'm fine," he said. "Do you need anything?"

She shook her head, which was a mistake because the movement made her stomach lurch. She wished she'd chosen a more casual outfit for the flight instead of the fitted silk suit she'd worn for the ceremony. Something loose and comfortable, like her pajamas.

"You don't look well," he said.

"Thanks."

"That wasn't an insult. I'm concerned."

"I'm just a little airsick. It happens sometimes. And it's kind of embarrassing, so if you don't mind, can we just drop it?"

"Sorry."

After that, they sat in awkward silence. During

their week together in D.C. they had seemingly endless conversations. Most people viewed her as a spoiled and witless debutante, and her father didn't help, perpetuating the rumors by pampering and coddling her. But Mitch had seen past that. He had listened to her, made her feel…special. Now she had no idea what to say to him.

How about something along the lines of, *By the way, did I mention that I'm pregnant with your child?*

She had planned to tell him in the limo on the way to the airport, but she'd been otherwise occupied, trying not to be sick all over the leather interior. She'd decided to wait until they settled into the villa in Greece. She didn't doubt the news was going to come as a shock, but she was sure that when he grew used to the idea, he would be happy to be a father.

As if reading her thoughts, Mitch said, "Maybe we should have a talk about our expectations in regard to our relationship."

She hoped he wasn't talking about sex, because that hadn't been part of the deal. This was supposed to be a business arrangement. She had no intention of being his concubine. "What kind of expectations?"

Her wariness seemed to amuse him. "Not the kind you're obviously thinking of. Our relationship stops at the bedroom door."

"Good," she said, feeling relieved. And strangely enough, a little disappointed.

"What I meant, for example, is that as a part of my business, it's required that I occasionally attend social functions. As my wife, I will expect you to accompany me, and of course I'll do the same for you."

That didn't sound so terrible. "I can do that."

"You'll also be expected to host several parties."

That was something that she was actually quite good at. "Of course."

"And since I'm not particularly fond of seeing my name in the tabloids, or being the source of the latest gossip, I think it should appear to everyone that we're happily married. If word gets out that this is part of a business deal, we'll never hear the end of it. I personally value my privacy."

Personally, she didn't give a damn what people thought. But for the baby's sake, it would be best if they kept up a ruse of wedded bliss, so the child wouldn't feel unwanted.

"As soon as we get back to the states we can start house hunting. Or if you prefer, we could build."

"What about your townhouse?"

"It's too small for our needs."

"If you think so," she said. She had never actually been there, but she couldn't imagine that someone as wealthy as Mitch would live anywhere that could be considered small. Although she couldn't deny that the idea of having her own home was a little exciting. All of her life she had lived in her father's Houston estate or D.C. townhouse. He hadn't even allowed her to decorate her own room, preferring instead to let a professional choose the decor. She had never had a place that was truly hers.

"Of course, you'll be in charge of the household," Mitch continued. "You'll be responsible for the hiring and dismissal of the staff."

"Will I be allowed to decorate?" she asked.

The question seemed to puzzle him. "Of course."

"I won't need your approval for every little thing I do?"

He looked confused. "Is there a reason you should?"

She had just assumed that, like her father, Mitch would deem her untrustworthy or incapable. Or maybe he was just saying these things to lull her into a false sense of security. Maybe he would be an overbearing tyrant.

And maybe you're paranoid.

"Other than the obvious financial requirements, is there anything specific that you expect from me?"

She wasn't sure what he meant by financial requirements. Did he think she would expect him to pay her a salary? "What 'financial requirements' are we talking about?"

"Credit cards, cash. As I assured you, you won't want for anything."

Despite what most people believed, she wasn't the spoiled, pampered heiress they described in the society pages of the paper. Her father had always provided her with a generous allowance for clothing and essentials, but otherwise kept her on a pretty short fiscal leash. He monitored her credit card statements to be sure that she wasn't spending his money on anything inappropriate, and he limited the amount of cash she was allowed. She'd always wondered what it would feel like to be financially independent, to not have someone scrutinizing her every move.

If Mitch did give her financial freedom, maybe this marriage deal wouldn't be quite as miserable as she'd expected.

"Come on," he said. "There must be *something* you want."

Though she was going to wait, he'd left the subject wide open, and she couldn't resist dipping her toes in to test the waters. "What about children?"

"What about them?"

"Well, I know this is just a business arrangement, but I've always wanted kids."

The dark expression that spread across his face chilled her to her core. He shook his head and said, "I think that would be a bad idea."

Oh, this was not good.

Maybe it was the act of conceiving the baby that he had a problem with. Maybe he no longer found her attractive. Their kiss after the vows couldn't have been colder or more formal. Maybe she had been so terrible in bed that first time, he had no interest in a repeat performance.

"If it's the intimacy you're concerned about," she said, "there are other ways—"

"It has nothing to do with that. I feel it would be unfair to bring a child into a loveless marriage."

Her stomach bottomed out. How would he feel if he didn't have a choice in the matter? Would he insist on a divorce? Tell her father the truth about what happened in D.C.? Or even worse, would he disown his child? Then where would she be?

A sense of panic filled her. There had to be a way to convince him, to make this right. "Maybe if we—"

"No," he said firmly, his mouth set in a stubborn line. "There is no maybe. I'll give you anything you want, Lexi. Anything but this."

Just because they didn't love each other, it didn't have to mean their child wouldn't be happy. Her mind worked frantically on a way to make him change his mind.

What if she did everything he asked of her and became the perfect wife? Then would he accept the idea of having a child? But is that what she really wanted? To live a lie?

At this point, did she even have a choice?

Mitch felt slightly guilty for denying Lexi something she obviously longed for, but she would just have to get used to not getting everything her greedy little heart desired. He was sure that no matter how much she thought she wanted children, she had no idea what kind of responsibility it would be. He knew from experience that spoiled debutantes like her didn't have time for anyone but themselves. She would grow tired of the burden, just as his mother had, and walk away. He refused to allow his child to grow up unable to count on the one person who was supposed to provide unconditional love.

They endured the remainder of the nine-hour flight engaged in occasional strained small talk, with Mitch always initiating the conversation. The way she had talked nonstop in D.C., he could only assume that she was now giving him the silent treatment. She probably wasn't accustomed to people not catering to her every whim.

Well, she would have to get used to it. He didn't intend to deny her happiness, but he wasn't about to pamper or spoil her, either. It was time she began living in the real world.

After a brief layover in London, which Lexi spent the majority of in the ladies' room, they boarded a flight for Athens. Lexi fell asleep the minute the wheels left the tarmac and didn't wake until they landed. A limo met them outside the airport to bring them to the port of Lavrio where they boarded the small passenger ship that would take them to the island of Tzia.

Two hours later, and sixteen hours after they left Houston, they finally arrived at the villa where they would spend the next week. About half a mile east, he could see rows of densely built houses that looked like windowed shoe boxes clinging to the steep slope that bordered the village of Loulida, and nothing but open countryside for at least half a mile in every other direction. When Lexi said the area was secluded, he hadn't realized just how alone they would be.

Mitch let Lexi have the top-level master suite and took one of the three guest bedrooms on the ground floor for himself. It was more than enough space for him, and a large sliding glass door conveniently led to the swimming pool, hot tub and pool house, where he guessed he would be spending much of his time. Just off the bedrooms was a spacious living room with a full bar and plush, comfortable-looking furniture. The middle floor held a modern and well-equipped kitchen with an adjoining dining room, while another comfortable sitting room led to the main terrace and the barbecue area.

The interior was a combination of vibrant colors and innovative designs that could have very comfortably housed half a dozen people or more. His preference would have been a place that was smaller, and more intimate. But someone like Lexi would want the biggest and most luxurious lodging available. Although he was a bit surprised that she hadn't hired a full staff to cater to her. She hadn't even arranged for a chef or a maid.

"I think I'll lie down for a while," she said, when he carried her luggage to her room for her. She was still looking a little green, and he couldn't help feeling sorry for her. He had never been one to suffer from motion sickness, but from the looks of it, the last day had been hell.

"Can I bring you anything?" he asked. "Something to eat? A cup of tea?"

"I think I just need to sleep for a while," she said, but looked at him a little funny, as though she couldn't figure out why he was being so nice to her.

That makes two of us, sweetheart. Must be jet lag, or temporary insanity.

"I'll be in my room unpacking if you need me," he told her, then he left her room, closing the door behind him. Something seemed different. Lexi was acting almost…humbled.

He shook his head. It was probably just due to the fact that she was feeling sick. He was sure she would be back to her entitled, narcissistic self by tomorrow.

As he walked to his room he pulled out his cell and dialed his brother, and though it was barely 7:00 a.m. in Texas, he answered on the first ring.

"You're supposed to be on your honeymoon," Lance said.

"I am."

"Then why the hell are you calling me?"

"I just wondered if there's anything new from Darius about the fire. Anything pointing to Alex Montoya."

"Nothing since you left, which was less than

twenty-four hours ago. And if I do hear something, I'll let you know."

In other words, don't call me, I'll call you. "If there are any problems at the office—"

"Mitch, forget about work and enjoy yourself. You're on your honeymoon. Go seduce your wife or something."

"You know as well as I do that it isn't that kind of marriage."

"You're a newlywed, and the way I look at it, that gives you certain rights. Like sex with your new wife on your wedding night. I guarantee you won't be disappointed."

Mitch knew that firsthand, but the question was, how did Lance? Then he realized: Lance must have slept with her when they were engaged.

Lexi certainly hadn't wasted any time hopping from one brother's bed to the next, he thought wryly. Maybe to her, it was just a game. Some kind of twisted challenge. At least Mitch knew for a fact that he had been first. And according to Lexi, that was exactly the way she'd planned it. What she hadn't counted on was Lance dumping her for someone else.

"I felt kind of sorry for her yesterday," Lance said.

"Why?"

"Having only her assistant at her wedding. You would think her father would have the decency to show."

"He's a busy man."

"Too busy to see his only child get married? Would you miss your daughter's wedding?"

No, but then, he wouldn't be having a daughter, or a son. He would just have to be content spoiling the children that he was sure Lance and Kate would have. "I'm sure the senator had his reasons."

"That doesn't make it any less lousy."

Mitch couldn't help thinking she got exactly what she deserved.

After he hung up with his brother, Mitch took a long, hot shower to wash away the travel grit, then collapsed naked between the cool silk sheets. He decided he would sleep for an hour or so, then get up and make them something to eat. But when he opened his eyes again the sun had already set, and the room was dark but for the light in the hallway shining through the open door.

Hadn't he closed the door before he'd lain down? He was almost positive he had. In fact, he *was* positive.

Then he saw a silhouette move across the room. He jerked up on his elbows, groggy and alarmed, but as his eyes adjusted, he realized the form was female. And not just any female.

It was Lexi.

Five

Lexi crossed the room to Mitch's bed wearing a floor-length, low-cut, white silk nightgown that shimmered in the light. Her pale hair lay in soft waves across her shoulders, cascading down to the swell of her breasts.

For a second he wondered if he was dreaming. What reason would she possibly have to be in his room? Was she sick? Or plotting to smother him with his pillow?

"Is something wrong?" he asked, his voice rough from sleep.

"Nothing is wrong."

Relieved, he dropped his head back down on the bed. "What are you doing in here?"

"This is officially our wedding night," she said.

Yeah, so? he thought, unsure of the significance. Then she lifted the gown up over her head and dropped it to the floor. She wasn't wearing anything underneath. Now he knew he *had* to be dreaming. But as she slipped between the sheets beside him, her body warm and soft against his, it was too vivid, too fantastic to be anything but real. Nothing about this made any sense.

"This wasn't part of the deal," he reminded her.

She leaned on one elbow, gazing down at him. In the dim light she looked like an angel, when he knew for a fact she was actually a devil in disguise. "I know."

She laid her hand on his chest, lightly stroking his skin, and his body responded instantly. She was obviously willing, so why couldn't he shake the feeling that something wasn't right? Why did he feel guilty, as though he was forcing her?

"We don't have to," he said, even though he wanted nothing more than to run his fingers through the silky ribbons of her hair and pull her down for a long, deep kiss. He didn't want her to feel as though she owed him, or was somehow obligated.

Uncertainty flickered in her eyes, and in that instant he had never seen a woman look more vulnerable or insecure. Deep inside of him something hard and unyielding softened a bit around the edges. Was it possible that she wasn't as confident and fearless as she liked people to believe?

She pulled her hand away and said, "We won't if you don't want to."

Was she serious? He couldn't think of a single other thing he would rather be doing. He took her by the wrist and guided her hand under the covers to his erection. "Does it feel like I don't want to?"

A smile crept across her face as she wrapped her hand around him and squeezed. The sensation was so erotic he nearly lost it.

"I want you, Mitch," she whispered.

That was all the convincing he needed. He caught her behind the neck, pulled her to him and kissed her.

One second Lexi was lying across Mitch's chest as he tangled his fingers through her hair and ravaged her mouth, and the next she was flat on her back on the bed looking up at him. The change of position was so swift it left her breathless and dizzy. Or maybe it was his kisses that were doing that. She just prayed, as he pressed his weight against her, caressing her skin with his hands and his mouth, that he didn't feel her trembling. She didn't want him to know how terrified she had been that he might reject her. She had no clue how to play the role of vixen, how to be the aggressor, but if she was going to convince him this was a real marriage, if she was going to make him fall in love with her, she had to play the part. What kind of wife would she be if she didn't please her husband sexually? Especially on their wedding night.

Although right now, he seemed to be the one doing all the pleasing, and she had almost forgotten how impossibly wonderful it felt to be close to him. How he made her feel as though she was the most beautiful, desirable woman in the world.

"I thought we were keeping this relationship outside the bedroom," he said, nibbling his way down her throat. On the contrary, it was her intention to keep him in bed as much as humanly possible while they were in Greece.

"Not that I'm complaining," he added. "Just mildly confused."

"We both have needs," she said. "I figure, if we have to be stuck with each other, why not enjoy it?"

He grinned down at her. "Lexi, isn't that supposed to be *my* line?"

"You know what I think?" she asked, and his brow perked with curiosity. "I think you talk too much."

His grin turned feral. "And I like the way you think."

She wrapped her arms around his neck and pulled him to her for a slow, deep kiss. They caressed and touched each other until she felt as though she would go out of her mind. She wanted him inside her so badly, she actually ached.

"Make love to me," she told him. "Right now."

Mitch looked up from the nipple he'd been teasing with his tongue. "I thought that's what I was doing."

"Maybe you could do it a little faster?"

"What's the hurry?"

All she knew was that it felt as though there was a big empty space inside of her that she was desperate to fill. He must have seen the desperation on her face because he opened the drawer on the bedside table and pulled out a condom. At her questioning look he said, "Doesn't hurt to come prepared."

She didn't tell him there was no point, that the damage was already done.

He rolled it on, then entered her with one slow but purposeful thrust. She gasped at the stinging sensation as her body stretched to accept him.

Concern filled his eyes. "Did I hurt you?"

"No," she lied, because it was a good hurt. Since that night at the hotel, she'd had the constant and nagging feeling that something was missing. She had felt...incomplete. Now, with their bodies joined, she finally felt whole again.

She arched up, taking him even deeper inside of her, wrapping her legs around his waist. Mitch groaned and grasped the bedcovers. It gave her a thrilling sense of power to know that he was losing control, and she was making it happen.

He rolled over so that she was on top, straddling him, their bodies still joined. Now that she was up here, she was unsure of what to do. What if she did it wrong and made a fool of herself? What if she was clumsy and awkward, and couldn't satisfy him? "Mitch, I don't—"

"Yes, you do," he said, as though he had complete confidence in her. "Just do what feels good."

She braced her hands on the mattress on either side of him and rose up, but she went too far and he slipped out. She made a noise of frustration, but Mitch didn't seem to mind.

"Don't worry," he said, guiding himself back in like it was no big deal. This time he rested his hands on her hips to guide her. "Take it slow."

She began to move slowly, eyes closed in concentration. At first, she was so afraid to make a mistake, focused so completely on her every move, she wasn't able to let herself enjoy it.

"Relax," he said, arching his hips up to meet her downward thrusts. They slipped into a slow, steady rhythm, and she began to lose herself in the sensation, in the sweet friction, until it began to feel as natural as breathing.

This was the way she wanted to spend the rest of her life. Acting on impulse, living by instinct. Doing things just because they felt good.

"Open your eyes," Mitch said, and when she did, when she looked down at him, she could see that he was barely hanging on.

With his eyes locked on hers, he reached down to where their bodies met and stroked her. Pleasure rippled through her from the inside out and an orgasm that was almost shocking in its intensity locked her muscles. She threw her head back and rode out the sensation, and through a haze she heard Mitch groan, felt him tense beneath her, his fingers digging into her skin.

Limp with satisfaction, Lexi collapsed against his chest, their hearts pounding out a frantic beat together. It just kept getting better and better. She had never felt as close to anyone in her life as she did to Mitch tonight.

This was going to work, she assured herself. Everything was going to be fine. But as he rolled her over and began kissing her, making love to her all over again, she couldn't help feeling like a fraud.

Mitch woke the next morning and reached for Lexi, but her side of the bed was empty. He glanced over at the clock, surprised to see that it was after eight. Jet lag had his schedule all jacked up, because he never slept a minute past 6:00 a.m., even on weekends. He sat up and looked groggily around the room, thinking that maybe Lexi had just stepped into the bathroom, but he could hear the clatter of pots and pans and dishes in the kitchen. He caught a whiff of something that smelled like breakfast, but he knew he must be imagining it, unless she had hired a cook after all.

He rolled out of bed, pulled on a pair of pajama bottoms and walked to the kitchen. Lexi stood by the stove, poking at something in a frying pan with a spatula. On the counter sat a plate with some sort of sausage.

She cooked?

Beside her, the state-of-the-art dishwasher was open and there were actually dishes inside. He didn't think a spoiled heiress even knew what a dishwasher was, much less knew how to use one.

Was it possible that he'd misjudged her?

"Good morning," he said.

She turned to him and smiled a sweet smile that made him believe she was genuinely happy to see him. "Good morning."

She was wearing the silk gown she'd had on last night and her feet were bare. Her hair was pulled back in a ponytail and her face was free of makeup. She looked young and sweet and pretty, but from the neck down, she was all woman. Full and firm breasts, perfectly proportioned hips. He had to fight the urge to scoop her up in his arms and carry her back to bed. Having a little occasional fun was one thing, but they shouldn't overdo it. He didn't want her getting the wrong idea.

"Are you hungry?" she asked. "I made breakfast."

"Starved," he said. They had skipped dinner last night. "Can I help?"

"I've got it. Do you want coffee?"

"I can get it," he said, but she shooed him away.

"Go sit down. Relax."

Ooookay.

He took a seat in the nook by a window overlooking the pool, while she filled a cup that was already sitting by the coffeemaker.

"Milk or sugar?" she asked.

"Black, please."

She laughed lightly and shook her head.

"What?" he asked.

"It's just weird," she said, crossing the room and setting the cup in front of him. "We're married and I don't even know how you take your coffee. I guess this just wasn't the way I imagined my life."

Amen to that. He never imagined himself ever getting married. He would have been happy playing the field the rest of his life. Having relationships on his terms. Living life by his own rules.

She walked back to the stove and he was mesmerized watching her hips sway, the curve of her behind under the silk gown. He couldn't help but wonder if she was commando under there. If so, it wouldn't take much to lift up the gown and pull her into his lap....

He gave his head a shake. He needed to stop with the fantasies and keep his hands to himself.

She scooped scrambled eggs onto his plate, added a few links of sausage and then set the plate in front of him. *"Bon appétit,"* she said, then sat down across from him and rested her chin on her clasped hands.

"Aren't you eating?" he asked.

She shook her head. "I had something when I got up."

He stabbed a forkful of eggs and shoveled it into his mouth...and nearly spit it back out. The eggs were so salty he almost gagged. He forced himself to swallow and chased it down with a guzzle of coffee, but almost choked. The coffee was so strong that if he didn't already have hair on his chest, it would have put some there. He tried to cover the bitter flavor with a bite of sausage, but it was so overcooked and dried out he could barely chew it.

The meal was a total and complete disaster. And one thing was absolutely clear. Lexi *did not* know how to cook.

If he had a choice, he would dump the whole thing down the sink, or do like he had when he was a kid and feed it to the dog. Unfortunately, they didn't have a dog, and she was gazing at him with such a hopeful look on her face, he didn't have the heart to hurt her feelings. He pasted on a smile and said, "Delicious."

He wasn't sure what brought on this sudden attempt at domesticity, but, mind-boggling as it was, he gave her credit for the effort. He forced down every last bite of eggs and sausage, stopping just short of licking his plate clean, and he even asked for a refill on his coffee.

"That was really good. Thanks." He stood to clear his place, but she stopped him.

"You sit. I'll do it."

She cleared away his dirty dishes and set them in the dishwasher. "I was thinking of making lamb for dinner," she said.

If it was even half as bad as breakfast, he didn't

think his stomach could take it. "Why don't you let me cook dinner?"

She frowned. "Why?"

He could see that he was walking a very delicate line here. One wrong step and he would hurt her feelings. "It's only fair that we split the household chores while we're here. Don't you think?"

"But I'm your wife. I'm supposed to take care of you."

That was the part he didn't get. Hadn't they agreed that this wasn't a real marriage? That this was a business deal? This was the last thing he expected. "Why, Lexi?"

The space between her brows furrowed. "Because that's what wives do."

Real wives maybe, not pretend ones. Maybe she had caught a bug and wasn't feeling well, or she was a little off due to jet lag. "You don't have to."

"But I *want* to."

What was he supposed to say to that? You can take care of me in the bedroom anytime you like, but otherwise leave me alone? That was just…sleazy.

It was obvious that a sexual relationship was a really bad idea. And he hoped like hell that this desire for domestic bliss would wear thin. They would get back to Houston and settle into a life of servants and chefs, and live amicable but very separate lives.

"If it means that much to you, you can make dinner," he said.

She sat back down at the table across from him, wearing a smile so full of relief it worried him.

What the hell was going on?

"So, what did you want to do today?" she asked. "We could walk to the village, or hire a car to take us on a tour of the island."

"Actually, I was thinking of just hanging out by the pool."

"Oh. Well, that sounds like fun."

He meant alone. As in, by himself. He hadn't even entertained the idea that she would want to spend the day with him. He figured they would just go their separate ways. But what was he supposed to say? Leave me the hell alone?

This was just too weird.

He rose from his chair and she stood up, too. "I'm going to take a shower."

"And I have to clean this mess. Meet you outside in thirty minutes?"

She looked so eager, so desperate to please him, all he could do was smile and say, "I can hardly wait." But he felt as if he'd climbed out of bed into an episode of *The Twilight Zone*.

Six

When Mitch was gone, Lexi collapsed back down into her chair, dropped her head in her hands and blew out a relieved breath. Talk about stressful. Making Mitch think this marriage was real was going to be a lot harder than she'd anticipated. Especially if he refused to cooperate. She had the feeling that in her attempt to impress him with her domestic skills, she might have overplayed her hand just the tiniest bit.

Thank goodness Tara had answered the phone when Lexi called—considering it had been after midnight, Houston time—and knew how to make scrambled eggs. Although it had still taken Lexi a dozen eggs and six tries to get it right. But part of that was due to the fact that she wasn't sure how to work the electric stove to get the proper heat settings.

It wasn't that she had never wanted to learn to cook, it was just that her father would never allow it. That was what they had servants for. He considered cooking and cleaning beneath her. She was sure it would be fun once she got the hang of it.

There was a leg of lamb thawing on the counter that Tara assured her would be a no-brainer, and tomorrow for breakfast, she might even try something complicated, like pancakes.

She walked to the stove, grabbed the pan of leftover eggs and was about to dump them down the sink when she realized her stomach was feeling marginally settled. She picked up a fork and took a bite, gagged and spit it directly into the sink.

They were awful. Yet Mitch had sat there straight-faced and eaten every bite. Even told her they were delicious. Though she wasn't supposed to have any, she poured herself a splash of coffee and gave it a taste. It was even worse than the eggs.

No wonder he'd suggested that he make dinner. He probably thought she was trying to poison him. She would have to be sure that she made dinner extra special. Maybe then he would think that breakfast had been a fluke and she wasn't completely useless.

She loaded the rest of the dishes and the frying pan into the dishwasher and filled the receptacle with the liquid dish soap she found under the sink, giving the dishes an extra squirt just to be safe. It took her a few minutes to figure out the digital display, but after randomly pressing buttons, she eventually got it running. It was amazing all of the things she didn't know how to do, but she was determined to figure them out. To be the perfect wife. The perfect partner.

However, one thing she definitely had to avoid was sleeping in Mitch's bed. She woke this morning with her stomach in knots, and barely made it to her own bathroom before she vomited. Mitch was bound to get suspicious if he realized she was tossing her cookies every morning. Every day she didn't tell him about the baby she risked making an even bigger mess out of things. But if things went according to plan, by the time she finally did tell him, he would be so happy, and love her so much, he wouldn't even care that she'd kept it from him.

Her baby's welfare depended on it.

Mitch showered, changed into his swim trunks, then headed to the kitchen to grab a soda on his way out to the pool. He stopped short in the doorway when he saw Lexi on her hands and knees, wearing a white beach cover-up, amid an ocean of thick white soap bubbles on the kitchen floor. She was trying frantically to wipe them up with a dish towel, but wasn't doing much more than pushing the suds around, and it was starting to overflow into the living room.

"What the hell happened?" he asked.

Startled, she looked up at him. "I don't know. Something is wrong with the dishwasher."

He looked over and saw that suds were continuing to ooze out from underneath the unit. He slipped and slid his way across the soapy floor and hit the cancel button. "Why didn't you shut it off?"

Only after the words were out, and he saw Lexi's wounded expression, did he realize how harsh he'd sounded. She looked at the dishwasher, then up at him and shrugged helplessly. It was then that he realized, she probably didn't know *how* to shut it off.

Keeping his voice calm, he asked, "How did this happen?"

"I told you, it's broken," she said. "I went to change and when I came back out, there was soap everywhere. You can bet the rental company is going to hear about this."

He had a pretty good idea what had happened, and it was in no way the rental company's—or even the dishwasher's—fault. "What kind of soap did you use?"

"The bottle under the sink," she said, in a tone that suggested he was dim for even asking.

He opened the cupboard and pulled out the soap sitting right in the front. "This one?"

"Yes, that one," she snapped. "Dish soap, for washing dishes."

"That's not for a dishwasher."

She frowned. "What do you mean? It says it is right on the label."

He reached back into the cupboard and extracted a box of granulated dishwasher detergent. "This is for the dishwasher. It doesn't suds up like regular dish soap."

"Oh," she said, pulling her lip between her teeth, looking mortified by her error. Once again, Mitch couldn't help but feel sorry for her. At least she was trying. How could he expect a woman who had probably never washed a dirty dish in her life to know how to run a dishwasher?

"Sorry," she said, her cheeks blushing bright pink.

He shrugged. "It's an honest mistake. No big deal."

She looked helplessly around at the mess she had created, as though she didn't have the first clue how to fix it. And though he felt like a complete degenerate for it, the only thing he could think about was getting her naked, laying her down and rolling around with her until they were both all slippery. Then he would…probably have his head examined.

"Why don't you go out by the pool," he told her. "I'll clean this up."

"It's my mess," she said.

Yes, and he had the feeling that if he left her alone to deal with it, she would only manage to make things worse. Besides, it would be advantageous to both of them if they weren't within mauling distance of each other.

"You're not here to wait on me hand and foot," he said. "You made breakfast, it's only fair that I clean up."

"Are you sure?" she asked, looking relieved for a valid excuse to bail on the situation.

"I'm sure. I'll have this cleaned up in no time."

"Okay." She rose to her feet, her legs all soapy, and tiptoed her way carefully across the floor, so she didn't slip and fall. "I'll see you outside."

No time ended up being over an hour, and he still hadn't been able to get all of the soap residue off the floor. He would just have to warn Lexi to be careful so she didn't slip while she was making dinner.

Though it wasn't noon yet, he felt he'd earned himself a cold beer. He grabbed one from the fridge, put his sunglasses on and headed out to the pool. Lexi lay in a lounge chair on the opposite side, sunning herself. Her eyes were shaded behind dark, designer sunglasses and she was wearing what looked like a very skimpy, pale bikini.

Wait a minute….

He slid his glasses down his nose to get a better look at her, and as his eyes adjusted to the bright sunshine, he realized she was in fact not wearing a pale bikini, skimpy or otherwise.

Lexi wasn't wearing anything at all.

Eyes closed behind her sunglasses, the late-morning sun drenching her skin at a very comfortable seventy-five degrees, Lexi tried to shake off the mortification of failing at the simple task of working the dishwasher. She should have called Tara before she went anywhere near it. She also should have stayed in the kitchen and helped Mitch clean, but she was too embarrassed. And no doubt if she had stayed, she would have done that wrong, too, and looked even more inept than she already did. How could she expect him to take her seriously, to consider her a good wife, if she couldn't even negotiate her way around a kitchen? She would have to make an absolutely perfect dinner.

More than an hour had passed when she finally heard Mitch open the patio door. She peeked through half-closed lids and saw that he was walking in her direction. A shadow robbed the sunshine as he hovered over her. "What the hell do you think you're doing?" he asked, his harsh tone making her jolt with surprise.

Was this some sort of trick question? "S-sunbathing?"

She could see by his exasperated expression that it wasn't the answer he wanted to hear.

"Yes, I can see that," he said. "What I would like to know is why you're naked."

"Technically, I'm not naked. I have bottoms on." More exasperation on his face, so she added, "I don't like tan lines. Besides, everyone in Europe sunbathes topless."

"You're a senator's daughter. I would think you'd know better."

She looked around. "Who's going to see me? We're in the middle of nowhere."

"That's not the point."

Then what was the point? What man didn't enjoy seeing his wife sunbathing topless?

The kind who married his wife for business. One who found her so physically unattractive, the only place he cared to see her naked was in a dark bedroom, where he could pretend she was someone else.

She felt sick all the way down to her soul. She pulled herself up from her chair, grabbed the towel she'd been lying on and wrapped it around herself. "I'm sorry that you find my body so offensive."

"Lexi, that isn't what I—"

"I'll be sure to keep it appropriately covered from now on," she assured him, nose in the air, giving him the cold and bitchy routine so he wouldn't hear the hurt in her voice. She turned to walk away, but Mitch wrapped a hand around her upper arm to stop her.

"I swear you're the most insecure woman I've ever met," he said. "And you're making it really hard for me to do the right thing."

The right thing? What was that supposed to mean? She tried to tug her arm free. "Let go."

Instead, he yanked the towel from around her and scooped her up. She let out a shriek as he flung her like a sack of potatoes over one shoulder and carried her toward the sliding glass door that led to his bedroom.

She wiggled, trying to get loose, but he only held on tighter. "What are you doing?"

"I could tell you that you're beautiful and desirable until I'm blue in the face, but you probably wouldn't believe me."

Okay, so maybe he didn't find her *completely* undesirable.

She pounded on his back with her fists, which was about as effective as hitting a boulder with a feather. "So, you pull a caveman routine instead?"

He slid the door open and carried her into his bedroom. Despite his brutish and uncivilized behavior, a shiver of excitement rippled through her. After all, it had been her plan to keep him in the bedroom as much as possible.

He slid her off his shoulder onto her back on the mattress and knelt beside her, a look of pure mischief in his eyes. "You won't listen to me," he said. "So, I'm just going to have to show you."

Mitch spent the rest of the morning and a good part of the afternoon showing Lexi just how beautiful and desirable he thought she was. And boy, was he good at it. Every time she tried to climb out of bed, he would pull her back in and start convincing her all over again. When she finally insisted she had to put the lamb in the oven or it wouldn't be ready in time for dinner, he reluctantly let her go. She wobbled into the kitchen on spaghetti legs, and every inch of her skin hummed with sexual satisfaction.

At this rate, it wouldn't be long before she could tell him about the baby.

Following Tara's instructions to the letter, Lexi seasoned the lamb shank and popped it in the oven. And though it took a minute of pushing buttons, the oven finally beeped and turned on. She peeled the potatoes and carrots next, then put them aside to add to the roasting pan forty minutes before the lamb was done. Until then, she didn't have much to do, so she went looking for Mitch.

She found him sacked out in a lounge chair by the pool, sleeping so deeply, he was snoring. It looked as though she'd worn the poor guy out. For a second, she considered all the creative ways she could wake him, most using her mouth, but he looked so peaceful, she didn't have the heart.

Instead, she stretched out in the chair beside him to get some sun, but her eyes felt heavy and in no time she drifted into a deep sleep, and had strange and erotic dreams about Mitch. Hazy, disjointed images of bare skin and feelings of intense sexual sensation flooded her. She could smell him, taste the flavor of his mouth and skin. She could feel the weight of his hands touching her, her hair tangled in his fingers, the flex of her muscles as she took him deep inside her body. The strum of sensation on her nerve endings.

Not a strum so much as a loud hum. And the hum grew louder, the sound filling her head until it was more annoying than arousing. A sharp, piercing bleat.

Her eyes flew open and she realized the sound wasn't in her dream. It was coming from the house, through the open door that led to the kitchen…and was that *smoke* she was seeing?

Wide awake now, she jumped from the chair, grabbed her cover-up and tugged it on as she dashed for the house. She was stunned by what she encountered in the kitchen.

Acrid smoke hung in the air, the oven sat open and empty and the pan the roast had been in was sitting in the sink under a flow of water. She could only assume that the black lump was the charred remains of the lamb shank. Mitch stood in the middle of the room in his swim trunks, fanning the smoke detector with a broom.

Oh, God, what had she done this time?

Mitch finally looked over and saw her standing there, watching him. He flashed her a smile and said, "The lamb is done."

After the dishwasher fiasco this morning, there didn't seem to be much point in trying to blame it on the oven. She had obviously screwed up again. Only this time, instead of flooding the house, it looked as though she'd nearly burned it down.

They had made some real progress today, and now

she'd ruined it. She couldn't even imagine what he must be thinking, and she wondered how long it would be before she and the baby were out on the street.

Mitch swung the broom around and, using the handle end, gave the smoke detector a solid whack. It gave one final bleat, then fell silent. Which was even worse than the deafening screech.

She opened her mouth to say something, apologize maybe, but words escaped her.

Mitch walked over to the sink and turned off the tap, looking down at the soggy remains of dinner. "We should probably open a few windows to let the smoke out."

"I'll get the family room," she said, eager to skulk away in shame. This could go one of two ways. He would be completely exasperated with her and make her feel like a total dope, or he would be understanding and sweet, all the while thinking that she was a lost cause.

She honestly wasn't sure which would be more humiliating.

When every window on the main floor was open, she walked back to the kitchen where Mitch was closing the oven and shutting it off. She couldn't tell if he was angry, or just resigned to the fact that he'd married a domestic disaster.

She gestured to the sink, taking a feeble stab at humor. "Was the lamb thirsty, or is this your way of telling me it's too dry for your taste?"

"I couldn't find the lid or fire extinguisher, so this was the only way to douse the flames."

Flames? It had actually been on fire?

Just when she thought she couldn't be more embarrassed, she discovered a whole new level of humiliation. "I don't suppose you would believe me if I said the lamb was supposed to catch on fire."

He cracked a smile.

"So, what did I do wrong this time?" she asked, even though she wasn't sure she wanted to know. She couldn't imagine he would ever let her near the kitchen again, much less cook something.

"The oven was on broil instead of bake."

Which meant what, exactly? She thought meat was supposed to broil. Her confusion must have been obvious because he added, "Bake warms the entire oven uniformly and allows food to cook slower. Broil is a direct flame right over the pan and cooks things much faster. Obviously."

Something she would have known if she'd ever used an oven before.

"I'm sorry I murdered dinner," she said.

He shrugged, again like it wasn't a big deal. "Unless you're a pyromaniac, which I seriously doubt, it was an honest mistake."

She wanted to believe he felt that way, but he had to be realizing how truly useless she was. What would her next honest mistake be? Accidental poisoning?

Maybe there was a reason her father had kept her so sheltered. Maybe he could see that left to her own devices, she was a danger to herself and others.

"I suppose it's obvious that I've never cooked before. Or used a dishwasher."

"Seriously?" he asked, trying to look surprised, but he was a terrible liar.

She shot him a look.

"Okay," he admitted. "I sort of had that feeling."

"I appreciate that you choked down breakfast despite how awful it was."

He shrugged. "It wasn't *that* bad."

"Yes, it was. We would probably both be safer if you cooked from now on."

"What makes you think I can cook?"

"You can't be any worse than me. I should stay as far away as possible from the kitchen."

"How are you going to learn if you don't try?"

"I did try, and I almost burned the house down! I'm useless."

He huffed out an exasperated breath. "What is it with you and this low self-esteem? You are not useless. And if you really would like to learn, when we get back to Texas we'll enroll you in a cooking class."

She shook her head. "No, my father would never allow it. He considers it beneath me."

"Your father isn't the one calling the shots. You're married to me now, and you have a say in your own life."

At first, she thought he was just making fun of her, but then she realized he was serious. Unfortunately, it wasn't that simple. "If he finds out, he'll be furious, and you still need his senatorial support."

"Let me worry about that."

He would risk his relationship with her father just so she could have a couple of cooking lessons? She narrowed her eyes, still not sure if she could trust him, wondering if this was some twisted game to him. "You're serious?"

"Yes. Very serious." He folded his arms across his chest and leaned against the counter. "Out of curiosity, what else has your father kept you from doing?"

She considered his question for a minute, then said, "It would probably be easier to tell you what he *did* let me do, since it's a far shorter list."

Mitch shook his head. "My father could be a real bastard, but I'm beginning to wonder if I didn't have it so rough, after all."

It was the first time he had ever said anything to her about his family. Of course, she had never really asked. "What did he do to you?"

"Suffice it to say, the slug to the jaw I took from Lance was nothing in comparison."

"Your father *hit* you?"

"On a regular basis. But it sounds worse than it was. I got over it."

Why did she get the feeling he really hadn't?

"So, what are we going to do about dinner?" he asked.

She looked over at the sink, at the remains of the lamb shank. "Don't look at me. I'm not going anywhere near the stove until I get those lessons."

"In that case, why don't we get dressed and go into the village?"

That sounded like the perfect solution to her. "Give me fifteen minutes."

Seven

What the hell was wrong with him?

Mitch walked with Lexi down the dirt road to Tzia, the local village, wondering what the hell he'd been thinking today when he carried her into his bedroom. So much for treating this marriage like a business deal. But when she'd accused him of finding her repulsive, and he realized she actually meant it, that she wasn't just manipulating him, the hurt look she wore had done something to his brain. What choice did he have but to show her how wrong she was?

And what was all that crap about cooking lessons? Where the hell had that come from? He didn't care if she could cook or not. But again she had looked so helpless and dejected. He couldn't help but feel sorry for her. Which was probably exactly what she wanted. But there was a small part of him that kept wondering, what if it wasn't an act?

She'd reached for his hand as they left the villa, and what was he supposed to do? Refuse to hold it? Tell her he didn't think it was appropriate? They *were* married. He could feel himself getting sucked into...something, although as genuine as her feelings seemed to be, he couldn't shake the suspicion that she had ulterior motives. They had agreed this was going to be business and nothing more, and he was determined to stick to that. As soon as they got back to Texas. He figured by then they would have gotten this nagging sexual attraction out of the way and would both be sick of each other.

At least he hoped so.

They reached the village just before sundown. As they passed under the arch leading inside, the beauty of the architecture stunned him. They strolled down cobbled streets lined with shops, crowded bars, and outdoor cafés. There was even a gallery whose front window boasted the works of famous Greek artists such as Tsarouhis, Fasianos, and Stathopoulos.

After some browsing, they chose a quiet café at the north end of the village and sat outside under a thick blanket of stars. He ordered an ouzo and though he tried to convince Lexi to try it, she opted for a bottled water, instead. In D.C., she had always had a glass or two of wine with dinner.

"Are you sure you don't want something to drink?" he asked after the server left the table.

"I'm sure."

"Wine or beer?"

She smiled, a warm breeze blowing the hair back from her face. "Why, are you planning to get me drunk?"

If he'd learned one thing in the past couple of days, it was that he didn't need the aid of alcohol to have his way with her. They ordered their food, both choosing authentic Greek favorites, but when it came, Lexi just picked at it.

"You don't like it?" he asked.

"No, it's good. I'm just not very hungry."

As far as Mitch could tell, she'd barely eaten anything since they left the U.S., and maybe it was his imagination, but she looked thinner than she'd been that night in D.C. He didn't remember her collarbones being so pronounced and her cheeks so hollow. He knew she was insecure, but would she drive herself to the point of anorexia? Or what if she was sick? Something more dangerous than airsickness and jet lag?

"Is something wrong?" he asked.

His question seemed to surprise her. "No, why?"

"You've hardly eaten a thing since we left Texas. Are you sick?"

There was the slightest pause before she smiled and assured him, "I'm fine, really." But he couldn't escape the feeling that she wasn't being completely honest with him. Although, what reason would she have to lie?

By the time they finished eating, most of the shops had locked their doors and the bars looked over-crowded and smoky, so they headed back to the villa with nothing but the full moon to light their way. The air had cooled and it was so silent, Mitch could hear the thump of his own heart.

Once again, she reached for his hand and rather than fight it, he twined his fingers through hers.

She surprised him by asking, "Did your father hit Lance, too?"

His father wasn't a subject he liked to discuss, but in all fairness, he had been the one to bring it up earlier. "Lance, me, our mother—until she'd had enough, packed her bags and left."

"Your mother left without you?"

"As Lance likes to say, she had her reasons."

"My father never hit me, but in a weird way I wish he would have."

"No, you don't."

"At least then I would know that he felt *something*. After my mom died he just…shut down. I did everything I could to make him happy, everything he ever asked, but I still felt invisible."

If what she said was true, maybe she didn't have the spoiled and pampered life after all. Maybe she was just as bitter and confused as everyone else. Or maybe she was one hell of a good actress. Either way, this conversation was getting a little too personal. She needed to understand that when they got back to Texas, things would change.

But what if she didn't understand that? What if, God forbid, she thought she was falling in love with him? He knew how it was for women like Lexi. They decided on something they wanted and went after it with a vengeance, all pistons firing. Right up until the second they got bored and found a new toy to amuse them.

"We should probably talk about how things will be when we get back to Texas," he said.

She gazed up at him, her skin luminous in the moonlight. "What things?"

"Us. Our relationship."

"Okay."

"I just think I should be clear about a few things. I'm a very busy man, and I like to do things, to live my life, a certain way. You should know that I don't intend to change."

She nodded silently, but he had the distinct impression he'd hurt her feelings. If he had, he was sorry for that, but it was important they were both clear on the way things would be.

"As we agreed before, this is a business deal. Nothing more."

"Of course," she said, but he could swear there

was a slight waver in her voice. An edge of disappointment. Maybe she really believed things had changed. Well, that wasn't his problem.

Then why did he feel so damned guilty?

She was silent the rest of the walk home. When they walked in the door, he expected that they would go their separate ways, to their own beds, but she stunned him by keeping hold of his hand and leading him to his bedroom. The sex was so passionate and intense, for a while he almost forgot that it wasn't real. As she lay naked beside him, her body curled around his, the idea of this ending seemed almost inconceivable. But he had never been one to mistake sex for affection or love. When she tired of the arrangement and pulled her inevitable disappearing act, he wouldn't be sorry to see her go.

Though Mitch's words stung and she seriously considered giving up, Lexi chose to disregard what he'd said about their marriage and forge ahead with her plan.

They spent the better part of the next six days in bed, or in various other places, having sex. And when they weren't climbing all over each other, or collapsing with sheer exhaustion, they sunned themselves by the pool or went for walks and explored the shops in the village. Sometimes they just talked about his work, or their families. There was so much about him she didn't know—and wanted to learn.

As the days passed, she slowly began to realize that not only did she have real feelings for Mitch, she was almost positive she was falling in love with him. But since she had never been in love before, she couldn't be one hundred percent sure. She only knew that it had to be something very special, and she didn't doubt that he was feeling it, too.

Since that night walking back from the village, he hadn't said a word about the marriage being just business. Instead, he'd shown his affection for her in a hundred little ways.

She was confident that in a week or so, if all continued to go well, she would be able to tell him about the baby. Then she could finally stop feeling as though she was walking on eggshells, constantly conscious of everything she said and did.

She could finally relax and be happy.

Their last night in Greece, she lay beside Mitch, listening to his deep, heavy breathing as he slept, knowing she should get up and go to her own room, but feeling too lazy to move. She always waited until he was asleep to slip away. As much as she would have loved to spend all night with him, she was still getting sick every morning. Soon though, he would know about the baby, and she could stop hiding. But for now, she really needed to get up.

Five more minutes, she told herself, letting her eyes drift shut and cuddling up against Mitch's side.

When she opened her eyes again, sunshine was

pouring in the windows. Mitch was behind her, his breathing slow and deep as he slept, but one part of his anatomy was already wide awake.

As she was considering the most pleasurable way to wake the rest of him, she felt a familiar lurch in her stomach. She broke out in a sudden cold sweat and a wave of nausea overwhelmed her. Swallowing back the bile rising in her throat, she slid out of bed as quietly as possible and pulled on her nightgown. There was no time to make it to her own bedroom. She had no choice but to use Mitch's bathroom. She reached the commode just as her stomach violently emptied. The spasms were so intense, she was convinced she would look down and find an internal organ or two floating around. When she was finished, her entire body felt limp and shaky. She sat on the floor and rested her face against the cool tile wall.

"Are you all right?"

Lexi's eyes flew open. Mitch was standing in the doorway, wearing only his boxers, his hair mussed from sleep, concern etched on his face. Damn it! She should have shut and locked the door.

"I'm fine." She reached over and flushed the commode, but it was obvious that she'd been sick.

"No, you're not." He grabbed a washcloth from the towel bar and soaked it with cool water from the tap. He wrung out the excess and handed it to her. She wiped her face with it, feeling the nausea beginning to pass. She would be completely fine in an hour or so.

He reached over to feel her forehead, but she held up a hand to stop him. "I don't have a fever. I'm okay."

"What's going on?" he asked.

"Must be something I ate," she lied, and she could see he wasn't buying it.

"I know something is wrong. You've hardly eaten anything all week, you've lost weight, and every morning you look pale and exhausted. I want the truth."

He knew. She could see it on his face that he'd already figured it out for himself. Or at least suspected. She had the feeling that her saying the words was a formality at this point.

Maybe this was a good thing. The longer she put it off, the harder it was going to be, right? The more it would sound like a lie. And he didn't look upset, exactly. More concerned than angry, so maybe it would be okay.

She took a deep breath, blew it out, and finally said the words she had been holding on the tip of her tongue for more than a week. "I'm pregnant."

"Pregnant?"

She could not have prepared herself for the look of dumbfounded shock on his face. Whatever he might have thought was wrong with her, pregnancy had clearly never crossed his mind. And if his reaction was any indication, everything would *not* be okay.

"You didn't think to mention this before?" he asked, his voice low and quiet, but she could see that he was ready to explode. And could she blame him?

He'd said it himself, he didn't want to bring a child into this. Had she really thought a week of fantastic sex was going to make him change his mind? Make him fall madly in love with her?

She felt as if she might be sick again.

"I only found out for sure a few days before we left," she said, knowing it was a pathetic excuse. "I was waiting for the right time to tell you."

"That's what this has all been about, hasn't it?"

"All what?"

"The cooking and the cleaning. The sex. Did you think you could manipulate me?"

Her heart sank. What was she going to tell him? No? Lie to him again? She had done that, just not in the way he thought. Not so sneaky and underhanded. "It wasn't like that, I swear. I wanted you to see that I could be a good wife."

He looked so disgusted with her, so…violated. "I didn't marry you so I could have a wife. I only did it for your father's support."

And that was her life in a nutshell. She was only as useful as her political connections. No words could have cut deeper or stung more.

"Does Lance know?" he asked.

Lance? Why would he think that she would go running to his brother? "No, of course not."

"And he never can," Mitch said.

His words took her aback. What the hell was that supposed to mean? How could he not find out, eventually? Did Mitch expect her to give the baby up, or even worse, terminate? Was he that cold and heartless, or so arrogant that he believed the choice was his alone?

What did his brother have to do with this, anyway? This was between her and Mitch. "Who cares if Lance does find out? What's he going to do about it?"

The veins at his temple pulsed. "You can't mess with people's emotions that way, Lexi. He and Kate are happy. Something like this could tear their marriage apart. I refuse to let that happen."

How could she and Mitch having a child ruin Lance's marriage? This didn't make any sense. "What are you asking me to do, Mitch?"

"We'll raise the baby as mine," he said.

Then it dawned on her. Their odd and confusing conversation suddenly made sense. He thought it was Lance's child. Lance, who she had barely kissed, much less slept with. It had never even occurred to Mitch that the baby was his.

Did he honestly believe that she would jump from Mitch's bed right into his brother's? Did he really have such a low opinion of her?

Obviously, he did. This past week, all the time they had shared, it meant nothing to him. He was using her for a good time, because he apparently believed that was all she was good for.

Her stomach lurched and she had to fight to keep from vomiting again. How had she gotten into this mess? Married to a man who considered her a garden-variety slut, one who jumped from one brother to the next as casually as she changed shoes. Even if she did try to tell him the truth, she doubted he would listen, or believe her. Or care.

She had been hoping they might have a real marriage. Not just hoping, but longing for it. She desperately wanted someone to really see her. To love her. But it was clear that Mitch would never be that man. He could never respect or love her, and all the pretending, all the seducing in the world would never change that. It would never alter the preconceived notion he had of her.

First rejected by her father, then by her husband. As long as she lived, she would never trust any man ever again.

Using the wall for support, she pulled herself to her feet. She swayed unsteadily for a second, then straightened her spine and faced Mitch. "If you'll excuse me," she said, brushing past him, but he grabbed her by her upper arm to stop her.

"From now on, I would appreciate it if you kept your hands to yourself."

She lifted her chin and met his eyes, so he wouldn't see how humiliated and cheap he'd just made her feel. "The truth is, you were hardly worth the effort. Looks like I married the wrong brother."

She could see that her arrow had hit its mark, but for some reason it only made her feel worse.

She yanked her arm free and stalked from the

room. She was stuck with a man who was arrogant, coldhearted and just plain mean.

On the bright side, she could spend the rest of her life making him as miserable as she was.

Mitch watched Lexi strut from the room, feeling more betrayed and disillusioned than he ever had in his life. He'd honestly believed that they had connected, that the dynamics of their relationship had shifted. He'd let himself consider that their marriage might be more than a business deal. But it had all been an act. She had used him.

How could he have been so foolish? How could he have let his guard down when all along he knew the kind of woman that she was? Because he had been thinking with something other than his brain, that's how.

Alexis Cavanaugh was a spoiled, heartless viper and that would *never* change.

At least now he knew why she had so readily agreed to marry him, and he was thankful that she had. Lance and Kate were happy and he refused to let Lexi's selfishness—her lack of concern for anyone but herself—ruin that. For all he knew, she might have conceived on purpose. Maybe she felt she needed a bargaining chip, a way to guarantee her marriage to Lance, but he had broken the engagement and married Kate. Mitch could only imagine what Lexi's next move would have been had he not offered to marry her, instead. Blackmail, maybe? Extortion?

He wondered what the senator would think if he knew what his daughter had been up to. Of course, for all he knew, she learned this sort of behavior from him. But Mitch couldn't let himself forget the old man's threat. *If you hurt my daughter, I'll ruin you.* He didn't have a choice but to make this work. For the company's sake.

She was his wife, God help him, and he was going to raise his brother's child the way he would his own, with the best of everything. He had never imagined being a father, especially at his age, but he didn't seem to have much choice. He had no reservations about running a multimillion-dollar company, but the responsibility of shaping a child's life terrified him. Probably because his own father had done such a bang-up job with him and Lance.

When Lexi grew bored and left them, which he had little doubt she would eventually do, he would reject everything he had learned from his own father and be the best single parent possible. He owed the kid that much. Someday, when the time was right, he would tell Lance and the child the truth, but until then, no one but he and Lexi would know.

That wasn't even the worst part. To keep up the ruse, so Lance didn't suspect the truth, Mitch and Lexi had no choice but to make their marriage look like a real one.

Eight

The trip home was the longest and most miserable in Lexi's life. It was raining as they boarded the ferry to the mainland and the ride was a choppy one, launching her already questionable stomach into turmoil. The first leg of their flight was delayed due to weather and they missed their connecting flight. They were stuck in the London airport for six hours waiting for the next available departure, and when they finally took off for Texas, the flight was so turbulent she spent most of it in the bathroom in a scene straight out of *The Exorcist*.

The entire time, Mitch didn't say a single word to her.

When they reached Houston, she was so relieved she felt like dropping to her knees and kissing the ground. She just wanted to go home and crawl into her own bed. But as they were climbing into the limo, Mitch reminded her that all of her things had been moved into his townhouse and that was her home now. On the bright side, he didn't seem any happier about it than she was. Her misery wasn't as hard to swallow when she knew he was right there with her.

Located on a golf course in what was by far the most affluent neighborhood in Maverick County, Mitch's townhouse was anything but small. The front door opened into a foyer and spacious living area. It smelled of furniture polish and faintly of Mitch's aftershave. The decor, to her surprise, was very homey and welcoming. Not what she would expect from a house occupied exclusively by a man.

There was a formal dining room and enormous kitchen with every modern device known to man. On the countertop sat a huge bouquet of flowers, two champagne glasses and a bottle of sparkling fruit juice chilling on ice. Beside it was a note penned in Tara's handwriting that read, *Congratulations and welcome home!*

At Mitch's questioning look, she said, "It's from Tara, my assistant."

He gestured to the nonalcoholic drink. "I guess it's safe to say she knows you're pregnant."

"She's my best friend. I tell her everything." Well, almost everything.

"That's sad," he said.

"What? That I tell her everything?"

"No, that you have to pay someone to be your best friend."

How did he always manage to hit the rawest nerve? But she refused to let him know that he'd hurt her feelings. She lifted her nose at him and said, "That's a little hypocritical coming from a man who had to buy his wife."

She braced herself for a sarcastic comeback, but instead, the hint of a smile tipped up the corner of his mouth, catching her off guard.

"Your room is on the second floor," he said. He backtracked through the house to where he left her bag by the stairs. He grabbed it and started up, and she followed him.

"Dry cleaning is picked up and dropped off Mondays and Thursdays. It will be your responsibility to see that it's left on the porch."

"Fine."

"I have a cleaning service in Monday, Wednesday and Friday."

"What about a cook?"

"I'm not home enough to warrant it. I usually eat out or order in. But if you want to hire someone, I won't object. And of course when we move, we'll need a full-time staff." He led her to the first room on the left. As far as she could see, there were three other bedrooms.

It was a typical spare bedroom, with gender-neutral furnishings and decor, but Tara had placed several of her things from her bedroom at her father's estate around the room. Photos and keepsakes mostly, as well as her books.

She peered into the walk-in closet and saw that Tara had also arranged all of her clothes and shoes, and in the bathroom she found her makeup and toiletries.

Mitch stood in the doorway watching her. "Is it satisfactory?"

It was more than adequate, but she said, "I suppose, if this is the best you can do."

He folded his arms across his chest. "Well, the master suite is larger, but then, you would have to share it with me."

Like *that* would ever happen. "Where is your room?"

"Why? Are you planning another midnight visit?"

"Actually, I need to know so I can avoid it."

He flashed another wry grin. "End of the hall on the right. The third floor is the den and my office. I would appreciate it if you didn't go up there."

Which meant that would be the first place she investigated.

"Just up the road is the community center. There's an exercise room and tennis courts. There's also a pool, although I'll warn you that bathing suits are not optional. Unless you want to get yourself arrested."

"Don't worry, I'll only walk around naked inside the house."

He didn't look as though he believed her, which would make actually doing it all the more fun.

"I'll need a space for Tara to work."

"She can have the room across the hall. I'll call my real estate agent so we can start house hunting."

She still didn't see the need for anything bigger than this, but he was the one paying the bills, so who was she to argue? "I'd like to unpack and change, and I have a few phone calls to make," she told him.

"Okay," he said, but he didn't move. At her questioning look he added, "Oh, did you want me to leave?"

"Please."

"I should probably check in with my girlfriend, anyway. Let her know I arrived home safely."

She wondered if he really did have a girlfriend, then figured he probably just said he did to annoy her. If he cheated on her and her father found out, Mitch could kiss his support goodbye. She smiled sweetly and said, "You mean the girlfriend who needs occasional reinflation?"

He smirked. "I'll be unpacking if you need me," he said as he left, closing the door behind him.

She sat on the bed and looked around. She would have to thank Tara for setting up her room. It made her feel a lot less like an interloper.

She turned on her cell phone and found she had half a dozen messages from her father and two from Tara. Since she wasn't quite ready to face her father yet, she called Tara first. They hadn't spoken since before the kitchen disaster—she'd been too embarrassed to admit how she had botched Tara's seemingly simple instructions.

She dialed and Tara answered on the first ring. "Welcome home! Did you see your surprise?"

"I did, thanks. And thank you for arranging all of my personal things."

"I'd love to take credit, but that was your husband's idea."

It was weird enough when she thought of Mitch as her husband, but to hear someone else say it felt like the final nail in her coffin. "That must have been before he decided he hates my guts."

"Oh, my gosh! What happened? I thought things were going really well."

"They were. He didn't even seem to care that I completely botched breakfast, flooded the kitchen, and nearly burned the house down making dinner. And the sex? Amazing. Everything was great, right up until the second I told him I'm pregnant."

"Oh, no, Lex. Was he really that upset?"

"I don't think it was the baby so much as the fact that he thinks it's Lance's."

"He what!?" she shrieked, obviously outraged. "You told him the truth, right?"

"There didn't seem to be much point. I doubt he would have believed me. He apparently thinks he knows the kind of person I am. I figure, why shatter his illusion?"

"Oh, Lex, I'm so sorry."

"I guess the worst part was that I thought for the first time in my life, someone really saw me, you know? I thought he cared." Lexi was mortified to realize that she was welling up. Enough of this. She had to pull herself together.

"Maybe if you told him the truth—"

"There's no point now. I can never trust him again."

"You're going to have to tell him eventually."

Yes, but for now, she would make him suffer a bit. Make him as miserable as she was. "Could we talk about something else?"

"Sure, Lex," she said, sounding hurt. Why did it feel as though whatever Lexi said or did, it was never right?

They talked briefly about setting up a temporary office for Tara in the townhouse, and then she called her father.

In lieu of hello, he snapped, "Why didn't you call? You should have been home hours ago."

It was on the tip of her tongue to say, "Hi, Dad, nice to talk to you, too." But she had never had the courage to speak to him that way. One wrong move and he might shut her out completely. Stop calling altogether.

"Our flight was delayed due to bad weather," she said. "We just got home."

"Well, I was concerned."

Just not concerned enough about her to come to her wedding, or call her while she was in Greece.

"Would a call have been too much trouble?" he asked sharply.

She could have asked him the same thing, but of course she didn't. "No, Daddy. I'm sorry."

That took the edge off his tone. "How was your vacation?"

"Greece was wonderful." It was the company she could do without. Although she couldn't deny that they'd had several very good days.

"You, Mitch and I will be meeting for dinner tomorrow evening at the Cattleman's Club," he said. *Demanded*, really.

"I'll have to ask Mitch if he's available."

"If he wants my support, he will be. Seven o'clock. Don't be late. I'm flying in from D.C."

He was flying all that way just to have dinner? She wondered what she and Mitch had done to deserve that. "We'll be there."

They disconnected and she set her phone down. She should probably give Mitch the good news.

She changed into a T-shirt and cotton capri pants, then went looking for Mitch. She started to walk toward his bedroom, then changed her mind and decided this would be the perfect time to snoop upstairs. She tiptoed quietly so he wouldn't hear her, and what she saw as she reached the top took her breath away. The entire floor was one large, open room. At one end was Mitch's office, which consisted of a slightly cluttered desk, file cabinet and bookshelves lining one wall. Across the room was a media center with a huge flat-screen television and a whole cabinet full of electronic equipment. Not to mention a wet bar. Everything was dark polished wood with comfortable-looking chocolate-brown leather furniture. One hundred percent male.

She crossed to his office area, running her fingers across the back of his chair, wondering if she should take a peek inside his desk. Just to annoy him, of course.

"I should have known I would find you up here."

She turned to find Mitch standing at the top of the stairs, arms folded over his chest.

"I thought we agreed you wouldn't come up here."

She shrugged. "I believe you issued an order. I never agreed to it. This is nice, though. Very macho."

"Is there a particular reason you're up here?"

To annoy you. "I was looking for you."

"Really? Because I told you I would be in my room, unpacking."

"I must have forgotten."

"What did you want?"

"To warn you that my father has invited us to dinner at the Cattleman's Club tomorrow night at seven."

"I'll have to check my schedule."

"That's what I told him. He said that if you want his support, you'll be there."

"Well, then, I guess I'll be there."

"That's what I told him."

"My brother left me a message. He said that Kate would like you to join her for a welcome-to-the-family lunch on Thursday."

"Family?"

"She is your sister-in-law."

Oddly enough, Lexi hadn't even thought about that. She had a family now—someone other than her father, that is. But she couldn't help wondering if it would be weird going out to lunch with the woman who had stolen her fiancé. "I'm not sure if that's a good idea."

His expression darkened. "You think you're better than her?"

"Of course not! Kate seems wonderful. I just thought it might be awkward."

"Fine, I'll tell Lance you don't want to go."

"I didn't say that. I'll go, okay?"

He shrugged, as though it didn't matter either way to him, yet she had the distinct feeling it did. "She said to meet her at the Cattleman's Club café at one."

She nodded, wondering how she was going to get there. If she asked Mitch to send a car for her, he would probably just accuse her of being spoiled. Unfortunately, her father had never allowed her to learn how to drive. Having his driver take her everywhere was just another way for him to keep track of her every move. Maybe Tara could drive her. And maybe, if she asked Tara nicely enough, she might teach Lexi to drive. She was twenty-four years old. It was high time she began asserting her independence.

"I talked to the real estate agent. We have a 10:00 a.m. appointment tomorrow. He said he has several properties to show us."

"That was quick."

"I called him last week and told him we'd be looking. The state of the economy being what it is, he said if we decide to buy, there's a huge selection right now. Building new would take considerably longer."

She shrugged. "Whatever you want. As long as I'm free by four."

"Why?"

"I have an appointment with my gynecologist."

His expression darkened. "Speaking of that, I think it would be best if we kept the...*situation* to ourselves."

She was tempted to tell him that the *situation* had fingers and toes and a beating heart, but she didn't see the point. He obviously wasn't ready to acknowledge the life growing inside of her. "Fine."

"Also, I think it would be best if people are led to believe that we're happy."

She pursed her lips. "Then maybe we should forget those cooking lessons and get me some acting lessons, instead."

"You don't give yourself enough credit. In Greece you had me snowed."

That's because I wasn't acting, you moron, she wanted to shout. But what good would it do? His mind was made up about her and she would never forgive him for it, so they were more or less at an impasse.

"Define happy," she said.

"I think we should act like newlyweds, show each other affection."

She narrowed her eyes at him. "How much affection?"

"I'm not suggesting we publicly maul each other. I'm talking about little things like holding hands, and maybe occasionally smiling at each other."

"But no kissing," she clarified. Not that she didn't enjoy kissing him. Quite the opposite. Every time his lips touched hers she got so hot her brain short-circuited. If that happened she might do something stupid, like sleep with him again. And because he did amazing things to her body, she knew once wouldn't be enough. If she slept with him too many times, she might begin to forget how awful he was.

"No kissing," he agreed.

Good.

So why did she feel disappointed that he hadn't put up at least a tiny fuss?

His cell phone rang and he looked at the display. "It's Lance. I have to take this."

"I'll be in the kitchen getting something to eat."

She brushed past Mitch and headed downstairs, hearing him call after her, "The fire extinguisher is in the pantry."

Smart-ass. She should burn the place down just to spite him.

"Welcome home," Lance said when he answered. "Did you get my message?"

"Yeah. In fact, I just talked to Lexi. She'll meet Kate for lunch." He didn't mention that Lexi hadn't looked all that thrilled with the idea. Mitch knew that she and her father looked down on people of Kate's past station in society.

"I'm glad," Lance said. "Kate is pretty excited about having a sister-in-law."

"Seriously?"

"The truth is, she credits Lexi for us finally getting together. If I hadn't planned to marry Lexi, Kate probably never would have quit, and I would still be walking around with my head in the clouds, not realizing how important she is to me."

That was an interesting way to look at it.

"Speaking of marriage," Lance said, "how was the honeymoon?"

"It was okay," Mitch told him, which wasn't a total lie. It had gone pretty well, right up until the moment Lexi showed her true colors. Unfortunately, if Mitch was honest about how truly miserable he was, not only would Lance feel guilty as hell, he might want to know why. It would be best for everyone involved if even Lance believed Lexi and Mitch were happy.

"Just okay?" Lance hedged.

"Better than okay," Mitch said. "I think this just might work out."

"I'm glad to hear it," he said, sounding relieved.

Mitch wasn't yet sure how he planned to handle the news of Lexi's pregnancy. Lance wasn't stupid. He would do the math and realize when she'd conceived. Mitch would just have to admit to his brother that he and Lexi slept together in D.C. He could lie and say they were drunk, claim they had been so out of it they had forgotten to use protection. He just hoped Lance wasn't too pissed at him, although Mitch wouldn't blame him if he was.

But that could wait a while, at least another month or two, until Lexi started to show.

"Any news about the fire?" he asked his brother.

"Whoever set it knew what they were doing. Darius hasn't been able to trace a thing."

"What does he think about Montoya? Is he even capable of pulling something like that off?"

"If he is, we'll find out."

Mitch couldn't help wondering if Lance was so determined to pin the fire on Alex Montoya that he would wrongly accuse an innocent man. "What if it wasn't him?"

"He's the only one with motive."

"We don't know that for sure, " Mitch countered.

"Hey, by the way," Lance said, "Darius asked that we meet him at his office next Wednesday evening."

"Did he say what for?"

"He said we had some business to discuss, but he wouldn't say more than that."

"Does it have something to do with the fire?"

"I don't think so."

"Sure, I'll be there." He was sure that by then he would need a night away from his wife—if they hadn't already killed each other.

Nine

The following morning Mitch and Lexi drove to the real estate agent's office to begin looking at houses. And though she still felt like death warmed over from a bout of kneeling to the porcelain gods, she put her best face on. The agent, Mark Sullenberg, was a friend of the family, which meant she and Mitch had to act happily married.

Unfortunately, he was really good at it.

There was barely a minute when he wasn't touching her, either holding her hand or casually draping his arm across her shoulders. He was so good, so charming and sweet to her, she started to forget they were only playing a role. It made her think of that week in D.C. and how perfect it had been, how naturally they had connected, which in turn made her feel depressed and lonely, because she knew she would never feel that way again.

She just prayed they would find a house soon, so they could go back to hating each other. But after looking at half a dozen homes, they hadn't found a thing either of them even remotely liked. They were all ultramodern in exclusive gated communities with lots of BMWs and luxury SUVs in the driveways. And they all looked the same. Lifeless and boring. By the sixth house, she could see that Mitch was getting frustrated and she was beginning to think that building new might be their only option.

"Can you show us something different?" Mitch asked Mark. "Something a bit more…"

"Traditional," she finished for him.

"Exactly," he said, looking surprised that she'd nailed it right on the head. "Something with some character."

"There is one property that recently came on the market," Mark said. "It's just outside of Maverick County. A renovated plantation house. The only problem is that it's located on ten acres of land, and you said you wanted to look in more of a suburban setting."

"How big is it?" Mitch asked.

"Fifty-five-hundred square feet. It used to be a horse farm, so there's a barn and stables."

That caught Lexi's attention. Her uncle on her

mother's side had kept horses when Lexi was a child. Though she had always wanted to learn to ride, her father would never allow it. Too dangerous, he'd decided. But her uncle would let her brush the horses and help feed and water them. The idea of owning a horse or two thrilled her.

She glanced over at Mitch, thinking she would reduce herself to begging if that was what it took to make him agree to at least look at it, but he appeared as intrigued as she was.

He shrugged and said, "Couldn't hurt to look at it."

They piled back into Mark's car for the twenty-minute ride, Lexi feeling uncharacteristically excited. For some reason, she had a really good feeling about this one.

"I'll warn you that it's a little run-down and over-grown," Mark told them. "When the owner died, there was a dispute with the will so it's been sitting empty for a while. It has a lot of potential, though."

They pulled off the road into a long, tree-lined driveway. He hadn't been kidding when he said it was overgrown. It would take a lot of work to get the yard in order. But Lexi couldn't keep her eyes off the house itself. It was…amazing. A huge, white Greek revival with pillars and balconies and black shut-tered windows. She could just imagine herself in the evenings sitting on the long front porch drinking lemonade and watching the sun set, or playing with the baby in the shade of the trees.

She knew without a doubt, this was the one. This was home.

Mark pulled to a stop and they all climbed out. As he'd done before, Mitch took her hand, lacing his fingers through hers. But this time it was different. This time he really held on, as though he was brimming with pent-up excitement.

"It was built in 1895," Mark told them, "and completely remodeled about thirty years ago. It's a little rough around the edges, but an excellent investment."

She and Mitch stood there for a moment, side by side, hands clasped, gazing up at the remarkable structure. Lexi didn't know about Mitch, but she felt as though this was meant to be. As if, for the first time in her life, she'd finally come home.

"So, what do you think?" Mark asked.

"We'll take it," they said in unison, then looked at each other, startled that they were in complete agreement.

Mark laughed. "Wow, how's that for a consensus? You haven't even seen the inside."

"Well, then," Mitch said, giving her hand a squeeze, "let's see it."

Lexi knew at this point that it was only a formality, but they followed Mark up the porch and through the front door. The interior was a bit shabby and outdated, the kitchen and bathrooms in particular desperately needed updating, but all Lexi could see was the potential. Mitch must have felt the same way. When they concluded the tour he told Mark, "Let's write up an offer," and when they got back to the office to fill out the paperwork, instead of bidding low, he offered several thousand above the asking price.

Though she didn't let it show, she felt almost giddy with anticipation. They were buying a house. A house whose renovations she would help plan, and whose rooms she would decorate however she chose. She could hardly wait to get started.

She had never felt so...*alive*. As though an entirely new and amazing world was opening up to her.

"I'll submit this right away and hopefully we'll hear something in the next day or two," Mark told them as they were leaving. "I'll be in touch."

Though she was practically bursting with excitement when they were in the car on the way back to the townhouse, Lexi tried to hide it. An automatic defense mechanism she'd learned from dealing with her father. If he knew something was important to her, he would use it against her as leverage. A true politician.

Then Mitch asked, "So, you liked it?"

She could no longer contain herself. She blurted out, "I knew I wanted it the second we pulled into the driveway. If I had every house in the world to choose from, that's the one I would have picked."

"It's going to need a lot of work. It'll probably be months before we can move in."

"I would be happy living in it just the way it is."

He shot her a sideways glance. "The interior is a disaster. We're going to have to gut it and start from scratch. The renovations will go much faster if it's unoccupied."

Although she would be happy moving in there today, he made a good point. Especially with the baby coming. The sooner it was finished, the better.

"I'll start calling contractors today," he said.

"Shouldn't we wait until we know for sure that we got it?"

"Don't worry," he said, his tone a little smug. "We'll get it."

There were definitely advantages to being married to a man who was used to getting what he wanted.

"I'd like to get a horse or two," she said, prepared for an instant argument.

But Mitch said, "We could do that." Then he added offhandedly, "It would be a good atmosphere for raising kids."

It was the first time since she'd told him she was pregnant that he'd acknowledged the baby. She wondered how he would react when she told him the truth. Would it change his feelings for her? Make him dislike her a little less?

Probably not. Knowing Mitch, he would be even angrier, and hold it against her for the rest of her life. It would probably be in her best interest to at least wait until they had signed a mortgage to tell him the baby was really his. Just in case.

"Did you want to go to my appointment with me today?" she asked, unsure of what his reaction would be, and wondering how she would feel if he refused.

He was quiet for a moment, eyes on the road, then asked, "Do you want me to?"

She realized that yes, she did. Even though he didn't know it yet, this was his baby and he shouldn't miss out on anything. From the first pre-natal visit to the birth, she wanted him to be there for every minute of it.

He hates you. He thinks you're selfish and spoiled.

But if she denied him this opportunity, wouldn't she be proving him right?

Before she could talk herself out of it, she told him, "I want you to."

"Then I'll come," he said.

He reached over and turned the radio on to a country-western station, ending the conversation, yet she couldn't help but feel as though they had made some sort of progress today. Although progress toward what, she wasn't exactly sure.

The doctor's appointment wasn't at all what Mitch had expected. In fact, he hadn't known quite *what* to expect.

He figured they would take her temperature and blood pressure, which they did, and she was asked to pee in a cup. Typical doctor-visit stuff. What he hadn't been expecting was the internal exam.

Though he'd seen Lexi intimately on more than one occasion, and his first instinct was to do or say anything to annoy her, this just didn't seem the place, so he turned his back while she stripped from the waist down and got up on the table.

Even though the process went quickly, he gained a whole new respect for what women had to endure during a routine exam. Between all the poking and prodding and the giant cotton swab the doctor used for God only knows what, he felt grateful to have outdoor plumbing.

Then the doctor pulled out a piece of equipment that looked a lot like some recreational sex apparatus. It was long and narrow with a cord coming out one end that was attached to a monitor.

"This is an internal ultrasound," the doctor explained. "So we can get a better idea of the baby's development."

Lexi looked a little nervous so Mitch took her hand.

As the doctor inserted it, she gasped and said, "Cold," then winced a little as he made adjustments. Suddenly, up on the monitor popped a hazy black-and-white image.

"There's the fetus," the doctor said, pointing to a white area on the screen. "And these are the arms and legs."

Mitch didn't see anything but a fuzzy blob at first, but as the doctor gestured to the different body parts, it began to take shape. With its oversize head and stubby appendages, it looked more alien than human.

"This flutter is the heartbeat," the doctor told them.

"Can we hear it?" Lexi asked.

He turned the volume up and the rapid whoosh of the baby's pulse filled the room.

Mitch had never even considered being a father, and here he was listening to his baby's heartbeat, looking at its tiny form on a monitor.

Lance's baby, he reminded himself.

In a way, he felt as though he was stealing something invaluable from his brother, an opportunity to see his child develop. But he was sure that Lance and Kate would eventually have children and he would experience it all with her. This might be Mitch's only chance.

"Everything looks great," the doctor told her. "I'll see you in a month."

When they were back in the car and on their way home, Lexi sat so quietly gazing out the window that Mitch began to think maybe something was wrong. He couldn't help but ask, "Are you okay?"

"Seeing the baby, hearing the heartbeat. It suddenly seems so...*real.*"

She looked so dazed and bewildered he wondered if the weight of the responsibility was finally sinking in. Wouldn't it be ironic if, now that he'd finally begun to accept the situation, she changed her mind and decided not to have it?

"You say that like it's a bad thing."

She looked over at him, surprise on her face. "No, of course not! I just…" She shrugged, then shook her head. "Never mind."

"Tell me," he said.

"You'll just make fun of me."

"I promise I won't make fun of you."

She studied him for a moment, as though she wasn't quite sure she could trust him. Finally she said, "I guess I'm just a little…scared."

He didn't think Lexi was scared of anything, and was surprised that she would admit it to him, of all people. "Scared of what?"

"Being a bad parent. What if I do everything wrong?"

It was on the tip of his tongue to say, "You probably will." But he didn't have the heart to knock her down when she looked so vulnerable and unsure of herself. She was opening up to him and he couldn't use that against her. Besides, there was always the very slim, one in a million chance that she would be a good mother and stick around. Maybe he should give her the benefit of the doubt.

So she would only disappoint him later? What was the point?

"You'll do the best you can," he told her, wishing he actually believed it, but Lexi seemed to buy it because she smiled.

A minute later, he pulled into his driveway and cut

the engine, but when he looked back over at Lexi she was frowning.

"What's wrong now?" he asked.

She turned to face him, looking almost nervous. "Mitch, there's something I need to tell you. Something you should know."

He had no idea what she was going to say, but he had the feeling he wasn't going to like it. "What?"

She hesitated, lip wedged between her teeth. Then she said, "About the baby…"

"What about it?"

"I thought you should know…"

She looked so nervous, he started to worry something was really wrong. "What are you trying to say?"

After another pause she finally said, "I just wanted to say thank you for coming with me today. For being a part of this."

And here he'd thought it had been something important. Half a dozen snarky comebacks were just dying to jump out, but instead he said simply, "You're welcome. Now, we better get inside and get ready or we'll be late for dinner. I get the distinct feeling your father isn't one to tolerate tardiness."

She smiled and nodded. "That's a fairly accurate assumption. I love my father, but to be honest, the sooner this evening is over and he flies back to D.C., the better, as far as I'm concerned."

Well, that was one thing they could agree on. So, why did he get the feeling there was something else? Something she wasn't telling him?

Ten

When Lexi and Mitch arrived at the Cattleman's Club to meet her father, her goal was to get in, eat dinner, and leave as fast as humanly possible. Which was odd because in the past she had cherished every moment her father would spare her. It seemed that lately she was no longer so desperate for his time or his approval. But Mitch needed his support, so she would be on her best behavior.

"Are you ready for this?" Mitch asked, holding out his hand for her to take.

She laced her fingers through his. Another few hours of pretending they were madly in love? She could hardly wait. At least now when he touched her it didn't feel so…unnatural. In a way it was kind of nice, even though she knew deep down that he hated her, or at the very least disliked her a lot.

"This way," the hostess said, gesturing toward the dining room door. They followed her, and as they entered the room, it took a few seconds for Lexi to process what she was seeing. Tables full of familiar people all smiling at them, balloons and streamers everywhere and a banner draped across the back wall that announced in huge block letters, *Congratulations Mitch and Lexi.*

Everyone shouted, "Surprise!" and the room erupted in laughter and applause.

She heard Mitch mumble, "Oh, shit," and thought, I couldn't have said it better myself.

Lance and Kate stood close to the door, beaming. He stepped forward and shook Mitch's hand.

"What did you do?" Mitch asked him.

"Don't look at me, bro. This was all Kate's idea. I couldn't talk her out of it."

"You had to have a wedding reception," Kate said, flush with excitement. She hugged Mitch, then pulled Lexi into a warm and affectionate embrace, and Lexi was so stunned she almost forgot to hug her back.

"But it wasn't just me," Kate said, nodding toward the door. "Your assistant was a huge help."

Lexi turned, and realized Tara was standing just off to one side of the door. She hadn't even seen her when they walked in.

She flashed Lexi a feeble smile and said, "Surprise."

She was the only one in the room who knew what a disaster the marriage was. No wonder she looked so apologetic.

"So, were you both surprised?" Kate asked.

Lexi nodded and Mitch said, "To quote the great Chevy Chase, if I woke up tomorrow with my head sewn to the carpet, I wouldn't be more surprised than I am now."

The room burst into laughter.

Someone handed Lexi and Mitch each a flute of champagne from a passing tray, and she realized everyone in the room already had their own glass.

Lance held his up in a toast. "To my little brother and his wife. May you live a long and happy life together!"

"Hear, hear!" everyone chanted, clinking their glasses together, and Lexi had no choice but to pretend to take a sip. As she studied the sea of faces before her, she couldn't help noticing that the one she had been expecting to see wasn't there. Her father.

Tara must have read her mind because she leaned close to Lexi and said, "The senator's secretary called a while ago to say he'll be a little late."

Didn't that just figure? He skips her wedding altogether and shows up late for the reception? She wondered why he bothered to show up at all. But she didn't have much time to think about it as a constant

flow of friends, relatives and club members stepped
forward to hug them or shake their hands and give
their best wishes. Darius Franklin and his fiancée
Summer Martindale, Kevin Novak and his wife Cara,
Mitch's best man Justin Dupree. Even Sebastian
Huntington and his daughter Rebecca were there.
And those were just the people she recognized. She
had no clue Mitch had so many friends.

A too-real wedding reception for a fake marriage.
Did it get much worse? Lexi couldn't help thinking
that this just might be the longest night of her life.
But as the champagne flowed and the music played,
she discovered herself getting caught up in the festivities. Mitch never once left her side, and if he
wasn't holding her hand or draping an arm around
her, he was touching her in some way.

Dinner was served around eight and halfway
through the meal, Kate started to clink her glass with
a fork, and then everyone joined in. Lexi had been
to enough wedding receptions to know that it meant
she and Mitch were supposed to kiss.

Mitch looked at her apologetically because he
knew as well as she did that they had to make this
look real. She held her breath as he cradled her face
in his hand, leaned forward and laid a kiss on her that
curled her toes and turned her brain to mush. The
guests applauded, and she heard a couple of wolf
whistles. After that, it seemed as though every five
minutes the clinking started, and Mitch would be

forced to kiss her yet again. Not that he seemed to mind, and she couldn't deny the man did fantastic things with his mouth.

He'd had several glasses of champagne with dinner, then after dessert, switched to whiskey. The more he drank, the more relaxed he became, and the more relaxed he became, the more affectionate he seemed to be. By the time they had their first dance together, he nearly had her convinced they were madly in love. The song playing was a slow one and he pulled her so close, gazed so tenderly into her eyes, she thought any minute he might drag her to the nearest broom closet.

"When we walked in here I thought this night was going to be a disaster," he said. "But I have to admit, it hasn't been so bad."

She'd thought the same thing, but she was actually having a great time.

"You might have to drive us home tonight," he warned her. "I think I may have had a few too many."

That could be a problem. "I can't."

He frowned. "You haven't been drinking, have you?"

"Of course not! What I mean is, I really can't. I never learned how to drive."

His eyes widened. "You're kidding."

She shook her head.

"Let me guess. Your father wouldn't allow it."

"It would have made it more difficult to keep me

under his thumb. I had a driver who took me wherever I needed to go."

Mitch shook his head in disgust. "No offense, but the more I learn about the senator, the less I like him."

His irritation stunned her, but she realized it was a nice change to have someone to defend her. "I can ask Tara to drive us."

"I'll call a car," he said. "And the first chance we get, I'm teaching you to drive."

"Seriously?" First cooking lessons, now driving? He was being almost too nice and understanding. Probably tomorrow, when he was sober, he would come to his senses and change his mind.

"Speak of the devil," Mitch said, gesturing toward the door with his chin.

She turned and saw that her father had arrived. He was watching Lexi and Mitch dance, and he didn't look happy.

"Is it my imagination," Mitch asked, "or does he look really pissed off?"

"It's not your imagination." She couldn't help wondering what she'd done this time, because when he looked like that, it was usually her fault. "I should go talk to him."

"You want me to come with you?"

"Maybe you'd better give us a few minutes alone." The last thing she needed was for her father to berate her in front of her husband. Not that she thought it was possible for Mitch to have a lower opinion of her than he already did, but why take a chance?

She crossed the room to where her father waited, forcing a smile, and said, "Hello, Daddy."

She hadn't expected a warm greeting, but she also hadn't expected him to clamp a hand around her upper arm and pull her to an unoccupied corner. He had never been one to get physical.

"What's the matter with you?" he said under his breath, but she had no idea what she'd done.

"I—I don't know."

Before the senator could respond, Mitch appeared at her side. He held a hand out for him to shake and her father had no choice but to let go of her arm.

"Senator Cavanaugh, I'm so glad you could finally make it." He was all smiles but his words had bite. He put an arm protectively around her shoulders and asked, "Is there a problem?"

"Yes, there's a problem. Lexi looks awful. Her skin is pale and she's obviously lost weight."

"You think so?" Mitch asked, looking down at her.

"I know my daughter, Mr. Brody, and I know something isn't right."

Sudden fear gripped her. With that invaluable senatorial support in mind, what if Mitch decided to break down and tell her father the truth? Instead, he looked at Lexi with one of those sizzling smiles and said, "She looks damned good to me." Then right in front of her father, he lowered his head and brushed his lips against hers, so soft and gentle and sweet that her knees went weak.

He eased back, and with his eyes locked on hers said, "Excuse us, Senator, but I'd like to dance with my wife."

Her father's stunned expression as Mitch took her hand and led her away gave Lexi far more satisfaction than it should have. When they were back on the dance floor, he said, "What the hell kind of man tells his daughter she looks awful at her wedding reception?"

"I probably looked happy."

"Isn't that the point?"

"I think it makes him feel threatened because when I'm happy about anything, he always says or does something to sabotage it."

"He's your father. He's supposed to *want* you to be happy."

Lexi shook her head. "The entire time I was growing up he talked about how he wished he'd had a son, but my mom died before they had the chance. He never said he resented me for being born a girl, but it was obvious he felt that way. As I got older, he started to talk about me getting married and giving him lots of grandsons. Like he only saw me as a baby-breeding machine or something."

"I guess that explains why he was so anxious to marry you off."

"Exactly." But he didn't want a grandson so badly

that he would tolerate her being an unwed mother. If she had a boy, she honestly wouldn't put it past him to try to take the baby and raise it himself.

"Is he still looking at us?" Mitch asked.

She looked past his shoulder and saw that her father was holding a drink and talking to Sebastian Huntington, but his eyes were on Lexi and Mitch.

"Yes, he's still looking."

A devilish smile curled the corners of Mitch's mouth and she was sure that any second he might sprout horns. "Then let's give him a good reason to feel threatened."

Before she could ask what he planned to do, he lowered his head and locked his lips with hers, kissing her so passionately, so deeply, she could swear she felt him hit her tonsils. She might have been embarrassed but her brain had ceased to function the instant his lips touched hers. When he finally pulled away, she was breathing hard and gripping his suit jacket with both hands.

"How did he like that?" Mitch asked, looking a little breathless himself.

She looked over just in time to see her father walk out the door. "Apparently he didn't, because he just left."

"Good riddance."

She looked up at him and smiled. "Thank you for rescuing me."

"You owe me big time," he said. "And I would be willing to accept sexual favors as payment."

She opened her mouth to speak, but before she had the chance he said, "Relax, I'm just kidding."

Oddly enough, she'd been about to ask, *What would you like me to do?* Instead she said, "Not that it wasn't fun to see my father knocked down a peg or two, but if you want his support you should really be careful what you say to him. He likes to play hardball, and he enjoys a good fight, but not at the expense of his pride."

"If getting his support means kissing his ass, I'm not sure I want it anymore."

Her breath caught in her throat. If Mitch didn't want her father's support, then why would he stay married to her? And if he left her, what would she do then? Crawl back to her father and beg him to take her in? What choice would she have?

"Of course, if I blow this, Lance will probably kill me," Mitch continued. "So, I don't really have much choice."

The surge of relief she felt was so complete she nearly collapsed. She couldn't help but feel she'd just dodged a bullet.

Mitch wasn't usually much of a drinker, but he had figured the more intoxicated he was, the less inclined he would be to attack Lexi the instant they stepped in the front door. And what a brilliant plan *that* had been. While he had managed to keep his hands to himself, he'd been lying in bed awake for the past hour staring at the ceiling with a boner that just wouldn't quit. But what did he expect when he spent half the night with his hands all over her and the other half with his tongue down her throat?

On the bright side, they seemed to have everyone at that party convinced that they were happy as clams and having the time of their lives.

He rolled over and the sensation of the sheets sliding against his hard-on was almost enough to set him off. He could always take care of matters himself, but how sad was that? Very, considering he had a gorgeous wife just down the hall and he couldn't make love to her.

Couldn't or wouldn't? He was the one making the rules. He had told her that their marriage wouldn't be more than business, and he was beginning to think that as far as dumb moves went, that just about topped them all.

He couldn't help but wonder if Lexi was lying in her bed, staring at the ceiling, feeling as sexually frustrated as he was.

He heard a noise coming from the first floor, the screech of the kettle whistling. He sat up in bed. Though normally boiling water wouldn't cause him alarm, he knew Lexi could find a way to turn even making tea into a disaster of biblical proportions.

He jumped out of bed, threw on his robe, and headed down to the kitchen to stop her before she set something on fire. What was she doing up at 1:00 a.m. anyway?

When he got to the kitchen, the flame under the kettle was off and Lexi was opening and closing cupboards. She was wearing that same long silk gown she'd worn in Greece, and all he could think about was getting her out of it.

"Looking for something?" he asked.

She spun around, startled. "What are you doing here?"

Her breasts swelled enticingly against the sheer fabric and he could see the rosy outline of her nipples. Maybe it was his imagination, but her chest looked fuller than it had just a week ago.

"Last I checked, I live here," he said. "What are *you* doing?"

"I couldn't sleep, so I came down to get something to drink."

"Were you looking for something?" he asked.

"Herbal tea," she said. "Sometimes it helps me sleep. I thought I might make a cup. Do you have any?"

"In the narrow cupboard above the coffeemaker." He watched, mesmerized once again by the sway of her hips under that silk as she crossed the kitchen and opened the cupboard. "Top shelf in the back."

She stretched for it, but even on her tiptoes she wasn't tall enough. She turned back to him and said, "I can't reach it."

He knew even before he took a step that he was going to regret this, but he couldn't stop himself. He crossed the kitchen, caging her into a corner, and to his surprise, she didn't object or try to move to one side. She smelled fantastic and she was giving off enough pheromones to bring a football team to its knees.

Resting one hand on the counter beside her, he reached up with the other to grab the box of tea bags. He told himself that getting this close to her without an audience was a bad idea, but the message was getting scrambled in his hormone-drenched brain. Instead of backing off, like he should have, his body was telling him to move closer.

Lexi's breathing sounded labored and he could feel her trembling. He wasn't sure if she was scared or excited, or a little bit of both.

"We shouldn't be doing this," she said, but she didn't try to stop him, didn't push him away.

"I know. But I get the feeling we're going to, anyway." He didn't just get the feeling, he knew for a fact.

She opened her mouth to speak, probably to tell him to back off, but since that was the last thing he wanted to hear, he lowered his head and kissed her instead. With his tongue in her mouth she wasn't able to do much but moan. Which was exactly what she did. Her arms went around his neck and she tunneled her fingers through his hair. If she'd been planning to stop him, she had obviously changed her mind. At this point, they were both too far gone to turn back, and he only felt slightly guilty for using her this way.

Wasn't it Lexi who had said that they both had needs, and suggested that since they were stuck with each other, why not have a little fun?

At that moment, he couldn't think of a single reason he shouldn't take her advice.

"Tell me you're not wearing panties under this," he said, gripping the silk in his hands.

She gave him a fiery smile. "Why don't you look and see?"

He pulled it up over her head. Nope, no panties. And damn did she look good naked.

"How about you?" she said, eyeing his robe. "Are you wearing anything under there?"

He grinned. "Why don't you look and find out?"

She undid the belt and shoved the robe off his shoulders, smiling when she realized he wasn't. For an instant, he considered carrying her up to his bedroom, but honestly, he didn't think he could wait that long. He wanted—needed—to be inside her. It hadn't even been a week since they'd last made love, but it felt like years.

Not love, he reminded himself. This was sex.

He lifted her up and set her on the counter. Without hesitation she hooked those long, shapely, perfect legs around his waist. He was inside her, buried just as far as he could go, before he even thought about using a condom.

But why bother? It wasn't as though he could get her more pregnant than she already was, right?

He wanted it to last, but she was so hot and wet and tight. The sensation of skin against skin had him hovering on the edge of a precipice, struggling to keep his balance, but Lexi was moaning and writhing and sinking her nails into his back. Then she gazed up at him with a look that was caught somewhere between shock and ecstasy, and her entire body started to tremble. Her muscles contracted around him and he couldn't have held back then if his life depended on it. He came so hard his knees nearly gave out and he had to grab the edge of the counter to hold himself up.

Lexi clung to him, her forehead resting on his chest, breathing hard. "We really shouldn't have done that."

"No," he said, his own breath coming in short rasps. "We probably shouldn't have."

He could always say the alcohol had impaired his judgment. What was her excuse?

She lifted her head and gazed up at him. "Now that we have that settled, you want to do it again?"

Eleven

Lexi woke the next morning at six-thirty and immediately felt that something was different. Something other than the fact that she was in Mitch's bed and she was curled up against his side while he slept soundly.

She lay there for several minutes, trying to put her finger on the change, then realized she didn't feel sick. She should be bolting to the bathroom by now, losing last night's dinner.

She lay there for another minute or two, sure that any second it would hit her, and still nothing.

Maybe she had to move a little, jostle her stomach, to get the ball rolling. She untangled herself from Mitch's arms and slowly pulled herself into a sitting position, waiting for that overwhelming wave of nausea, for the cold sweats and the abrupt rush of bile to her throat. Instead she felt something else in the pit of her stomach. She felt…*hungry*.

She usually couldn't choke anything down until closer to lunchtime, yet here it was not even seven and she was famished.

The doctor had told her chances were good the morning sickness would ease up, but she'd had no idea it would end so abruptly.

Mitch touched her back and in a groggy voice, asked, "Are you okay?"

"I think so." She had warned him last night, when he refused to let her get up and sleep in her own room, to expect her abrupt departure from bed.

He peered up at her through sleepy eyes, his hair adorably mussed. "Should I get you a bucket?"

She gave him a playful shove, even though she liked that he was worried about her. "I don't think that will be necessary. I actually feel pretty good. Like I could eat breakfast." Which meant he would have to make it since he'd asked that—until she started those lessons—she please not cook anything. Although she had managed to boil water last night without incident.

He looked over at the clock and groaned. "It's too early to eat."

"Don't you have to get up and get ready for work, anyway?"

"Since someone kept me up half the night, I was planning on sleeping in and going in late."

"*I* kept *you* up?"

"You were insatiable. I feel so…used."

She wasn't the one who kept dragging him back under the covers every time she tried to go back to her own room, or kiss her awake when she would start to doze off from sheer exhaustion. "You just keep telling yourself that," she said. "But we both know what really happened."

He grinned up at her. "Since you're not sick, how would you feel about it happening again, right now?"

She huffed impatiently, and said in her best exasperated voice, "I suppose breakfast can wait."

When he finally let her out of bed it was closer to lunchtime. She showered and dressed, and when she went downstairs to the kitchen to find him, he was fixing them something to eat. She had expected him to be in a suit, ready to go to the office, but he was dressed in casual slacks and a polo shirt.

"Don't you have to go to work?" she asked.

He shrugged and said, "They'll manage without me one more day. Besides, I promised you a driving lesson."

She had just figured, since he'd been intoxicated at the time, that he would have forgotten about the driving lessons. The thought of actually getting behind the wheel of a car, especially with Mitch watching, had her heart skipping a beat. "Maybe we shouldn't."

"How else will you learn?"

"What if I do it wrong?"

"You probably will at first, but that's all a part of the learning process."

"What if I do something terrible, like run us off an overpass or something?"

"I promise I'll keep you on solid ground until you get the hang of it."

She chewed her lip, wondering what she could say to talk him out of it without sounding like a total chicken.

Mitch reached over and took her hand. "Have a little faith in yourself, Lexi, and you'll do just fine."

That was the problem. She had been taught to believe that she couldn't do things on her own, but he was right. She had to stop being so afraid of everything, so willing to depend on other people. It was time she started living her life, and not just sitting back and watching the world pass by around her.

She took a deep breath and blew it out. "Okay. Let's do it."

"After we eat, we'll take you out for your first lesson."

At least this way she didn't have to ask Tara to do it.

Mitch's cell phone rang and he unclipped it from his belt to answer it. "Hey, Mark, what's up? Did they accept our offer?"

Lexi's heart jumped when she heard the real estate

agent's name. She held her breath while Mitch listened quietly, his expression hovering somewhere between curiosity and concern. He'd all but said he would do anything to get the house, but what if the owners changed their minds and refused to sell it?

"I understand," he said. "I'll talk to you later." He hung up and clipped the phone back on his belt. "That was Mark."

As if she hadn't already figured that out. "What did he say?"

"He heard from the seller."

"And?"

A slow smile spread across his face. "They accepted the offer. The house is ours."

Lexi screamed and threw herself into his arms. She had been so afraid that something would go wrong, she hadn't let herself hope it would really happen. Now she was so excited she could barely contain herself.

Mitch laughed and hugged her back. "I guess I don't have to ask if you're happy."

"I am," she said, resting her head against his chest, squeezing him tight. For the first time in a long time she was really, really happy.

Something had happened last night. When he took her hand and they walked into that party, something in their relationship had changed. She was sure of it. They could say that this marriage was nothing more than a business deal, but she knew it wasn't true. He was the man she'd spent that amazing week with in D.C., the one she had fallen in love with. And despite a few rocky patches, she knew that deep down she had never really stopped loving him. And he loved her, too, even if he hadn't said so.

"We close in a week," he said.

"We?" she asked, looking up at him.

"It's your house, too."

Her house. The idea made her almost giddy with excitement.

Everything was perfect. Even better than perfect.

Except for one thing. She still hadn't told Mitch the truth.

Lexi had assumed her lunch at the Cattleman's Club café would be just her and Kate, but when Tara dropped her off at the club and the hostess led her to the table, she saw that they were being joined by Summer Martindale, Cara Pettigrew-Novak, Alicia Montoya, and Rebecca Huntington.

Lexi wondered if she was walking straight into the lion's den. Kate had been incredibly sweet the other night at the party, but what if that had been an act? What if she resented the fact that Lexi had been engaged to her husband and she'd lured her here to humiliate her?

Kate saw Lexi approaching and rose from her chair, a huge smile on her face, and said, "Hey, sister-in-law!" Then she proceeded to wrap Lexi up in one of those warm and affectionate hugs.

Well, that was unexpected.

"Sit down," Kate said, gesturing to the empty seat beside hers. "I think you know everyone here."

As she sat, the women smiled and greeted her warmly, and Lexi began to think that maybe this would just be a friendly lunch with the girls after all. Which for her would be a totally new experience. She hadn't been allowed to have many friends or associate with people who weren't the top shelf of society—she couldn't have contact with anyone who could be a potential danger to her father's political aspirations. He never would have approved of a friendship with someone like Kate, a lowly assistant, or a dancer like Cara. In fact, there wasn't a single person at the table, besides Rebecca Huntington maybe, whom he would deem acceptable. And for the first time in her life, she didn't care what he thought. Lately, the past couple of days especially, she'd been feeling rebellious and independent, and she *liked* it.

A waitress appeared at their table to take Lexi's drink order. Lexi saw that everyone else had an alcoholic beverage, and boy did she wish she could have one, too, but she ordered an iced tea instead. For a second, she worried someone might question her choice, but no one said a word.

"We try to meet at least once a month," Cara told her, "so we can discuss all of the latest gossip."

Lexi wondered if she had ever been the topic of conversation.

"Today we're also celebrating," Summer said, and all heads turned her way.

"What are we celebrating?" Alicia asked.

Summer held out her left hand, so everyone could see the enormous diamond ring and diamond-encrusted wedding band she was wearing. "Darius and I eloped!"

Excited squeals and congratulations followed.

"I'm so jealous!" Rebecca said. "It seems as though everyone is getting married but me."

"Marriage is hard work," Cara said, then added with a smile, "but well worth it when you finally get the gears running smoothly."

The waitress brought Lexi's tea and set a basket of fresh bread and rolls on the table. Lexi was absolutely famished—the last few days it seemed as though she was constantly eating—so she dove right in and grabbed a roll.

"What's the latest with the refinery fire?" Rebecca asked Summer, and Lexi couldn't help noticing that everyone glanced at Alicia. At first she wondered why, then remembered that it was Alicia's brother Alex who was being looked at for the arson.

"Is Darius any closer to finding out who did it?" Kate asked.

Summer shrugged apologetically. "He doesn't say too much about his work."

"I know what everyone thinks," Alicia said. "But Alex would never hurt a soul. He didn't set that fire."

"I believe you," Rebecca told her. "Alex is a good person." Lexi noticed that the woman looked at Rebecca with surprise. "Based on what I've heard, I mean," she added, blushing slightly.

"What about the rezoning in the Somerset district?" Kate asked. "I heard Alex was behind it."

"He is, because someone had to do something to pick up revenue. I know that no one wants to believe it, but the town is in trouble," said Alicia. "With Alex's help, I'm working on a project to create an 'Old Towne' tourist attraction downtown. It will bring jobs and add tourist revenue to the city, not to mention preserve history, which, as curator of the museum, is important to me."

"Sounds like your life lately has been all work and no play?" Cara asked with a strange smile on her face.

"Well, not *all* work," Alicia said cryptically.

"Did you meet someone?" Rebecca asked excitedly.

Alicia flashed them a smile. "Maybe."

"Girlfriend, are you holding out on us?" Summer asked.

"Let's just say I'm afraid I'm going to jinx it. But I will say that I have a date this Friday. He said he wants to take me somewhere special."

"You have to come to Sweet Nothings," Rebecca insisted. "A special date deserves sexy underwear."

Alicia laughed. "I could spend my entire salary in your store, Becca."

"You're one of those people who can eat anything and still stay pick thin, aren't you?" Cara said. Lexi was surprised to find that Cara was talking to her, and mortified when she realized why. While everyone had been chatting, Lexi had almost wiped out the bread basket by herself.

"Sorry," she said, setting down the roll she'd been devouring. She could feel her cheeks turning pink. "I skipped breakfast."

"I just have to look at food and my butt gets bigger," Rebecca said.

"I hate to think what I'd look like if I weren't dancing all the time," Cara said.

After that, Lexi was careful not to draw attention to herself. She ordered a salad with the dressing on the side, then only ate half, even though she was hungry enough to eat three times that much. Maybe the next time they met—if she was even invited next time—she would be able to tell them about the baby.

It was getting to the point where she *had* to tell Mitch the truth. She had almost said it the other day after they found the house, but she'd chickened out at the last minute. She knew, though, that it was time. She'd begun to believe that now he would be thrilled to learn that the baby was his. Because even though he hadn't said it out loud yet, Lexi was convinced that he loved her. He showed her every day in a hundred little ways. Most of them in the bedroom.

Though she knew better than to mistake sex for love, she was sure that this time it was different.

The alternative was no longer an option.

Twelve

Mitch found it ironic that when he had agreed to meet at Darius's office, he'd figured he would be thankful for the time away from his wife, when in reality, he would much rather be at home with her. For a self-proclaimed workaholic who loved his job above all else, he'd been taking a lot of time off since they got back from Greece.

At first he tried to convince himself that it was just the sex, and then he told himself that he felt guilty leaving her alone, or was worried that she might try to use the stove and burn his house down. But now, as he sat in the conference room of Darius's security firm with Darius, Lance, Kevin and Justin, he couldn't deny that he simply missed her company.

As hard as he tried to tell himself that she was a spoiled, heartless brat who cared about no one but herself, her actions said he was way off base. If what she'd told him about her father was true, and after seeing the senator in action he was pretty damned sure it was, it was a miracle that Lexi had any self-esteem at all. He now believed that she hadn't hopped from his bed to his brother's as some sort of vendetta, but because she was desperate to be accepted and loved. She *deserved* to be with someone who could love her. But Mitch didn't do love.

In a few weeks, he'd gone from thinking that he was somehow superior to her, a better human being, to thinking that he just didn't measure up. But he had to stick it out for the baby's sake, the niece or nephew growing in her who deserved to be raised by family, not some stranger.

"So, when is this meeting going to start?" Kevin asked Darius.

"As soon as the last person I invited gets here." No sooner had the words left his mouth than the confer-ence-room door opened and Alex Montoya walked in.

In an instant, Lance was up and out of his chair. "What is he doing here?"

Alex shot Lance daggers with his eyes.

"I asked him to come," Darius said. "As a Cattle-man Club member, this concerns him, too."

Mitch sat up in his chair, in case he needed to hold his brother back, but after a tense moment, Lance took his seat and Alex found a chair on the opposite side of the table. Mitch didn't like Alex, but he gave him credit for having the guts to show his face.

"I called you all here," Darius said, "because I have suspicions that someone may be cooking the club books."

"Are you suggesting that someone is embezzling from the club?" Justin asked.

"That's exactly what I think."

"What led you to think that?" Kevin asked.

"When I set up the new billing system for Helping Hands, something strange happened. The club cut us a check for expenses, but it was made out to Helping Hearts. I called the office and talked to Sebastian Huntington and asked him to fix the error. I just assumed he'd used the wrong name, but he said that he'd sent the wrong check by accident."

"I didn't know there was an organization named Helping Hearts," Mitch said, although admittedly, he didn't pay much attention to the club's finances.

"I didn't either," Darius said. "But I was curious so I did a bit of research, and after some digging, I found that Helping Hearts doesn't exist."

"As club members we have the right to examine the books," Alex said, looking as concerned as the rest of them.

"I suppose you think you should be the one to investigate," Lance snapped back. "How do we know you're not the one behind it?"

Alex glared at him. "First you call me an arsonist, now you accuse me of theft? Perhaps you would like to blame me for the stock market crash as well."

"I know," Darius interrupted, before fists started flying, "that it can't feasibly be someone in this room. Only a member higher up in the ranks could pull this off."

"Like who?" Kevin asked.

"I'm not ready to point any fingers yet. And Alex is right, we need someone to examine the books. I think that person should be Mitch."

Suddenly all eyes were on him. "Why me?"

"I can handle setting up a simple billing system," Darius told him, "but you're the financial whiz kid of the group. If anyone would be able to spot discrepancies, it's you."

"I agree," Justin said.

"I do, as well," Alex agreed, which earned him a sharp look from Lance.

Kevin added his vote. "Me, too."

"So it's unanimous," Lance said.

Mitch wasn't sure if he was comfortable with this, but it seemed he didn't have much choice. "And if I find something?"

"We'll demand an audit from an outside firm. According to the bylaws, the club has no choice but to comply."

"I'm still having a tough time believing someone would steal from the club," Kevin said.

"So was I," Darius assured him. "I never would have come forward with this if I wasn't sure. You'll keep us posted, Mitch?"

"Of course."

The meeting broke up after that, Alex wisely being the first one to leave. On his way out, Justin asked Mitch, "You want to head to the club for a drink? Watch some soccer?"

Normally, Mitch wouldn't have hesitated to spend a few hours with his best friend, but he didn't feel right leaving Lexi alone. Besides, he had promised they would talk about contractors and the renovations they wanted to make on the house. "I can't tonight," he told Justin.

"Have to get back to the old ball and chain?"

Mitch didn't justify that with a response, he just shot Justin a look.

Justin laughed and shook his head. "Damn. I never thought I'd see the day when Mitchell Brody settled down."

"You could be next," Mitch said, which only made Justin laugh harder.

"I wouldn't advise holding your breath. Now that you're tied down, that just means more available women for me."

Leave it to Justin to rationalize it out like that. Although it surprised Mitch to realize it, he didn't miss playing the field. Maybe later that would change and he would begin to feel restless. But for now he was quite content being a one-woman man.

When Lexi answered the knock at the front door, the last person she expected to see standing on the porch was her father. As far as she knew, he was supposed to be in D.C.

"Daddy, what are you doing here?"

"I need to speak with you," he said, entering without waiting for an invitation.

"Of course," she replied, stepping aside. Maybe he was here to apologize for the way he'd acted at the party.

He gazed around the foyer looking unimpressed. Probably not big or grand enough for him. "Is your husband here?"

"No, he had a meeting." She gestured toward the kitchen. "I was just making myself a cup of tea. Would you like one?"

"You're making it? Does your husband not even have the decency to hire a housekeeper?"

She shrugged. "It's not a big deal. In fact, I sort of like doing things myself for a change."

He shook his head. "It's even worse than I thought."

Clearly that apology wasn't going to happen. "What's worse than you thought?"

"Your life. What Mitch has reduced you to."

Reduced her to? On the contrary, it felt as though

she had been introduced to a world she never knew existed, with opportunities and possibilities she had never dreamed of. "I'm fine, Daddy. Really."

"Nothing about this is 'fine.' After the degrading display the other night at the party, I've decided not to give the Brody brothers my support."

Her heart sank. "You can't do that."

"I can and I will. I still can't believe the way he was groping you. Do you have any idea how it looked to everyone else in the room?"

"Probably like we were a newlywed couple so madly in love we couldn't stand being apart."

"Well, the charade is over, so there's no need for you to stay here any longer. Pack your things and I'll take you home."

She didn't want to leave. "You promised them your support."

"I also told him that if he hurt you, I would crush him."

She began feeling a little frantic. Her father was being completely unreasonable. "But he *didn't* hurt me."

"He sullied your reputation, which is even worse, as far as I'm concerned."

"Reputation is more important than my happiness? I love Mitch."

He spit out a rueful laugh, and regarded her as though she were the village idiot. "You can't possibly be that naive. He only married you for my support."

The lengths he would go to, the things he would say to make her feel bad about herself, knew no bounds. But she knew exactly what this was about, even if he wouldn't admit it. It had nothing to do with reputation or Mitch's behavior at the party. He only wanted her to leave Mitch because she wanted to stay. He wanted control of her life back. Married to Mitch, he could no longer manipulate her. But this time she didn't have to listen to him. "You really can't stand it, can you?"

"Stand what?"

"To see me happy."

He scoffed. "That's ridiculous."

"Then why would you say something like that to me? I say I love Mitch and you accuse him of using me?"

"I said it because it's true. You know that I've never believed in coddling you."

"How do you know Mitch hasn't fallen in love with me?"

He shook his head sadly, as though she were even more pathetic than he realized.

"Do you believe I'm that horrible?" she asked. "That unlovable?"

"I didn't say that. But he isn't right for you."

"A month ago you seemed to think he was."

"Well, I was wrong."

If he couldn't accept that Mitch loved her, that was his problem, not hers. Mitch was going to be furious when he found out that her father had reneged on their deal, but she was pretty confident that he wouldn't hold it against her.

"Charade or not, I can't end the marriage."

"Why not?"

She shouldn't say it, but as soon as she told Mitch the truth everyone would know anyway. "I'm pregnant."

"Pregnant?" The anger disappeared and to her surprise, a look of wonder overwhelmed his face. "I'm going to be a grandfather?"

She had expected him to be furious. But it made sense that he would approve now that he was getting something he wanted out of the deal. And he had always wanted a grandson.

She smiled and nodded.

"That's...incredible."

"We had even discussed naming him after you," she said, even though they had done no such thing. They didn't have a clue what the baby's gender would be, much less what they planned to name it.

But he seemed to buy it because he beamed with pride. "I suppose a divorce *is* out of the question now, but we can figure out a way to make it work."

She smiled, thinking it was time to go for the throat. "You can start by giving Mitch and Lance all the senatorial support they need."

His smile faded. "I can't do that."

"You will if you want to see your grandchild."

He was so stunned that for a moment, he didn't seem to know what to say. It was the first time she had ever seen him rendered speechless and she enjoyed every second of it. When he found his voice, he asked, his tone soaked in disbelief, "You would use your own child against me?"

She sighed. "If I have to. Of course, I have plenty of other things I could hold against you."

"What things?"

"Things that could make your life very difficult when you're trying to get reelected."

The color leached from his face. "Did you just threaten to blackmail me?"

She sure as hell did. For the first time in her life she stood up to him and it felt wonderful. She flashed him a "Bless your Heart" smile. "Daddy, blackmail sounds so…uncivilized. Up on Capitol Hill I believe they call it extortion."

"I can't believe you would do this to me."

She shrugged. "I guess you could say that I learned from the master."

She waited for the anger, for him to explode, but to her surprise, it didn't happen. He just stood there, perplexed, as though he simply could not grasp what had just happened. That his compliant little girl had finally grown a will of her own. God knows it was about damned time. Then the front door opened and Mitch walked through, the vestiges of a cool early-autumn breeze following him inside.

"I thought that was your car outside," he said to her father as he walked right past him without shaking his hand or anything, pulling Lexi into his arms and kissing her. "Sorry it took so long, sweetheart."

Long? He'd barely been gone an hour. She had assumed "meeting" meant maybe twenty minutes of business followed by a few hours of drinking and bullshitting with the guys. Sort of like her lunch with Kate, but with more profanity and testosterone.

"Daddy stopped in to say hello," she told him. "Wasn't that nice?"

He obviously knew something was up, and he played along, saying in a Southern drawl that she had never heard him use before, "Why, yes it was. Can I get you a drink, Senator?"

"Unfortunately, he was just leaving," Lexi said. "But thanks for stopping by, Daddy."

Looking shell-shocked and confused, her father mumbled goodbye and let himself out of the house. As soon as he was gone, Mitch turned to her and, the drawl gone, asked, "What the hell just happened?"

Thirteen

Mitch lay in bed several hours later, Lexi against his side, her body warm and soft. He couldn't stop smiling. "I wish I could have seen the look on his face when you threatened him. That must have been priceless."

"I keep waiting to feel guilty. I never dreamed of saying something like that to him. Instead, I feel…liberated."

"I don't mean for this to sound condescending, but I'm proud of you," he said, and he could feel her smile.

"I'm proud of me, too. And I don't think you ever have to worry about losing his support. It's a real possibility that he won't ever speak to me again, though."

"How do you feel about that?"

"Not as bad as I expected. In a way, I kind of feel relieved. I don't need him anymore." She was quiet for a moment, then said, "Mitch, there's something I need to tell you. Two things, actually."

He rolled on his side to look at her. "What?"

"First, I lied to you. I said something really awful that wasn't true."

He frowned. "What?"

"It was the morning after we slept together in D.C. I thought…" She paused and bit her lip.

"You thought what?"

She took a deep breath. "I was so naive. I woke up, and I thought that you were going to beg me to marry you instead of Lance. I thought you…loved me. And you have no idea how long I'd waited for someone to feel that way about me. But the first thing you said that morning was that sleeping together had been a mistake. I was crushed. I lashed out and said the most awful thing I could think of."

"That you used me?"

She nodded.

In an odd way he was relieved, and at the same time it disturbed him. Not because she lied—he understood why she'd done it, and couldn't really blame her—but because she had just cemented the fact that he had totally misjudged her.

"I know we had barely spent a week together, but I loved you, Mitch. And I think…I think I still do."

He knew what she wanted, what she desperately

needed, but as much as he wanted her to be happy, he couldn't bring himself to lie to her. "I care for you, Lexi. I really do. I just can't…"

She rolled onto her back, but not before he saw her face fall, her happiness crumble. "I understand."

"It's not you. It's me."

She shrugged. "You don't have to explain."

He waited for her to get angry, or to cry. To do something. But she just lay there quietly and he felt like the world's biggest heel. She deserved better than this. Better than him. She should be with someone who loved her. Who was capable of love.

"What else?" he asked.

"What do you mean?"

"You said there were two things you had to tell me."

"Oh," she said softly, turning away from him to lie on her side, pulling the covers up over her shoulder. "It wasn't important."

He considered pushing the issue, but figured maybe he was best off not knowing. He lay awake for what felt like hours, marinating in his own guilt and self-loathing.

When he woke in the morning and reached for Lexi, she wasn't there. He got out of bed and pulled on his robe. He figured Lexi was downstairs in the kitchen making tea, but he found her in her bedroom, packing. She was leaving him.

He was more disappointed than surprised. "Going somewhere?" he asked.

She turned to him, looking tired and sad. "Good morning."

He doubted that. "You don't have to do this."

"Yes, I do."

He had half a mind to beg her to stay, to swear that things would change, but that would just be cruel and selfish. The best thing he could do for Lexi was let her go.

"Are you going back to your father?"

"God, no. I would never give him the satisfaction."

"Good. He doesn't deserve you. And don't worry about money. I'll see that you and the baby are set for life."

"I appreciate that, but I can't spend the rest of my life with other people always taking care of me. I need to do this on my own."

"Where will you go?"

"Tara said I can stay with her until I'm on my feet."

He was tempted to insist that she stay with him, at least until the baby was born. By then, the house would be ready and she could stay there. But if she needed to prove something to herself, he wasn't going to stop her. Maybe she would realize how hard it was to be on her own, and come back to him.

But Lexi was tough, and he had the feeling she would be just fine. He would miss her, and always care about her, but the truth was she deserved a better man than Mitch Brody, and he hoped someday she would find him.

* * *

Lexi had never been so humiliated in her life.

Her father had been right all along. Mitch didn't love her. He "cared" for her, which she was pretty sure translated into caring about her father's senatorial support. Just as her father had warned her.

She could be a bitch about it and see that her father did everything in his power to crush them, but she just wasn't the vindictive type. After all, it wasn't Mitch's fault that Lexi had fallen in love with him. She had done that herself, creating her own fantasy world. Mitch had told her time and time again that their marriage was just business, but she hadn't listened.

"You have to tell him the truth," Tara said, handing her a steaming cup of tea. She took a seat in the armchair across from the couch where Lexi sat. "It's his baby. He deserves to be a part of its life."

"I will tell him. Eventually."

"When? After the kid is out of college?"

"After I get back on my feet, when I don't need his help." Which might be a while considering she had no job skills, no driver's license and all she'd had the will to do the past four days was sit curled up on the couch in Tara's condo, feeling sorry for herself.

The prospect of supporting herself and the baby was beyond overwhelming, but she was determined to figure out a way.

"He's going to have to pay child support," Tara said.

She knew that was inevitable. He would insist, because that's the kind of man he was. But she wasn't ready to accept his help. Not yet. Although at this point, there was no way he would be anything but furious with her when he found out the baby was his, and he would be completely justified. She should have told him the truth that day he assumed the baby was Lance's, whether he believed her or not. At least then she could say that she'd been honest. But she had procrastinated and put it off and painted herself into a tiny little corner that she had no hope of getting out of unscathed.

When all was said and done, everything was her fault. She had made this mess, done this to herself, and she was the only one who could fix it.

But right now, she just wasn't ready.

Mitch sat in his office, staring out the window, finding it impossible to concentrate on his work. Since Lexi had left him, he hadn't been able to think straight. Hell, he'd barely been able to function. He just couldn't stop thinking about her, *missing* her. He'd stripped his bed and pillows, even sprayed air freshener, but he could still smell her, still feel her presence in the room. He couldn't drive his car without picturing her behind the wheel, so adorably nervous, but determined to learn. He couldn't walk into the kitchen without re-membering the night they had made love there.

He had lost all interest in buying the house. Part

of what had drawn him to it was her excitement, the thought of them being a family. Now there didn't seem much point in leaving his townhouse, even though he was miserable whenever he was there.

She had been indelibly ingrained in every part of his life, and he couldn't help wondering if this feeling he was having, the crushing ache, the longing he felt every time he thought of her—which was pretty much all the time—meant he loved her.

"Why don't you just call her?"

Mitch turned to find Lance standing in the doorway, arms folded across his chest. He sighed and asked, "Is it that obvious?"

Lance grinned. "You look just like I felt when Kate left me. And trust me when I say, if she loves you, she'll forgive whatever you did."

Lance was a good brother. He had always been there to protect Mitch, had always taken care of him and supported him no matter what. He owed him the truth. He'd already waited too long. "Come in, and close the door."

Lance did as he asked. "What's going on?"

"Lexi is pregnant," he said.

Lance laughed. "Already? You two sure didn't waste any time."

"It's not what you think. The baby…it's not mine."

He frowned. "What do you mean, it's not yours?"

"She's more than three months."

"Three months? That would mean she got

pregnant…" He trailed off, so Mitch finished the sentence for him.

"Right around the time you two were engaged."

He shook his head in disbelief. "Son of a bitch. All that time I felt so guilty for going behind her back with Kate, and she was cheating on *me?*"

His brother could not be that dense. "She wasn't cheating on you, you idiot. The baby is yours."

Instead of looking shocked or humbled, or even angry, Lance laughed and said, "No, it isn't."

He must have been in some serious denial. "Yes, Lance. It is. She told me herself."

"Then she was lying."

"How can you know that for sure?"

"Easy. Because I never slept with her."

"What?"

"I only kissed her once and believe me when I say that it wasn't all that red hot for either of us."

"Then why, on my honeymoon, did you tell me that if I slept with her it wouldn't be a disappointment?"

He shrugged. "A guess. It wasn't, was it?"

"Of course not, but…" This didn't make any sense. "Why would she tell me it was you if…?" Realization hit him with a force that knocked the breath from his lungs. "Oh, shit."

He must have gone white as death, because Lance asked, "Jesus, Mitch, what's wrong?"

How could he have been so stupid? "I'm an ass, that's what's wrong."

"I'm sorry, but you've completely lost me."

Despite what he'd believed at first, he knew without a doubt that Lexi hadn't been capable of hopping from Mitch's bed to Lance's. And that could only mean one thing.

"It's mine," he said, and at his brother's confused look added, "The baby. Lexi is having *my* baby."

"Then why did she tell you it was mine?"

"She didn't. When she told me she was pregnant, I just assumed it was yours."

Lance looked more confused than ever. "I thought you said she was three months. How could it be yours?"

Mitch dropped his head in his hands. He had no choice but to tell Lance the truth. He looked up at his big brother. His protector. "There's something I have to tell you. Something I should have told you months ago."

"What?" Lance asked.

"Remember that week I spent with Lexi on your behalf?"

Lance nodded. "Of course."

"That last night, before you proposed, we... I slept with her." Mitch waited for the impending explosion.

"I'm not an idiot," Lance said calmly. "I saw the way you two acted after the D.C. trip. I kind of figured something happened."

Mitch couldn't believe that Lance knew, or at least suspected, this entire time. "You're not mad?"

"It wasn't a real engagement."

"But you're my brother. You were going to marry her."

"But I didn't. If it would make you feel better, I could punch you again. Although it looks like you're doing a pretty fair job of beating yourself up."

"I deserve worse, believe me."

"Let me get this straight. She told you she was pregnant, and you just automatically assumed it was mine?"

He nodded.

"So, what you were saying to her was that you believed she slept with you, then turned around and hopped in the sack with your brother?"

Mitch pinched the bridge of his nose. "Yeah, pretty much." Lexi must have been furious. Not to mention humiliated.

"Why didn't she just tell you the truth?"

"She probably thought I wouldn't believe her."

"Would you have believed her?"

"Probably not."

"I hate to say this, Mitch, but you are an ass."

He wanted to be furious with Lexi for not telling him the truth, for lying by omission, but the only person he could muster any anger for was himself. All of this, this entire jumbled-up mess, was his fault. Yes, Lexi had lied about using him, but he had spent a week wining and dining her, and yes, seducing her, only to turn around and say it was a mistake. Could he really blame her for being hurt and lashing out? If he had known her better then, he would have realized she wasn't capable of what she'd claimed. She would never use anyone.

Ironically, if he had been honest with his brother from the start, he would have learned the truth and they could have avoided this entire mess.

"What I still don't get is *how* she got pregnant," Mitch said.

His brother smirked. "You don't really need me to explain that to you, do you, Mitch?"

Mitch sighed. "I know *how,* I'm just not sure when it could have happened. We were careful."

Lance shrugged. "Birth control has been known to fail."

"I think… I think I love her."

"You think?"

No. He *knew* he loved her. It was the only explanation for how miserable he was without her. He rose from his chair. "I have to go see her."

"It's about time."

Mitch grabbed his jacket and headed for the door. Then he remembered there was a slight hitch to his plan. He had no idea where she was.

Lance must have read his mind because he said, "She's staying at her assistant's condo." Mitch looked confused. "Wives are an excellent source of information."

Hopefully, Mitch would be finding that out for himself. He was going to ask Lexi to marry him, and this time they were going to do it right.

Fourteen

The doorbell rang, and since Lexi was home alone and not expecting anyone, she peered out the front window to see who was standing on the porch. Her breath caught and her heart started to hammer a million miles an hour when she saw that it was Mitch.

What could he possibly want?

He must have come right from work because he was wearing a suit. He glanced her way and though she dropped the curtain, she wasn't fast enough. He saw her.

Damn it!

He knocked on the door and called, "Come on, Lexi, I need to talk to you."

She was going to shout back that everything they needed to say had been said, but it was a lie. Instead, she unlocked the door and pulled it open. "What?"

"I finally figured it out."

"Figured what out?" she asked, stepping aside so he could come in.

"When it happened."

She shut the door and turned to him. "When what happened?"

"When you got pregnant."

His words nearly stopped her heart. She hoped he didn't mean what she thought he meant. "W-when?"

"The third time, in the middle of the night. For a few minutes we didn't use a condom. Am I right?"

Stunned, she asked, "How did you…?"

"I figured it was time to tell my brother the truth. Imagine his surprise when he found out that he was having a child with a woman he never slept with."

She chewed her lip. "I never actually said—"

"That you slept with him. I know."

"I was going to tell you—"

"But you didn't trust me," he finished for her. "I get it. I was an ass."

Huh? What was he saying? "You're not angry?" Lexi asked.

"How can I be angry at you when this entire mess is my fault?"

What? This was her fault. "This whole thing started because I lied and said I used you."

"Lexi, this whole thing started because *I* told *you* we made a mistake, because I didn't want to admit that I was falling in love with you."

He *loved* her?

No, of course he didn't. She knew exactly what this was. Now that he knew about the baby, he wanted them to be together. Or maybe he was worried that he and Lance would lose the senator's support. Either way, it was obvious he would say anything to get his way, even if that meant lying about loving her.

"Aren't you going to say anything?" he asked.

"Like what?"

"Hell, I don't know, maybe something like, you love me, too?"

"I won't stay with you just for the baby's sake."

"I don't recall asking you to. This is entirely selfish. I want you to stay with me for my sake. Because I love you."

"If you're worried about losing my father's support, I'll see to it that you don't."

"This has nothing to do with that. As far as I'm concerned, he can take his support and shove it where the sun don't shine."

"I don't believe you. It's the only reason you married me."

"Maybe it was," he admitted. "But it's not why I want to marry you now."

"We're already married."

"I know, but I was thinking that it would be nice if we had a big wedding, did it right."

"No. What would be nice is a neat and tidy divorce."

He folded his arms across his chest. "You still honestly think I'm doing this for your father's support?"

"Among other things."

"You don't believe I love you?"

She shook her head.

"Okay," he said. "I guess I'm just going to have to prove it to you."

Good luck with that.

He pulled out his cell phone, dialed a number and put it on speaker.

"Who are you calling?" she asked. If she wouldn't believe him, did he think she would believe someone else?

"Senator Cavanaugh's office," she heard her father's secretary say.

"It's Mitch Brody, could I speak with the senator? It's urgent."

"One moment, Mr. Brody." She put him on hold.

"What are you doing?" she asked.

"They say actions speak louder than words."

Oh, no. He wouldn't.

Her father came on the line, his tone exasperated. "What do you want, Brody?"

"Hello, Senator, I just wanted to tell you to take you support and sh—"

"Mitch!" she screeched. She snatched the phone away from him and snapped it shut. "Are you crazy?"

"No. I love you."

His phone immediately began to ring, but Lexi ignored it. "Why would you do that?"

"How many times are you going to make me say it? It isn't about the baby, and it's not about the senator. You could be carrying the postman's baby and I would still love you. And my business, my life, means nothing if you aren't in it."

Would he say all that if he didn't really mean it? If he didn't love her?

"You love *me?*" she asked.

"Yes, *you.* You know, we really have to work on this self-esteem issue you have."

She bit her lip and nodded, afraid that if she said anything, she would burst into tears. Mitch must have realized, because he pulled her into his arms and held her. She could hardly believe it was real— that after everything they had been through, this was actually going to work out.

"You know, you could say it, too," he said.

She smiled up at him. "I love you, Mitch. I've known since that week in D.C. that I wanted to spend the rest of my life with you."

He gazed at her, his eyes so full of love and affection she had to swallow back a sob. He caressed her cheek and said, "I can hardly wait for us to be a family."

Tears slipped from the corners of her eyes and he brushed them away with his thoughts.

"Those better be happy tears," he said.

She grinned up at him. "Absolutely."

He grinned and kissed the tip of her nose. "We had kind of a bumpy start, I guess."

"A little," she said, but she knew that from now, it would only get better.

* * * * *

Don't miss the next book in
THE MILLIONAIRE'S CLUB *series,*
The Maverick's Virgin Mistress,
available next month from
Mills & Boon® Desire™.